THIS MUCH TO GIVE

JEAN S. MacLEOD

This Much to Give

Originally published as *Special Nurse*, Harlequin Romance #597

CRAIG

Harlequin Books

TORONTO·LONDON·NEW YORK·AMSTERDAM·SYDNEY·WINNIPEG

Original hardcover edition published by Mills & Boon Limited

SBN 373-00597-0

Harlequin edition published June, 1961,
under the title *Special Nurse # 597*

This **Harlequin's Collection** edition printed 1976

Printed in Canada

CHAPTER ONE

I

THE BRIGHT LIGHT above the operating table shone down
upon the surgeon's bowed head.

The silence deepened and the junior nurse on the other
side of the table shifted her weight from one foot to the
other. Her eyes above the white mask were on the surgeon's
hands, deep blue eyes under straight dark brows which
were drawn together now urgently as she watched the most
critical stage of the operation being performed by this
man who was fast becoming one of the most imposing
figures in the medical profession. Lindsey Hamilton realized
that she had not yet passed the stage where her thoughts
wandered for a moment to the patient, that still, pros-
trate form lying on the high table unconscious of the
working of the miracle of modern science. For an instant
she allowed her eyes to travel to the small, masked figure
of the anaesthetist sitting at the top of the table surrounded
by his apparatus, saw the surgeon glance at his colleague
and the old doctor's answering nod, and then her eyes
were back upon that tall central figure again, watching,
marvelling.

She had seen Stewart Harvey operate twice before, both
intricate brain cases owing their success to the cool daring
of his work, and she understood why he was admired and
respected and often envied by his colleagues in the profession. Before she had come to the Alexandra Infirmary
she had read articles by him in many medical periodicals
and always his name had carried weight and authority.

The surgeon straightened, standing back as his assistant inserted the last few stitches, and to Lindsey it seemed that there was a certain weariness about him, although his tall figure was still erect, his eyes sharp and clear above the concealing mask .

Then, with a brief nod to the anaesthetist, he moved away from the table to make room for the matron and the theatre sister, and Lindsey followed him swiftly into the anteroom, pulling off the fine rubber gloves which encased his hands. As he untied his mask their eyes met and held for an instant, but he turned to the task of scrubbing up without a word, and she hurried back to the theatre to take her further instructions from Matron.

She was carrying the last saline bowl into the anteroom when Sister Jeffries left the theatre and a veritable babel of talk broke out. It was like the sudden turning on of a giant tap, a rushing spate of exclamations and remarks.

"Two and a half hours without a break! I'd never be able to face it without collapsing ignobly at someone's feet," Molly Nicholl declared breathlessly as she replaced a dettol flagon on the shelf over the sluice.

"Preferably Stewart Harvey's?" a cynical voice inquired from the doorway of the theatre. "I wonder what *his* reactions would be?" The owner of the voice laughed unpleasantly. "Could you imagine him dropping everything and stooping gallantly to the rescue?"

"Personally, I don't think he ever stoops."

"Not mentally, anyway," the red-headed Molly retorted. "One just couldn't imagine Mr. Stewart Harvey being small about anything. He's splendid, and I only wish I had been in the theatre this afternoon." She turned to Lindsey, who was stacking bowls away in the cupboard. "You were, Hammy, weren't you? What was he like?"

Lindsey smiled.

"As aloof and enigmatical as ever, but still wonderful for all that," she answered, and then more seriously: "It's a joy to watch him operate."

"And an honor just to untie his mask afterwards in the hope of a smile as a reward?" suggested the cynical one.

She was pointedly ignored.

"R. Stewart Harvey," Molly Nicholl mused. "I wonder what the R. stands for. Robert, perhaps. It couldn't be Reginald, do you think?"

"I haven't an idea," Lindsey laughed, "and I wouldn't worry about it if I were you, Nicky. We're never likely to get as far as Christian names!"

"No, I guess not." Molly's ready smile flashed out as she linked an arm affectionately through her friend's. "Why did you have to get transferred, Hammy? We're all going to miss you terribly, especially me."

"Shortage of staff at the new hospital, I suppose," Lindsey suggested.

"As if there wasn't a big enough shortage here! You'll write, though, won't you? And perhaps we'll be able to meet in Glasgow if you leave. St. Ronan's is a military hospital, isn't it?"

Lindsey nodded.

"It's going to be lonely enough after Glasgow," she admitted ruefully, "but I feel that I'm going to like the work." Her eyes were suddenly shining. "I've read up such a lot about occupational therapy and I heard yesterday that St. Ronan's has a wing entirely given over to the treatment. I've always longed to do that sort of work, Nicky."

"I overheard Jeffries saying the other day that you were cut out for it," her friend confided. "She, of course, has no use for anyone who isn't flat out for surgery."

"I've always had the feeling that Sister Jeffries wasn't particularly fond of me," Lindsey mused, as she opened the door of the nurses' common room, "but I've never lost sleep over the fact or let it unduly depress me."

Molly chuckled.

"She's making the presentation tonight."

"Presentation?"

"Yes. Haven't I kept the secret admirably? You're to have a presentation." Molly's laughing eyes sobered. "It's just a small gift, Hammy—something to remember us by."

"As if I could ever forget you!" Lindsey said, her voice suddenly husky.

Molly thrust her into the room where a dozen girls in uniform were gathered in groups or reading at small tables set against the walls.

"Hullo, Hammy!" many of them greeted her eagerly. "How did the last operation go? They certainly did you well having Stewart Harvey on the job!"

"You'd almost think I'd been the patient!" Lindsey countered. "He was swift, cool and sure, as usual, and

7

Stewart Harvey doesn't see anything in an operating theatre but the iodined patch on the patients skull, so you needn't worry about his reactions over me being there!"

"What of *your* reactions, though?"

"I have none in the theatre—except the still-persistent desire to be sick, I don't think I'll ever get over that."

"There'll still be operations where you're going," someone warned

"I know. I'm hoping I may be put into the occupational wing, though I know I'd best prepare myself for a disappointment, in case not."

"You're lucky getting away from this hole. Where exactly is St. Ronan's?"

"Somewhere on the Kyles of Bute, I think. I haven't had my travelling instructions yet. I have a week's leave to take before I report."

"Lucky you!"

"I wish it were me."

"I certainly wouldn't like to be incarcerated in the Kyles of Bute. I'll expect to hear of your death by boredom, Hammy, in less than six months."

"It's kind of you to give me so long!" Lindsey moved towards the door. "I must tidy up before supper. Are you coming, Molly?"

Lindsey changed her wrapper and put on a fresh apron and was coming out of her room when Molly scuttled back along the corridor from hers. She was a small, bright girl whose one good feature was a pair of fine brown eyes which went oddly with her rust-colored hair and fair complexion, and she was often accused of chattering incessantly, although she was a good nurse and her few intimates knew that there were deeper channels for her thoughts on occasion.

"The bell's just gone. Not feeling nervous, are you? Jeffries won't say a word until after supper, so you'd best forget the presentation and make the most of your sausage and mash. It's sure to be sausage and mash on a Friday."

"I hope Jeffries won't be too long-winded," Lindsey said. "I'm expecting a long-distance call from Norman tonight."

"I thought he was in hospital?"

"I haven't had time to tell you," Lindsey explained hurriedly. "He's coming home." Her eyes darkened. "Evidently he's been invalided out. That breakdown he had in the spring seems to have left his nerves faulty, and

8

I don't suppose he'll be much good in the R.A.M.C., suffering from nerves. It's going to be a dreadful disappointment to him, Molly. He lived for his work."

"Will he take up practice again?"

The look of concern in Lindsey's eyes deepened.

"He wasn't practicing when he joined up. He had a hospital post. Someone once told Father he'd make a great surgeon one day." Her voice broke. "That was Norrie's ambition. We—it was a bit of a struggle for Mum and Dad to send him to the university," she went on to confess. "We weren't very wealthy, and Mother had been practically an invalid with arthritis for many years before she died. Norman didn't want to go at first, but we knew his heart was in it and he justified any sacrifices we made. He came through, if not brilliantly, with a very high percentage." She paused reflectively. "I suppose there are very few really brilliant students, and then they stand out for ever afterwards, like Stewart Harvey, for instance."

"Yes, I suppose they are few and far between," Molly agreed. "One can't imagine Stewart Harvey having had to struggle for anything, though. He's the sort of person that you'd know his background was secure as soon as you met him. He's got that *look* about him—remote, yet assured. I expect his people are wealthy enough."

"I don't know. Nobody seems to know much about him except that he's one of our coming men and, as such, there will always be an atmosphere about him and matrons and nurses will continue to stand in awe of him." Lindsey smiled, though not bitterly. "It's the done thing, I suppose, to place your chief consultant on a pedestal and bow the knee humbly as you approach!"

"With Stewart Harvey I don't mind, but some of the others. . . . That odious little Smerk man, for instance, just makes me boil!"

"Sh-h!" warned Lindsey. "Here comes our worshipper-in-chief!"

Sister Jeffries favored them with a bleak smile as they came abreast.

"Your last evening, Nurse," she remarked to Lindsey. "I hope you won't be late getting down to supper."

"We're on our way down now."

"I won't be many minutes." She smiled. "We have a little surprise for you, Nurse."

Molly and Lindsey walked on, more sedately now, conscious of their senior's eyes following along the corridor, and when they reached the dining-hall the benches along the tables were almost full, broken here and there by the odd vacancies where a nurse had already gone on duty.

A place had been reserved for Lindsey near the top of the table and she took her seat nervously, glad that Molly Nicholl found a seat almost facing her and that Sister Jeffries' vacant chair was some way up the table.

"Hammy," her neighbor remarked, "didn't you say you were going to St. Ronan's?"

"Yes. Why?"

"You're going to have a friend there." The speaker's black eyes sparkled in the glare of the electric light directly above her head. "Matron told Jeffries this morning that Stewart Harvey is going down there next month—as visiting consultant, I suppose. We're to see much less of him in consequence."

It was more than Lindsey could do to control the deep color which spread over her cheeks at the news.

"That will be very fortunate for St. Ronan's," she was able to say before Sister Jeffries came in to take her seat at the head of the table and say grace.

During the meal her nervousness increased, but when the Sister rose at last to command silence for 'a few brief words' she took herself in hand, forcing herself to an outward calmness which her fast-beating heart denied. She even managed a small and quite witty speech in reply to Sister's rather dry tribute as she handed over the green leather writing-case, but she was glad when the last good-byes had been said and she was alone with her friend in her own room, at last.

"It's only nine o'clock," Molly observed, glancing at the watch strapped to her wrist. "We've time for a stroll and perhaps a coffee at the Corner Shop. Feel like it?"

"I feel like a breath of fresh air," Lindsey agreed. "But there's Norman's 'phone call. I promised to wait for that."

"I'd forgotten. Suppose we wait in the hall? It can't be very long now."

The porter turned from the telephone booth as they descended the stairs, their coats loosely over their shoulders.

"Call for you, Nurse Hamilton."

"Oh, thanks, Joe. I won't be long, Nicky."

Molly Nicholl stood at the foot of the stairs waiting, and when her friend came out of the booth at last she was quick to recognize the troubled look in Lindsey's eyes.

She did not question her, however, waiting until a confidence should be offered, as was her way.

"Norman's not going to be the same," Lindsey said quietly, at last, turning into the main carriage-way, which led like a straight white stream between the dark trees of Kelvingrove. "I think I can guess the reason, too. He feels that he has been thrown back on us—if not exactly on the scrap heap, at least as a temporary responsibility. He's sound in wind and limb, of course, but I've a feeling he thinks he'll never operate again." She drew in a deep breath. "And I know just what that's going to mean to him."

"Perhaps it isn't as bad as you think," Molly encouraged. "He's probably got a stiff dose of depression, but he'll get over that. When does he get home?"

"Tomorrow. Almost as soon as I do."

"You'll be able to talk him out of it. You're good for people with the blues, Lindsey."

"I hope this is only 'the blues.' " Lindsey tried to smile in the starlight. "How about the coffee? Have we time?"

"Just, I think. Strange how we can always tuck away another meal in less than an hour after the hospital 'banquets'!"

Molly led the way into a small cafe where they were both well known and where they had spent many odd half-hours in free periods when there was not enough time to go farther afield, and they talked over the past year at the Alexandra, reviewing the days when their acquaintance had ripened into friendship, a friendship which neither wanted to see broken by this separation.

Since Molly would be on duty on the wards when Lindsey left the Infirmary next morning, their good-byes had to be said in Molly's room, and the final word was Lindsey's.

"My very first leave, Molly—we'll meet and swap experiences at the Corner Shop!"

Lightly she made the promise, but it was to be with a heavier heart that she kept it, for there were some things which remained locked in the secret places of that heart which she could not share even with Molly.

The week of her leave stretched before Lindsey and she viewed it with eager anticipation, although she realized that it would not be, strictly speaking, a holiday. Mrs. Birch, her father's cousin and housekeeper, had decided to visit relations at Dunbar, and she had just left the house when Lindsey arrived at Shawlands on the Saturday morning.

Ten minutes later her brother came up the path to the front door and she ran to meet him, standing in the vestibule while he went back to pay his taxi, and conscious, with a little sickening stab of anxiety, of the change in him. His uniform seemed to hang on him and there was no lightness in his step as he came up the short path again, his pale face thin and drawn and his eyes remote in spite of the smile on his lips.

"Hullo, Little-Un!" he greeted her in the well-remembered, bantering tone. "Got home before me, I see. Where's the Birch Tree, and why isn't she on the reception committee?"

"She decided to be received instead—by some relation in Dunbar, so you'll have to be content with me, at least till one o'clock when Dad gets in from the office."

She had spoken lightly, trying not to betray her concern for him, knowing that he might resent it being thrust immediately upon him.

"You'll do," he declared, giving her an impulsive hug. "If I had known you were all alone, we could have met in town and had a meal there."

"With all this junk?" She was helping him with his kit, trying not to remember that this must be all of it and probably the last time she would carry a khaki grip into his familiar room. "Can we put some of it in the hall cupboard? It will take up all your floor-space in here."

"I guess so. I'll have to get round to sorting it all out. Just now I haven't the energy."

The admission shocked her. Norman without energy, that vital, eager figure who had left them three years ago with a cheery smile and a wave of his hand as if he were just going round the next corner.

"I'll help you later," she promised, relieving him of his coat and the heavy Sam Browne which he had unbuckled, looking at it with a peculiar smile twisting his handsome mouth, as if he saw the shedding of it as a last symbol of his usefulness. "Are you desperately hungry," she hurried on to ask, "or can you hold out till Dad comes?"

"I can hold out," he said, putting thin hands on her shoulders and turning her to the light to look at her more fully ."You're looking well, Lindy. Hospital work seems to be agreeing with you all right."

"Probably because I like it so much. I told you in my last letter that I was leaving the Infirmary, didn't I? Do you know anything about St. Ronan's, Norrie? What sort of place it is? All I know is that it's one of newest and best-equipped hospitals we have up this way and that it's reputed to be easily the loneliest!"

"That shouldn't worry you much. You always liked the country. No, I don't know much about the latest hospitals. I've been a patient for the last three months, you know."

Her eyes met his steadily.

"You'll soon be well again, Norrie. Don't give up hope of a complete cure. It will come gradually. I know what a slow process it must seem, but you'll have good care here. The Birch Tree isn't so bad, and she's at her best when there's anyone sick around."

His hands dropped from her shoulders as he turned away, and she saw his lips tighten.

"I've no intention of sponging on the old man, even for a short while," he said firmly. "I'll get a job of some sort. I'm perfectly fit, or they wouldn't have discharged me yet."

"Then"—her eyes brightened—"you can go back?"

"Not exactly." He turned to face her. "You see, Lindy, it's not going to be so easy as that. I can't go back into surgery, I've lost my nerve. I'll never operate again."

"They've been very decent about it all," he went on. "They've offered me a clinical job here in Glasgow. I suppose I should be grateful. I am, in a way. As it is, I'm glad all the old man's sacrifices won't be entirely in vain. I can make something of myself yet."

He had spoken rapidly, and she knew he was talking to relieve the deeply rooted sense of loss which overshadowed his life and all his ambitions.

"You'll make it all right, Norrie," she said huskily. "This job—it will just be a new start. You'll pick up quickly once you're on the right road again."

He made no reply to that, and she sensed the scepticism to which he would not give expression and how deeply life had disappointed him.

Her father came in shortly after one o'clock, his lined face wreathed in smiles at sight of them both.

"You'll soon put on weight now you're back home," James Hamilton told his son cheerfully, trying to ignore the fear in his heart. "You'll not start work for a bit, though. We must arrange to get you into the country for a good rest. How would Dunbar suit you? Madge has some relations there who might be willing to take you.

I believe she said they ran a small boarding-house, and they'll be quiet enough now."

"I've got a half-promise of a job," Norman told him, rising. "It's here in Glasgow, so I'll be at home a good deal. It seems to me that the sooner I get into harness again the better. I've had six weeks in which to recuperate and I feel quite capable of holding down a job like this one. It's light enough, heaven knows."

Two days later he went for his interview. Lindsey awaited his return anxiously, running to the door at each summons of the bell, quite forgetful that he now possessed a latch-key. In the end he came through the close, entering the flat by the side door and calling to her quite cheerfully as she ran into the hall.

"Well, it's all over. I've got the job. Put on your hat and coat and we'll go out and celebrate."

"What about 'phoning Dad and meeting him in town for lunch?" Lindsey suggested. "He'll want to hear the good news right away. What is it, Norrie? Observation work?"

"More or less. I seem to be pretty good at taking temperatures and plotting a chart."

She put a sympathetic hand on his arm.

"Don't take it too hardly. It'll all come right yet. I know it will."

"I must try to have some of your faith—or is it just optimism?"

"I like to call it faith." She smiled at him as she tucked her nut-brown hair into her cap and drew on her gloves. "Who did you see? Anyone important?"

"The physician in charge, a Doctor Merrill. He was a genial old buffer, full of enthusiasm and in a flurry of excitement because they were having a visit from one of the big fellows. Seemingly Stewart Harvey takes an interest in this particular little clinic. His late chief established it on a small scale several years ago and Stewart Harvey is now its patron. It is his special charity and he does a good deal of work there. There's a home connected with it, too—somewhere in the country, and he operates there. . . ."

He paused, and Lindsey followed his tortured thoughts, forgetful for the moment of the surprise which the mention of Stewart Harvey's name had occasioned and the queer, uneven beating of her heart. Would this be a good thing for Norman, she wondered, working in the shadow of achievement such as he had longed for?

The thought pursued her through the remainder of that busy week when they went on long excursions into the country round Bearsden or out over the Fenwick moors, climbing on the high Campsie roads as far afield as Killearn, or walking almost to Kilmarnock, where they would be forced to capitulate and take a bus back home.

Norman's regret that he could not see her off to St. Ronan's at the end of the week was genuine. He had to report at eight o'clock and had left the flat as she was dressing. He had secured her a taxi, however, and her father went with her to the station.

"Write as soon as you can," he urged, "and I hope it's not going to be so long before you have leave again. I'll be missing you popping in now and then, girl!"

She kissed him tenderly.

"Norrie will be popping in instead," she reminded him. "I'll be writing often enough, I expect. There will be nothing much else to do. Take care of yourself, Dad."

"Norrie and I will take care of each other."

The journey by train to Wemyss Bay was a familiar one and she read the morning papers most of the way, but once on board the steamer and out upon the grey waters of the Firth she went on deck in spite of the fine drizzle of rain which disappointingly obscured the view, to walk up and down till they reached Rothesay, and thereafter her whole interest was given to her surroundings.

Looking ahead, she wondered where her destination would be. Could it be one of those lovely old houses built of stern grey stone and half-obscured in autumnal-garbed trees? Or was it farther inland, deep in the heart of some unseen glen?

A car would be waiting for her at the pierhead, she had been informed before leaving Glasgow, and she found it there when she got off the steamer and deposited her hand-luggage at the gates to pay the pier dues.

A tall girl approached, summing her up with a pair of candid blue eyes.

"Are you for St. Ronan's?" she asked. "I expect you are, since you're the only nurse on board."

Lindsey smiled.

"I seem to have an awful lot of luggage," she apologized. "You look fairly full up in the back there, too," she added, glancing at the boxes piled high in the rear seats of the little car.

"We'll manage somehow," the other returned. "I've been down collecting stores. St. Ronan's is fairly far out, and when a car comes down to the pier we generally find plenty waiting to go back."

Lindsey helped to stack her belongings on the boxes and got in beside the driver.

"I don't speak when I'm driving," she was informed. "It throws me off balance, somehow. One thing at a time, y'know, so you'll have to look around for yourself. as we go along. If there's anything you particularly want to know, though, you can sing out and I'll stop the car."

Lindsey was quite content with that. First contacts were generally a difficulty with her, but once the ice was broken she could be an interesting companion and a staunch friend, as Molly Nicholl had proved after an uneasy first week as Lindsey's room-mate at the Alexandra.

The country through which they travelled was densely wooded and the car ran silently over a veritable carpet of pine needles and fallen leaves, with here and there vivid glimpses of bright water where sun, struggling through the rain-clouds, set its glittering seal upon the Kyles.

"I'm going to love this place," she remarked aloud, and was not perturbed when her companion did not answer her.

They drove for half an hour at a good speed and then the car swung abruptly to the right down a private avenue between hedges of high, clipped yew and shining juniper until it slowed down before a stretch of the greenest park-land Lindsey had ever seen. The grass terminated at the water's edge, and behind them an old grey house slept quietly among the trees.

"Well, here's our 'haunt of ancient peace,' if you like things that way!" her companion remarked. "What do you think of it?"

"It's lovely. It's like a mediaeval castle!"

"Too like one for my taste!" The tall girl laughed. "I've got to take the car around now, but you can leave your luggage and it will be taken to your room later. I think you'd better go in and see Matron first. She'll be waiting with the stop-watch in her hand!"

Lindsey went in by the central doorway, finding herself in a vast entrance hall, arched and paved with stone and lighted by a beautiful mullioned window half-way up a massive oak staircase. She hesitated, and almost as if her presence had been sensed, an orderly came forward from the dim cavern beneath the stairs.

"You're waiting to see Matron?" he asked. "Will you come this way, please?"

She was conducted along a short passage-way to an oak door set in the end wall, and her guide knocked and waited.

"Come in."

The orderly opened the door, and Lindsey found herself in the presence of the Matron of St. Ronan's.

The woman sitting in the chair by the window rose as she entered, towering above her and making her feel nervous and ill at ease. She must have been at least six feet tall, with a superb carriage, and emitting an air of efficiency and criticism which was, to say the least of it, disconcerting. Lindsey felt, however, that this woman might be fair in her judgments, and knew that she had come from the Alexandra with a good record, which probably lay in the desk before the Matron of St. Ronan's at this very moment.

The interview was brief. Lindsey thought she had answered most of the questions put to her with reasonable intelligence, but there was a sense of relief and escape within her when she was finally dismissed.

"Nurse Granger will take you to your room," said Matron, indicating a fair-haired girl who had answered her summons on the bell on her desk. "She'll show you round, and you'll report to Sister Drummond in the morning. You'll be on day duty for your first week."

Lindsey followed her guide out of the main building, through a covered passage-way, and in at a swing door to a one-storeyed annex which had been recently built to accommodate the nurses. The common room was a cheerful place of bare, pine-lined walls and scrubbed floors, with a few rugs scattered here and there. The bedrooms

17

opened from the small, circular entrance hall, and when Lindsey had settled her few belongings in her own room, she went out in search of her guide.

Celia Granger greeted her with a smile that illuminated her plain, thin face and gave it a certain attraction.

"Come and meet everyone," she invited, drawing Lindsey towards the common-room doorway.

That first week at St. Ronan's became a confused memory to Lindsey. It seemed to her that all hospitals housed much the same types of her old colleagues at the Alexandra. Margery Wake, the pretty scatterbrain, who eluded detection over minor errors with a skill that was almost miraculous, had her opposite at the Alexandra in blue-eyed, vivacious Connie Forbes; Olive Menzies and Mary Green were model nurses who would gladden any matron's heart, their only interest being in their work, and Alicia Halton was the hard-featured, cynical counterpart of the Alexandra's Gwendoline Royce. There was Sheena Smith, known familiarly as "Smithy," who reminded her of Molly, and who she thought would make a sincere friend; and Florrie Webb, who had dropped her identity in that of "Spider." She thought, in fact, that she would like them all, with the possible exception of Edna Halton, Alicia's twin. Alike in outward appearance, the two girls cultivated an air of superiority in their different ways, but to Lindsey Alicia's cynicism was the least objectionable. Edna was patronizing, and she was heartily disliked in consequence, although one or two of the nurses had been awed into a pretence of admiration because it was generally known that their father was Bailie Halton the wealthy shipowner, and one of the governors of the Alexandra Infirmary.

Edna Halton had pointedly ignored Lindsey during that first week, which was her way with newcomers, and so it was with some surprise that Lindsey found herself waylaid by the tall, dark-haired nurse one morning as she was going on duty.

"You were at the Alexandra, weren't you?" Edna asked coldly.

Lindsey nodded.

"For over a year. It was wonderful experience."

"I suppose so." Edna considered social background a much more valuable asset than years of training. "You'd know Richard Stewart Harvey, then?"

"Not personally. I've seen him operate, of course. He was a visiting surgeon at the Alex."

"Yes, I know that. My father is one of the governors, and he and Richard have been friends for many years. It's really quite exciting to be going to have Richard here."

Lindsey did not know quite what to reply to this confession, and Edna favored her with a peculiar little patronizing smile and passed on.

"Well," said Sheena Smith, who had come along the corridor behind them in time to hear Edna's parting comment, "if that was meant as a warning that Stewart Harvey is Miss Halton's property, it was superfluous. No one could imagine an ordinary nurse daring to raise her eyes to anyone so remote and unapproachable as a visiting consultant!"

"I don't think he's actually unapproachable, Smithy," Lindsey returned thoughtfully. "He has a kindly manner with his patients and I've thought him quite unassuming. I think a good deal of this 'remoteness' where surgeons are concerned is mainly due to the attitude of our nursing higher-ups. Certainly there's a certain amount of respect due, but sometimes it's carried too far."

"It's not quite so bad here," confessed Sheena. "Of course, there's always an aura about visiting celebrities, and Stewart Harvey is a big shot, after all. His brother is here, you know," she added. "It's rather a sad case. He was in the R.A.F.—a pilot—and he crashed, smashing himself up rather badly. Stewart Harvey brought him here as an experiment, and he's over in occupational therapy just now, but it doesn't seem to be having a great deal of effect."

Suddenly Lindsey was thinking of Norman and the thought brought with it an acute feeling of sympathy for Stewart Harvey.

As they passed Matron's office she was surprised to be called into the sanctum.

"Ah, Nurse Hamilton, come in a minute, will you?" Matron signed a last report and turned to Lindsey, surveying her critically. "Nurse, I shall want you in the occupational wing tomorow morning. Sister Grey needs more help there, and I think you may prove the right type of person for the work. We have a special case there at present—Pilot Officer Harvey. His brother is one of our consultants, and I want you to help with the case while Nurse Beaton is on sick leave."

"I'll do my best, ma'am," Lindsey promised. "I have always taken a deep interest in that sort of work, though I have never had any practical experience."

"Better go across this afternoon and get settled in, then," she was told briskly. "We are expecting Mr. Stewart Harvey some time tomorrow, and Sister Grey won't want anyone to look like a new broom while he's going through the wards, so you'd better get acclimatized."

Lindsey's heart was suddenly beating fast and high in her breast. Here was the chance she had always wanted, the type of work she had long sought.

3

Lindsey's first few hours in the bright atmosphere of the accupational wing convinced her beyond all doubt that, here was the work for which her heart yearned, the work for which she had long known she was best suited.

"We have four very difficult cases," Sister Grey explained at the end of the day. "There is, of course, a case history behind each one, but often it is necessary to go further than that. Professor Baer is our regular consultant, but recently we have had Mr. Stewart Harvey here taking a great interest in our methods. He is the surgeon of course, but he looks upon this as 'after care,' the necessary follow-up of a difficult case."

Lindsey listened attentively as she gathered up the tools on the carpenters' benches.

"It's wonderful work," she acknowledged, "and most of these boys are so very young that surely even the difficult cases will respond in time?"

Emily Grey lifted a small fretwork saw, holding it between her shapely hands, and her eyes were suddenly remote.

"We have had failures," she admitted, "but the percentage of cures is encouragingly high."

"I see," Lindsey said quietly. "It's all in striking the right path, holding the interest."

"Fundamentally—yes. But there can be tortuous ways towards the right path. It isn't all straightforward, by any means. You have temperament—and often just temper! —to contend with, and heredity sometimes comes into the question. Experience of our difficult cases has been the greatest teacher, and you will learn by experience and the gift of patience."

She lay awake on her uncomfortable bed that night long after lights out, thinking of the new work which lay ahead, thinking of the men she had seen that day, men happy in their release from fear, and wondered about the 'difficult' cases, which she had not seen.

"Do you know anything about gardening, Nurse?" was Sister Grey's first question when she went on duty next morning.

"A little, but only as a amateur," Lindsey warned. "We have a little patch of garden at home where Dad grows roses."

"You might go down to the gardens this morning, I think." Emily Grey's manner proclaimed her absorption with another interest. "Things are running very smoothly there, and each of our patients has a small plot of his own which he runs entirely on his own lines." She glanced down at a list in her hand. "I want everything running absolutely smoothly this morning. Mr. Stewart Harvey is sure to look round. I'll leave you to see to the gardens, then, Nurse."

Lindsey turned away to find her cloak, for although it was sunny outside with all the appearance of warmth, there was a cold wind blowing from the north-east and the sea was fretted by little white-crested waves.

Going down to the small enclosure where several plots had been set out as an experiment she found two ardent gardeners busy at work. It seemed that this simple gardening might prove an introduction to the broader fields of marketing or even to an interest in farming in a bigger way, and in the sphere alone there was a wide choice of careers and a deepening fund of interest.

A man down on his knees on an old sack raised his fair head as she came forward. He was younger than he had appeared from the distance of the boundary hedge, and there was an arrogant lift to his head, though when he smiled his eyes revealed a gleam of light.

"Grubby work for a white apron, Nurse," he observed, surveying her with interest.

Lindsey smiled.

"I'm only supervising, this morning. When I really come to help I shall don overalls and look like the job!"

"Good for you!" He continued to study her keenly with the alert look of the deeply interested. "You're new, aren't you? Do you think you're going to like it here?"

21

"I think so. You see, I'm specially fond of gardens."

"Funny," he mused, "I wasn't until I saw how it all worked. I had always considered it an old man's job." He sat back on his heels, looking thoughtful, as if he had not attempted to put his experiences into words until now. "I believe—before I came here—I had the idea that the old maxim of 'what ye sow ye reap' was a bit out of date, but now—well, it's as if life and gardening were all mixed up. You've got to do the spade-work—to dig deep and plant true—before you can expect results. I never read Kipling much," he added with an apologetic grin. "and what I had to read at school went in one ear and out the other, but since I've been here I've had time to read—and to think." His face sobered and his sea-blue eyes were suddenly remote. "I had ideas about what my life should be like—the place the world owed me—and I kicked mightily against the pricks when things didn't work out quite so fine, and then someone put a spade in my hand and brought me down here, and I wasn't much use at first, because I didn't put my back into it, or very much interest. Then, in the rest-rooms I got to reading Kipling and that bit about some potting begonias and budding roses and those others that were 'hardly fit to trust with anything that grows.' . . ."

" 'But they can roll and trim the lawns and sift the sand and loam,' " quoted Lindsey softly, feeling deeply touched by his unexpected confession. "I'm glad," she added a little unsteadily, "that you found that out."

"Oh yes, it was all there. Kipling could put his finger on the quick pulse of living, even if some highbrows don't consider him an exceptionally good poet."

The rather arrogant lines of the young face were softened by his smile as he turned back to his plot.

"After I go out I'm putting what money I have left into market gardening," he said, after a pause in which he eased up the rich brown earth with a hoe. "When I think of all the money I have squandered. . . ."

Lindsey's heart beat more quickly as she went on from plot to plot, realizing that this thing was bigger than she had thought, and the next hour was in the nature of a revelation to her as she docketed her types in the orderly spaces of a tidy mind, deciding with swift insight exactly what approach would be most useful with each individual.

She came back to her Kipling enthusiast as the first warning bell for lunch rang through the quiet gardens, and

22

as she walked down the sheltered pathway she became aware of a fluttering white head-square on the far side of the yew hedge and Matron's voice raised in conversation with someone as yet unseen. Then, suddenly, the sound of a deeper voice reached her, a voice that was instantly familiar, and even before his tall figure appeared round the end of the hedge she knew that Richard Stewart Harvey was on his tour of inspection.

He came down the pathway behind his guide, his thoughtful eyes on the work going on in that quiet, sequestered acre, missing no detail of men or things, his interest in the experiment deep and genuine.

"This is a new departure, I think," she heard him say as she stood aside. "Your Sister-in-charge has just been telling me that she has had a good percentage of success with her gardens."

He had halted beside the young naval officer who had now risen to his feet and was confronting him over 'the glory of the garden.'

"You will have found the season wet for potatoes," he remarked. "What have you in there? Golden Wonder? Isn't it about time they were pitted?"

"I'm starting on them tomorrow morning," Ralph Hastings returned, his blue eyes eager with anticipation. "I've promised Matron the first boiling!"

Matron laughed with the ease which endeared her to all her patients, and warmed the heart of the young nurse standing in the background.

"I'm quite sure I shall never have tasted potatoes like them, even in my native Arran!" she returned nobly. "Mr. Stewart Harvey will be here for lunch again tomorrow, so he can also pass his opinion, Ralph."

Richard Stewart Harvey was smiling, and as he turned to walk farther along the gardens his eyes met two appreciative blue ones beneath a spotless coif. As he looked at Lindsey it seemed that he struggled with a memory.

Matron preceeded him along the well-kept paths, explaining and pausing here and there to let him have a word with her patients as the gardeners gathered up their tools and stored them in the potting sheds. When he followed her back to the house there was a thoughtful expression in his grey eyes, which remained there throughout lunch in her study, where they discussed the general affairs of the hospital, exchanging views and notes on results. At two o'clock he rose to go.

"I have some other work to attend to in the district," he explained, "but I shall be back tomorrow morning, and after that I shall probably be visiting you fairly frequently. I have been deeply interested by all you've had to show me here."

"I'm so sorry we hadn't a better report of your brother's condition to offer you," she returned, regretfully. "Nothing we seem to do will rouse him from that queer apathy, although Nurse Beaton did feel that she was getting somewhere with that handicraft idea of hers. He lost interest after the first design was completed, however—when it was all worked out to his satisfaction."

"It's rather a pity Nurse Beaton went on to the sick list," he remarked, a question forming in his eyes. "Perhaps there is someone else," he suggested.

The tall woman facing him regarded him with deepening interest. She had never been quite able to make up her mind about Stewart Harvey. He appeared remote at times, anxious to keep his dignity and his distance, while at others it occurred to her that he might quite easily be that rare thing, a shy and sensitive genius.

"I hope all this isn't inconveniencing you," he went on, "but I really think my brother would be better with a special nurse—someone who could be relied upon to appreciate the delicacy of his case, someone who would put everything into the effort, and, above all, someone with a definite fund of patience."

Although Lindsey Hamilton had been little more than a week at St Ronan's her name sprang immediately to the other woman's mind

"I think I have a suitable person in the wing now," she answered "I'll speak to Sister, and we can try Nurse Hamilton out. She appears the right type—capable, reliable, conscious of the importance of her work, and seemingly willing to put it first in order to achieve results. She came from the Alexandra in Glasgow a week ago, but you wouldn't remember her. . . ."

"We'll try your experiment, Matron," he said and almost immediately on his departure Lindsey found herself summoned to the office and was given her instructions.

"This is a most difficult case, Nurse, you understand? I want results if it is humanly possible to get them, and you will keep in touch with Sister, reporting even the slightest improvement."

"Yes, ma'am." Lindsey turned to the door. "Sister thought I should go on duty right away."

"If you've had your tea."

"I haven't, ma'am."

"Then, go along to the dining-hall now. You can report to Sister immediately afterwards."

Lindsey went swiftly through the connecting passage-way to the big, raftered dining-room where splendid paintings still hung upon the walls as they had done when the owner to St. Ronan's had lived there himself, to find most of the other nurses already seated before the plain deal tables which looked so incongruous in that place of shadows and dim gilt frames. The conversation at the tables appeared to be general, and as she took her usual place next to Sheena Smith, she heard her own name mentioned. Sheena looked round at that moment and made room for her.

"Well," the dauntless Smithy addressed the others at the long table, "here's Lindy now. You can ask her, and so satisfy your curious little souls!"

Lindsey looked round.

"Ask me what?"

"If it's true you're going down to occupational in Beatons' place—to be special for Pilot-Officer Harvey at the request of his brother?"

In spite of every effort to control it, a deep color surged up into Lindsey's cheeks.

"Not at Mr. Stewart Harvey's request, I'm sure," she said, her voice betraying something of her confusion. "I don't really know why Matron picked me for the job, unless it was because I'm such a duffer in the operating theatre, and not quite quick enough on the wards."

"You don't believe that, of course!" It was Edna Halton's coolly detached voice which broke into the silence before any of the others could answer. "Are you suggesting that they sent you down from the Alexandra for incompetence?"

The question held all the sting of suggestion, and Lindsey had to bite her lip to stem a crushing retort. What was the use of making bad blood right away over one girl's attitude when her work in the other wing would isolate her from them all except at meal-times?

"Well," said Vera Gower, "I think it's most romantic if he did!" Everything was 'romantic' to Vera. "He's just the sort of man to remember if a nurse looked capable or not, and of course, Lindsey's worked with him before."

25

"But not in a capacity in which he would be likely to remember me, far less recommend me," Lindsey told her, reaching for a slice of thinly jammed bread.

"Well," Katherine Bannerman remarked, "if Nurse Hamilton knows her work and does it efficiently, why are we arguing about the change—if we are arguing?" Katherine, plain, dark-haired and almost over-studious, was known in the dormitories as 'Florence' because, in Smithy's words, she never failed to 'hold aloft the lamp.' "How can it possibly matter," she concluded, "whether or not it was Mr. Stewart Harvey who recommended her?"

The remark brought a little silence in its wake, in which Smithy's grin broadened and she beamed upon Edna Halton, who had risen from the table, scraping her chair back with an impatient movement.

"It's nice to know you all seem so pleased about it," the high, sarcastic voice of Mae Winton put in at last. "Personally, *I* wouldn't like to discover that I had been chosen for a special job because some man favored me."

"There's not much fear," Smithy declared cruelly, although her enjoyment was mostly at Edna's discomfort, "unless he were blind and stone deaf!"

"It's something though," continued Nurse Winton, ignoring Sheena's rudeness with lofty disdain, "that there's one of us he does like. I suppose that will always be something to brighten our days—or, at least, Nurse Hamilton's!"

Lindsey, with her experience of these unforseen little gales which invariably blow up when a number of people of vastly differing temperaments are cloistered together for a long period without sufficient respite, ate the remainder of her meal in silence and, with a word to Sheena, went swiftly back to the occupational wing.

Sister Grey was waiting for her, standing at the open doorway leading into a long conservatory, where peach-trees climbed the stone wall of the house and big, feathery chrysanthemums stood in pots, making a sea of white and bronze and gold at the far end where a second doorway led out into the garden.

At this far end a slim figure sat in a cane chair, his legs thrust out on the low rest in a curiously unrelaxed attitude that gave his whole body the appearance of tension. His back was towards them and only the top of a dark curly head was to be seen, yet Lindsey thought that there was something familiar about the shape of it, something that brought a whiff of ether and disinfectants even into that flower-scented atmosphere, so strong was her memory of the Alexandra and Richard Stewart Harvey's dominating personality.

This, then, was his brother. She followed Emily Grey's meagre figure down the conservatory with a strange trepidation born of nervousness, and was conscious that her patient did not stir as they approached, though he must have been aware of their presence.

"This is your new nurse," the sister said brightly, as she came round the chair. "Unfortunately, Nurse Beaton has contracted pneumonia on top of the other trouble, and won't be back on duty for some time, but you'll soon get to know and like Nurse Hamilton. She has come from Glasgow—from the Alexandra—to be with us a time."

To all this there was no reply, and as if she had hardly expected one, Emily Grey moved quietly away leaving Lindsey alone with her new charge.

For a moment she hesitated, exceedingly conscious of her nervousness and the sudden knowledge that she was ill-equipped to deal with these cases, and then she moved resolutely forward so that they came face to face.

His was a handsome face, with long, clean lines and straight, dark brows over fine eyes whose expression was marred at the moment by a look which hovered between impatience and actual resentment. The lips, she noticed, were close set and the chin determined, and there were lines about both eyes and mouth which were the tell-tale marks of pain. A sudden swift rush of pity filled her heart, sweeping down the barriers which might have been erected by his first remark.

"I wonder why they can't leave me alone. I'm heartily sick of special this and special that, and now they saddle me with another 'special' nurse." He eyed her fiercely. "Can't they see that all I want is to get back inside a 'plane again!" Suddenly he began to laugh with cynical force. "I suppose they can see, and it's considered kind of them not to tell me I never shall, but their kindness is utterly lost on me. I know I'm finished! If they only knew how much 'kinder' it would be to tell the truth—that I'm out for the count— . . ."

"But you're not out for the count." Lindsey's voice was quiet, but it held firmness, too. "You only *think* you are, and perhaps you feel a little sorry for yourself, as I probably should do if I had lost something in life that I had cared so much about. . . ."

She hesitated, and he said bluntly, lifting the book he had been reading when she had come into the conservatory:

"You don't know what you're talking about. A woman's life can't be cut up like this. It's foolishness attempting to draw comparisons."

"Not always." She stooped to pick up some magazines and a newspaper which had fallen from the paper-rest on his chair. "Some women have achieved great things—and known frustration, and others have faced what you are experiencing now by just the loss of someone near and dear to them. It isn't an individual experience, as I see it."

"Well," he asked bitingly when she hesitated, "why don't you go on? Surely the next part of your charming little speech should point out that such disappointment—such frustration—must be conquered? 'It *can* be conquered, if only we have the will!' Isn't that it? Well"—dryly—"I haven't the will, and I should have thought that would have been an end to it."

She put a hand on his arm.

"Lieutenant Harvey, you're young." It seemed ridiculous that she should be saying this to him when, by terrible experience, the years had been stamped so clearly on his face, yet she knew he was little more than twenty-three.

"And I have all my life before me," he suggested. "For what?"

"To live to the full. Perhaps in a different way than that in which you had planned it, but it is not always by our own choosing that we achieve completeness in life."

"Who taught you all this?" he asked derisively. "Or have you been reading your text-books, word for word?"

Lindsey flushed.

"I'm new to this work," she confessed, meeting the rebellious eyes squarely. "I'm trying to understand."

"You never will. A woman could never understand."

"Perhaps you are wrong there," Lindsey said, without moving. "Perhaps if you had given someone a chance to show that they understood. . . ."

His eyes met hers, still resentful and faintly derisive, though somewhere in them was a vaguely questioning look.

"Why should I?" he asked. "Women haven't much time for misfits."

"You thought that flying might become your life's work?" she asked, ignoring his remark.

"I planned it that way."

"And now your horizon has gone a little grey?"

"Grey? It's gone completely black!"

"I'm sorry."

He laughed at that, bitterly.

"Why should you be? I'm only a case to you, a pretty hopeless case, and perhaps I should warn you right away that my brother has done all he can for me, and what Rick can't do must be pretty hopeless."

"Your brother is a brilliant surgeon."

"You know him?"—with a little more interest.

"Not personally."

"Of course, you came from the Alexandra. Forgive me for over-looking the fact, after Sister's efforts on your behalf." He smiled, and it was not quite the mirthless thing which had flitted across the mask of his face when they were discussing more personal issues, but something warmer that proclaimed his deep attachment to his older brother. "Rick was always the brilliant member of our family. He left us all far behind at school without being a complete bookworm and a bore, which is no small achievement. I remember the first year he was the Arnott prizeman, how proud we all were of him, and how quietly he took his success."

Lindsey's eyes were fixed on a point slightly above the dark head.

"Don't you think that it must be a great disappointment to your brother to feel that he can't complete your cure?" she suggested boldly.

He looked at her sharply, the old suspicion and bitterness flying back to his eyes.

"He's done his part. I guess I owe what I have left of life to his surgical skill, but I won't submit to another operation, and—we're not going to discuss it, if you please. It's a complete waste of time, I assure you—your time as well as mine."

It was as if a door had been deliberately and not too politely closed in her face, but through that door he had permitted her to see—unwittingly—a glimpse of something worth while, and she meant to search until she found the key which would unlock it for her again.

Strange, she mused, as she turned away to prepare his tea-tray, how she felt so convinced that she would one day find it!

The days passed slowly for Lindsey after that, almost as slowly as they did for her patient, and never by word or indication did Douglas Harvey recall that first conversation in the conservatory. He appeared to view life impartially, without taking a great deal of interest in anything apart from the books of which there was an endless supply, and seeming almost to resent the intrusion of the other patients.

For the most part Douglas sat outside in the sheltered loggia behind the conservatory, and although Lindsey did her best to introduce various subjects in a covert manner that would give no indication as to where they led, she knew that she had not even gained an inch of ground since that disappointing first contact.

At times she even thought that he was endeavouring to be so trying that the whole staff would lose patience and he would be left to go his own way, which, she realized, wasn't a very clearly defined way. But she carried before her the word 'Patience' emblazoned on a little silver shield and would not let him have his way.

She had been in the wing a fortnight before the personal note crept into his voice again as he asked, apropos of nothing, while they sat reading in the sheltered end of the loggia one afternoon:

"Have you always been a nurse?"

"Only for the past two years. Before that I was at home looking after an invalid mother."

He raised his eyes from his book, veiling the fleeting look of interest in them almost immediately.

"So that's where you get your amazing fund of patience from."

"Sometimes I don't consider myself very patient."

"That's why you were chosen for this job."

She flushed, and he laughed abruptly.

"I've had about six different nurses since I came here, all exemplary women, but none of them able to stay the pace, with the possible exception of Nurse Beaton, and if she had gone down with nervous prostration instead of pneumonia, I should not have been surprised." Again he flashed her that keenly observant look. "How much longer do you intend to stand your ground?"

"I don't consider it so much standing my ground as performing my duty," Lindsey told him easily. "I like the work."

"Shut up here with me when you might be in the classrooms making fretwork toys for Santa Claus or out in the grounds picking weeds?"

"It doesn't very much matter what one does."

"Will you tell me that you don't think your talents could be used to better advantage elsewhere?"

"I don't think so. Neither does Matron."

"She's pleased with me! Because I haven't had a black mood for more than a fortnight? Incidentally, since you came on the scene, but I can assure you that it is nothing more than coincidence. Where are you going?"—since Lindsey had risen from the seat by his side and was preparing to move away.

"To tidy up in the library."

"Are you always as methodical as you seem to be in the library? I suspect you have a depressingly tidy mind—everything and everybody neatly docketed."

"Eventually I suppose I do 'docket' people," she admitted, putting a new book where he could reach it without rising, "but I never place people on first acquaintance."

"Have you known me long enough to place me yet?" he asked unexpectedly, and then, presumably regretting the impulse, he added with unnecessary force: "Not that it matters two hoots, since it probably wouldn't interest me, anyway."

"Probably not," Lindsey agreed, walking away with the knowledge that he had raised himself on his elbow in order to look at her.

Making her way to the library, she was able to read there in comparative seclusion the letter which had come that morning from her father. He was worried about Norman, he confessed after the usual greetings. His son, he believed, was 'not himself these days.' It was a thousand pities that his health had suffered such a set-back. Nerves were a queer thing; you didn't know you had any until something went wrong with the system and then they made up for lost time. He didn't know whether Norman was happy in his new job or not. He said he was, but there was 'a something.' . . .

Lindsey, deeply aware of the nature of that 'something,' felt her heart contract with pain in sympathy with his disappointment, a disappointment that was being so gallantly hidden. Her mind turned sharply away from comparisons as she thought of Douglas Harvey. Their cases were not parallels. Norman had, at least, something of his old work left to him, though what it meant to see all his ambitions in the field of surgery scattered by the force of an adverse wind was well known to her.

She refolded her letter, turning to the task of arranging books which had been hurriedly replaced, and found herself smiling at the thought of Douglas Harvey's accusation about her 'tidy' mind.

When she went back to find him he was standing at the door of the conservatory pretending not to be waiting for her while he leaned heavily on his stick.

"I'm going for a walk," he intimated bluntly.

"If you can wait two seconds till I get my cloak, I'll come with you," she suggested.

"I don't need a watchdog."

"Not when you can growl like that!" she agreed.

He was still waiting however, when she came back, and he fell into step with her, although he did not speak more than a dozen words to her as they traversed the wide green slope that went downwards to the sea. Avoiding the gardens by his expressed desire, they returned to the house by the main avenue in time to see a car drawing up at the main entrance.

Two men got out, and Lindsey's eyes were suddenly chained to their tall figures as they approached the steps.

"Hullo!" her companion exclaimed, "there's old Rick! Now that I come to remember, he said he might be down today." He looked sharply at Lindsey, who seemed rooted to the spot. "What's the matter? Have you recognized someone?"

She nodded.

"The other fellow?" he asked almost sharply. "Who is he?"

"My brother."

It was Norman, there on the steps of St. Ronan's with Stewart Harvey, talking and smiling to the older man as if they had already become friends. Her heart suddenly contracted with overwhelming happiness, bounding forward from the moment when it had seemed to stop completely, and as they moved forward Richard Stewart Harvey turned on the top step and saw them.

He came swiftly down the steps again to greet his brother, while Norman, recognizing Lindsey, smiled his greetings from where he stood.

"Well, old chap, it's good to see you again," the young surgeon said. "I've brought some books I thought you'd like to read and the tobacco you asked for." No direct reference to the state of his patients' health, Lindsey noticed, although the keen grey eyes probably saw all that was necessary at a glance. "I've brought a friend down with me this trip, a colleague of mine, and I'd like you to meet him." He turned towards Norman, who had moved down the steps. "Doctor Hamilton—my brother."

"Another doctor?" Douglas' frown was ungracious, although his eyes rested on Norman's face a fraction of a second longer than they generally did when presented to a stranger. "The name seems to be in the air," he added dryly, turning to where Lindsey stood in the background. "My nurse, is one of the Hamilton clan."

"The same clan, as a matter of fact," Norman laughed easily. "I had no idea my sister would be nursing you, though I had certainly hoped to meet her."

Richard Stewart Harvey turned towards Lindsey and was holding out his hand.

"I, also, have been wondering if we'd meet, Nurse Hamilton," he said. "But now I know we have already met, on two previous occasions, I'm sure."

The grave friendly smile in the well-remembered grey eyes set Lindsey completely at her ease.

"I worked at the Alexandra for a year," she said, "and I have watched you operate on several occasions."

"From a front seat in the stalls," he laughed; but his glance had gone quickly to Norman when she had mentioned his surgical work and she knew instantly that he had gained her brother's confidence.

"Were you going in?" he asked Douglas, who seemed to have lost interest in the conversation.

"I suppose we were. It must be almost time for tea."

"I must pay my respects to Matron," the young surgeon said. "Will you come along, Hamilton? I'd better introduce you in orthodox style since you'll probably be coming down here quite a lot, and not always under my wing." He turned back to his brother. "I'd like to have tea with you, Doug., old man. Do you think you could hold out till I put the suggestion to the lady in command?"

33

"An hour is neither here nor there in this place," Douglas answered briefly.

"We won't keep you waiting an hour. I'm sure Hamilton, here, is ravenous after our journey down!"

They went off, Norman grinning back at Lindsey and looking happier than she would have believed possible in so short a time, although he probably would have termed himself a 'surgeon's lackey,' with a wry smile that sought to minimize his bitter disappointment. Lindsey was convinced, however, that it was not in this capacity that Stewart Harvey had taken him up, and she wondered, hopefully, what would come out of this unexpected friendship. That it was a genuine friendship, she realized beyond any shadow of a doubt, and that no finer guiding influence could have come Norman's way on his journey back to normal was also apparent to her eager eyes.

"Well, do we move, or are we fixtures here?" her patient asked sharply. "I suppose we can count Matron in on our tea-party now when she has a stranger to impress. You didn't tell me that you had a brother in the profession and that he knew Rick."

"I had no idea that your brother had taken an interest in Norman," Lindsey said, as they went back to the small private room in the west wing where the tea-tray had already been carried in and stood on an occasional table near the one comfortable arm-chair beside the fire. "I knew, of course, that your brother consulted at the clinic where Norman was sent."

Douglas prowled to the window, coming back to stand over the tea-tray.

"He's not the fellow Rick told me about who was invalided out of the Army, is he?—Nerves all to pieces, or something like that?"

"Yes, he had a complete breakdown, and even now he is only partially recovered."

Douglas Harvey's sudden laugh sounded through the quiet room like the crack of a whip.

"That's probably as far as he'll ever get—partially."

"I hope not."

"You're looking for a miracle. Do you believe in miracles?"

"Miracles of science are happening every day," Lindsey declared, "and there are miracles with which science has nothing to do. Even in this hard, modern world we are often confronted with them, perhaps more in the operat-

34

ing theatre than anywhere else. My brother," she added huskily, "believes that he will never operate again. The loss to a surgeon of his confidence in himself—his nerve— is a terrible handicap, and Norman wanted to be a surgeon from the moment he was old enough to think about these things."

Douglas received this information in silence while Lindsey plugged in the electric kettle and went to find the necessary extra cups and saucers in the event of Matron honoring the tea party.

When she came back along the corridor with them on a tray, Richard Stewart Harvey was standing in the doorway, his tall, broad-shouldered frame filling up the square of it, as she had seen him stand so many times in the doorway of the little anteroom at the Alexandra.

"If you'll excuse me?" she murmured, and instantly he turned, taking the tray from her, a little to Lindsey's dismay when she encountered Matron's eagle eye at the other side of the room. She was in conversation with Norman, while Douglas stood leaning one arm along the low brick mantelpiece with that air of being remote from all that was going on around him which could have been so exasperating if it were not so infinitely pathetic.

"You can infuse the tea now, Nurse," Matron said briskly, and Lindsey performed her task and withdrew, hoping that the tea-party and the fresh contacts would cheer her patient up a little, and wondering if she would be able to have a word alone with Norman before he left.

She was summoned back to the private sitting-room less than an hour later by a rather imperious ring of Douglas Harvey's bell, although it was his brother who met her in the doorway.

"We are going for a short stroll in the grounds, Nurse," he said. "I wonder if you will bring a warm coat for my brother."

"Certainly. It's chillier now. I'll get one right away."

When she came back into the room she saw that Matron had gone, probably on her late afternoon round of inspection before dinner, and she was surprised that Stewart Harvey had not been persuaded to accompany her. Probably he had come mainly to see his brother, however. She held out the coat for her patient.

"You'd better tag along, Nurse, just to complete the picture," said Douglas, though not quite so ungraciously as he had spoken previously, and it seemed that he had been sustaining some sort of conversation with Norman, because he walked on a little way ahead with her brother, leaving slightly embarrassed Lindsey to bring up the rear with the young surgeon.

"You would have gone out with my brother in the ordinary way?" he asked in a friendly tone which put her instantly at her ease. "I believe a special nurse is really necessary at this stage," he went on as they moved through the conservatory and Lindsey slipped her cloak over her shoulders. "I'm glad I've been given this opportunity for a few words with you in person, Nurse Hamilton. My brother's case is not in any way a straightforward one. He was always rather 'difficult,' to use a hackneyed word these days, and he has suffered a crushing disappointment. I know," he added swiftly, "that there are thousands like him even worse off, but that unfortunately doesn't make matters any easier for Douglas. He has always been the impulsive, go-ahead type, and I regret most deeply that some of his finer characteristics—true humor and a sense of fun, spontaneous kindness and light heartedness—have been submerged by this disaster."

"But surely only temporarily?" Lindsey said quickly. "This just couldn't be all life has to hold for him."

"I hope not." He drew a deep breath. "It has been the greatest disappointment of my career not to have been able to effect a complete cure; but some cures are not brought about through surgery alone. There are some instruments more delicate even than the knife, and the problem of mental ill-health is, in some ways, one of the greatest and most complicated with which we have to deal. Unfortunately, psychiatry has been handicapped by the extravagant claims of some of its devotees, but it has also a fund of established knowledge to offer, and we are endeavouring to probe even further here at St. Ronan's."

"There's so much being done," Lindsey said eagerly. "This work—even the briefest detail of it—is the most engrossing I have ever known. Surely, somewhere, there will be a cure for your brother, release from his unfortunate bondage."

"I believe," he said slowly, "that Douglas' case is one of a lack of adequate adaptation to life. He has been obsessed by an idea—the desire to make his mark as a flyer—and he can't let go. All this adds up to mental conflict of the most serious kind and here we have our most important factor as far as occupational therapy is concerned. If

36

it is going to answer at all, it must give him that other interest, and with Douglas it will have to be an all-absorbing interest."

"So far we have found only the reason for the conflict," Lindsey mused, so deeply engrossed that she had ceased to feel awkward or even shy in this man's presence. "And so far there has been very little evidence that the symptoms have been even diminished."

He considered this for a moment.

"I wondered when I first saw him walking in the garden this afternoon if there wasn't just a show of interest." He paused, and she looked round to find him gazing down at her. "It was obvious that the best general test of mental health is sustained capacity for activity and interest, and that's what we must develop for him in some way."

He seemed to underline the last three words with quiet deliberation, yet Lindsey knew that to be the whole idea behind occupational therapy—interest, adaptability, and the right guidance.

"It will be a stiff, uphill fight." He halted at the top of the incline leading down to the shore, turning to face her more fully. "May I say that I am glad he has been entrusted to your care, Nurse, and you will understand if I add a warning that I do not think the personal touch would be very beneficial just now."

A quick color flooded Lindsey's cheeks, but her eyes remained steadily on his.

"I have been trained as a nurse," she said quietly and without resentment, because the warmth of being taken into his confidence far outweighed any other feeling.

"I am more grateful than I can say for all the interest that has been taken in my brother here at St. Ronan's," he continued after a brief pause. "Here in the quiet of those hills one could very well let life go past for a while." He smiled at her, and again she saw what seemed a weight of weariness lifted from his spirit. "We are lucky to have such places as this put at our disposal."

"Have you seen our home farm?" Lindsey asked. "It is run on expert lines, and some prizes have come St. Ronan's way this year, I believe."

"So Matron tells me, and I'm very interested in farming," he added on a more personal note. "It is a real treat to see everything run so expertly as it is here."

He made a movement to walk on and they followed Norman and Douglas to stand on a rocky ledge overlooking the sea, where the spray was like fine rain. They stood smoking contentedly, revelling in the salt tang in the wind and the exhilarating feeling produced by the walk in the keen air.

"This is a grand place, Lindy!" Norman exclaimed. "I'm glad I've had this opportunity to come down and see you at work."

"It won't be the last one," Stewart Harvey remarked, and Lindsey caught the light which gleamed suddenly in her brother's eyes before doubt extinguished it again.

"Where are you going from here?" Douglas asked, as they walked back together over the short, tufty grass.

"We have another call to make before we go back to Glasgow." The young surgeon glanced at his watch. "Which means we must be pushing off now. I had no idea how late it was, Hamilton," he added, turning to Norman.

He put a friendly hand on Norman's shoulder; and some heaviness that was in Lindsey's heart when she thought of her brother was lightened as she watched them drive away together.

CHAPTER TWO

I

As IF BY sudden reaction, Douglas Harvey dropped into a period of what he chose to call 'black moods,' and Lindsey was to realize, perhaps for the first time in her whole career, how greatly the mental state can affect the physical. He lay for long periods of each day relaxed and lifeless looking, neither caring to read nor talk, and rejecting all suggestions from all comers.

Lindsey's attempts to entice him into the grounds met with blank refusals or frequently no answer at all, and then, without warning, he would be up and away, so that when she followed at a discreet distance she would often find him a considerable distance from the house, down on the shore, perhaps, beyond observation from St. Ronan's many windows, or deep in the heart of the wood that covered the hill behind the home farm. And always there would be that brooding look in his eyes, a dark look that held her sullen fear.

His reaction to her appearance was pretty much the same on each occasion. There was resentment and impatience, which would sometimes change to cynical tolerance of her as the watchdog and sometimes flared to unrestrained anger.

Of the two moods Lindsey thought that she preferred the latter, because it was at least a quick, spontaneous emotion, burning through that soul-obscuring veneer of apathy with which she could do nothing.

"How is the special patient progressing?" she was frequently asked at meals, but she felt that she could not discuss Douglas Harvey in the crowded dining-hall where some of the nurses' remarks were often of the most flippant kind.

"You'll be Sister-in-charge through there before you know where you are," she was told sarcastically on one occasion. "I hear Matron has a very high opinion of the work you are doing," Mae Winter continued in her high-pitched voice, "and it's going some to be pleasing her, especially when a consultant's brother is at stake."

Lindsey's chin went up and a little spark of anger kindled in her eyes.

"It wouldn't make the slightest difference to Matron who my patient was," she averred. " 'Special' in the sense means a special case, not a special individual."

"You don't say, Nurse!" The mocking voice had a bitter cut in it, the sting of childish anger. "Don't tell me you hadn't a few strings to pull when you came down here, not after walking round the grounds with Stewart Harvey and your brother the other day."

Lindsey was conscious of a pair of hard blue eyes levelled upon her from the other side of the table, and knew that Edna Halton, who had appeared absorbed in her breakfast since she had come in at eight o'clock, had looked up from her plate and was fixing her with a questioning stare.

"My brother has only been assisting Mr. Stewart Harvey for the past fortnight," she returned coldly.

"That's one of your 'strings' cut, Winter!" Sheena Smith put in between spoonfuls of porridge. "Pass the milk, if you please, Nurse Halton," she grinned, adding in an aside to Lindsey: "It has probably turned sour now. Just look at Halton's face!"

"I had no idea you were personally acquainted with Richard," Edna said frigidly, addressing Lindsey while completely ignoring the grinning Smithy. "The other day you practically told me you had never met."

"Which was the truth at the time," said Lindsey with dignity. "My brother introduced us."

"Well, what does it matter, anyway?" interrupted Vera Gower, attacking a last slice of bread and margarine. "There are sixty-odd patients in the hospital, so why argue over one? I'm sure I don't envy Lindsey her job with Pilot-Officer Harvey, though he's most devastatingly handsome to *look* at. Eva Beaton told me he had a dreadful temper and sulked for days on end."

Lindsey rose from the table feeling upset and wishing that she had not given way to that little gust of anger, even though it had been provoked. "Patience," Matron had said, and she couldn't even be patient with a jealous colleague, for it was no secret that Mae Winter had fancied the job in the occupational ward as Douglas Harvey's nurse.

"Never mind them, Hammy," said Sheena Smith, as they went down the corridor together to their respective wards. "Winter's pipped because she wanted occupational and no night duty. She's as lazy as they come, that girl, and her cheap brand of sarcasm makes me want to scream. Who said it was the poorest form of wit? Whoever it was, I'd like to shake hands with him! Is the Harvey boy really sulky?" she ran on without pause, which was her way. "I thought you were getting on famously with him when I saw you both out in the grounds so much."

"I was, but there are relapses, Sheena. Mae Winter just doesn't understand. It's the most tragic experience, and I want to help all I can. If I could only do something for him, something that would jerk him out of that dreadful apathy."

"Aren't there accepted ideas—all sorts of vocational suggestions constantly being put forward?"

"Yes, but that brick wall of apathy must be broken down first, and it's just that very wall that we are up against now." She smiled. "But don't worry. It'll come right somehow. I feel it in my bones. Are you going to the dance tonight?"

"I hope so. I'm on the list, if I don't blot my chart before then and now! Are you?"

"I'd like to, if I can get away."

"Read him his bedtime story an hour earlier," Sheena advised, disappearing through the doorway of the main ward.

Lindsey went about her own duties, going into Douglas Harvey's room at ten o'clock to find him in bed, though not asleep. She crossed to the window, drawing the curtains farther apart to look out.

"Aren't you going to get up?"

"What's the use? I can read in bed."

"If your leg isn't paining you, you should get up. Your leg's the only excuse you can make for staying in bed these days."

"Are you giving orders?"

"Yes."

"And if I refuse to obey them?"

She turned to look at him.

"You won't refuse, simply because you know you won't be unsporting enough to let Matron come down on me like a ton of bricks."

"Being 'sporting,' as you call it, doesn't apply here."

"No?" She looked surprised, her eyebrows slightly raised. "Do you know, I always thought it belonged everywhere, from when we first learned to own up about who dipped the sugar spoon in the jam to taking it on the chin for the other fellow when a 'plane crashed, for instance."

"You don't know what you're talking about"—surlily. "I didn't 'take it on the chin' for anyone."

"You brought your 'plane down when you could have baled out with the rest because you saw that it would crash on a coastal town."

He looked angry and uncomfortable.

"I can't see what that has to do with getting out of bed because it's time for you to fuss around tucking in corners and setting pillows at the prescribed angle."

"It hasn't anything to do with it, though it did crop up over the word 'sporting,' didn't it? I thought you wouldn't let me down."

She turned away, going quietly from the room, but before she had passed out of earshot along the corridor, she heard the bed creak and knew that he was scruffling about on the floor for his slippers. When she returned he was shaving, glaring at himself in the mirror above the wash-hand basin, but he went out without speaking, and to her surprise she found him in the library an hour later, scrutinizing the book titles along a high shelf, the scowl still marring his brow, though it had chased that vague look out of his eyes for a moment.

Leaving him alone, she went to look at some tapestry work which had been copied from a model screen in one of the window recesses. Since her arrival in the occupational therapy wing this work had held a fascination for her, and she had been eager to learn the intricate art of weaving those delicate pictures which could be as faith-

42

ful to life and detail as any that brush might apply to canvas.

In her spare time she had started a little screen of her own, a copy of an old sampler with a few variations which she considered improved the general design, and she picked it up now, comparing it with the more advanced work of a man who was soon to leave St. Ronan's to take up a situation in a large textile factory in the Midlands.

She did not see Douglas again until after the midday meal when she went into the conservatory to find him sitting in his usual chair gazing into space.

"Book not too interesting?" she asked.

"It will do." He opened it, pretending to read while she produced her frame and prepared to work on the unfinished corner of the screen. "Have you been bitten by the desire for employment in a textile factory, or has the work here merely driven you to try something else?"

"Neither. This is in the nature of a recreation. I'm not an expert knitter, and endless sewing tires me."

"You surprise me. I believed you possessed of all the womanly virtues."

"I hope you are not too greatly disillusioned."

He did not answer that, lowering his eyes to the printed page again, but presently she saw him move restlessly and lay his book aside, as if it had failed to hold his interest. She worked on, not wholly absorbed in her task, because she was aware that he rose and crossed the room, making a wide and unnecessary detour before he came back to stand behind her chair.

"What's this going to be?" he asked when he had studied the little picture for a while. "This hazy area in the corner here, I mean."

"A group of trees." She put her head on one side, considering. "Beech, I should think. Beeches in early autumn when they first begin to turn a tawny gold."

"Your ploughed field will be wrong, then"—dryly. "You'd better stook corn on it."

"It isn't ploughed, it's stubble, but I've to work it in yet. My corn is gathered and safely in the stackyard over here."

"It looks simple enough, after you've got the general outline."

"It isn't really. There are all sorts of pitfalls, but surmounting them is the exciting part. I'm not too good at backgrounds yet. They take such a lot of filling in."

43

"Your trees are quite good, and the steading. It might almost be—a real farm."

There had been something in his voice that she had never heard there before, an interest in things past, maybe, which was often a first step to an interest in things to come.

"Would you like to try?"

For a moment she thought that he was about to refuse as flatly as always, and then, with a smile as if he were humoring a tiresome child, he took her place before the frame.

"Don't blame me if I spoil it for you."

"I won't. It isn't expert stuff."

She watched him keenly as he brooded over the outline of the trees, her heart beating excitedly. Was she getting somewhere at last, and where would this road lead?

He worked for perhaps half an hour, seemingly forgetful of her presence in the room, and the light of hope burned even more brightly in her eyes as she watched. He worked awkwardly at first, and made mistakes, but she left him alone, conscious of something about him that went deeper than an interest in tapestry work, although she could not explain it, sensing that the work before him was but a medium through which he might be led to a more definite end.

The excitement of the thought stirred the rich color in her cheeks, and her eyes glowed with the deep radiance of achievement, even although it was in such small measure.

Abruptly at this point Douglas Harvey sprang up from his chair, carrying the little frame to the light at the far end of the conservatory where the vine leaves above his head thinned, letting in a beam of wintry sunshine. Lindsey rose and looked over his shoulder.

"Not so bad for a first attempt. You've helped with the stubble field, anyway, and I wondered how I was going to deal with such an area of it!"

Suddenly he turned, casting the frame on to the chair he had vacated, where it fell with a little rending sound, as if in protest.

"What interest have I in stubble fields, or any other kind of field, for that matter!" he demanded harshly, so that she knew there was an interest somewhere deep within him. "This is child's play—a damned waste of time, and I'll thank you not to bother me with your stupid ideas again."

He swung round, making for the door, his face livid, his mouth working spasmodically, and then he halted, brought up face to face with the man who stood in the doorway blocking his exit.

"Good heavens, Rick! What brought *you* here?"

Richard Harvey made no direct reply, but the eyes which had witnessed the display of passion were unfathomably dark and smouldering. He held the younger man's gaze for a second or two longer, and then he turned to Lindsey.

"Will you be good enough to leave us, Nurse?" he asked briefly.

Lindsey went quietly from the conservatory, her heart beating wildly. What had she done? The sternness of the young surgeon's manner towards her hurt in a curious way that she could not understand, but over and above this personal feeling was the fear that she had injured Douglas in some way, and had so retarded the hope of some other successful approach to his problem.

Richard Stewart Harvey was far from thinking along those lines, however. When she had left the conservatory he stood for a moment or two in an effort to gain control of emotions which had almost overridden his will to keep them in check, and then he said quietly:

"You're not going to get anywhere behaving like that, Doug., my boy. If you get some queer sort of satisfaction in lashing out at someone, why do it with a person you like, who is trying her best to help you?"

"What makes you think I like her?"

"For two reasons which we won't bother to go into now." He crossed to the chair, picking up the discarded tapestry frame to look thoughtfully at the little picture. "Quite a pretty little rural picture."

He ceased speaking almost abruptly, his keen eyes alertly conscious of the pictured scene before him and something he seemed to see beyond it.

"I wonder . . ." he murmured at last, as he laid Lindsey's unfinished picture aside.

Half an hour later he was talking to Matron in her office in the main part of the building.

"I confess I kept my temper with difficulty," he owned "I did not really think that he gave way to bursts of unreasonableness like that, and it is, to say the least of it, not good for him."

"Perhaps," the matron suggested tentatively, "a change of nurse is called for."

"No." He was quite definite on that point. "Nurse Hamilton is doing well enough. I had high hopes of this treatment, and I must confess that I expected some sign of improvement before now, but I really don't think a change of nurse at this stage would be in the least beneficial. It means that we must be patient a little longer. Just now—in the conservatory—I thought I had stumbled upon something, and if you don't mind I think I would like to give it a chance to work out. Results may prove me wrong, of course, and he must still undergo that operation before he is finally cured."

"We must explore every avenue," she assured him, seeing with deep understanding his affection and care for his brother.

When he had taken tea with her he went again to the conservatory, hoping to find Douglas there. Instead he came upon Lindsey gathering her patient's books together.

"Oh!" She looked startled. "Lieutenant Harvey has gone to lie down. His leg has been troubling him this afternoon."

"Is it very painful, or was it just an excuse?"

"He walked quite a long way yesterday. I was afraid it might be too far."

"To rest it is easing it, though?"

"It seems to be."

"I'll go in and see him presently."

Presently? Lindsey wondered if she was about to be reprimanded for the scene in the conservatory before tea, but the kindness had come back into his eyes again, like a lamp burning steadily, and she had to return his smile.

"I'm sorry about this afternoon, Nurse," he said. "I had no idea he was ever like that with people he approved of, but I see you have the patience and tact necessary to overlook these things." The smile had left his eyes, but they were still kindly. "It was good of you to persevere with the tapestry, and I have an idea that may interest you. Perhaps we can discuss it if I am down again at the week-end."

Lindsey hesitated. The coming week-end was to have been her first time off duty since she had arrived at St. Ronan's, and she was looking forward to a hurried visit to Glasgow to see her father and, possibly, Norman, who was a very poor correspondent and of whom she had heard nothing since his unexpected visit to the hospital.

"Leave?" he asked with a twinkle.

"I could cancel it," she offered immediately.

"No need, really." He hesitated, and then went on quickly: "Since it is just to talk over this idea of mine, couldn't we meet in Glasgow? I suppose you will be going home?"

"Oh yes." Confusion spread over her like an engulfing wave. "I was going on Friday afternoon—till Monday."

"Then, we can meet somewhere? You'll want to spend Sunday with your family, and probably you have already arranged your first evening at home. Can I hope that you might have an hour to spare on Saturday?"

Utterly bewildered by this unexpected proposal, Lindsey heard herself say:

"Saturday? Yes, I could come on Saturday. Would you like me to meet you at the clinic?"

He smiled at that.

"I thought we might meet in town—have dinner somewhere, perhaps?"

She supposed it was foolish to look so completely taken by surprise, but she had not dreamed that he was proposing they should spend the evening together to have dinner and talk. The prospect sent her pulses beating a little faster, though she said quite simply:

"That would be nice. Where shall I meet you?"

"I'll call for you, if I may? I've been to your home once before with your brother."

"Oh! I had no idea. Norman is a disgraceful correspondent, and I am quite looking forward to this week-end's leave so that I can hear all about the latest of him."

"I hope you will think it good news. He seems to be picking up remarkably well, and I'm quite convinced about his complete cure."

"You mean—he may be able to operate again—to take up surgical work?"

"I've a feeling that his nerve isn't really gone, that all he needs is the necessary confidence—renewed confidence."

"But where is he to get it from if it doesn't come from within?"

"It will come from within, sooner or later. Have no fear of that."

"You are so sure, yet . . ."

"I know he has had the finest care in the world, but sometimes a doctor can do nothing. It rests with the patient himself."

Lindsey flushed.

"I didn't mean to infer that your skill was inferior to others'."

He looked down at her with those grave eyes.

"I didn't even think of it that way," he assured her.

"Norman's not the type to go down easily before trouble. He must have fought this in the beginning," she went on. "Even now he is doing his best to look beyond his misfortune."

"I know, and that is what I admire so much about him, and that is why I believe he has the grit in him to pull out completely."

"It would mean so much to him—to us all."

"I see that." He took her hand, holding it in his for a second or two. "Good-bye, Miss Hamilton, until Saturday, at six shall we say?"

"Yes. I'll be ready then."

He left her, and Lindsey stood gazing after him as he went out of the conservatory in search of his brother, her heart racing madly, her eyes aglow.

On the Friday morning she did an early duty on the main ward and at twelve o'clock was ready to go out to the car which would take her to the pier when she turned to find Edna Halton, coming down the steps towards her.

"I heard you were travelling up today," she said distantly. "I have a special pass. Dad has been organizing a concert in the St. Andrew's Hall, and he wanted one of us to be there tomorrow evening. Alicia is simply fuming; she thought she should go, but Matron thought otherwise after the sluice incident yesterday." She drew on her gloves, giving Lindsey's week-end case a deprecating glance as she picked up her pigskin grip. "Well, we seem to be all they're waiting for," she concluded, "so we'd better get in. I thought 'Spider' Webb might be going up. I'm relieved, of course, that she's not. That girl gives me a headache every time I look at her, with her crude make-up and protruding teeth."

Lindsey did not reply, letting Miss Halton climb into the seat beside the driver while she occupied the rear of the car beside the two pieces of luggage.

"Smoke?" Edna asked, handing back a gold-and-blue enamel case.

"Thanks."

The case was withdrawn and the car proceeded on its way without further conversation. Lindsey looked out of the window on her side, watching the little white-crested waves chasing each other across the sand and the steamer cutting across them, leaving a long churned wake behind it.

The journey across to the mainland was uneventful. Edna went straight down to the cabin 'to travel in comfort,' but Lindsey preferred to stay on deck, revelling in the gusts of wind that blew strongly against her, and the circling gulls, and the sea, and the blue sky which stretched now over all the hills.

As they went up towards the platforms at Wemyss Bay, Edna remarked:

"I don't suppose you'll be travelling first? I could never bear to travel any other way, of course."

Mischief woke and danced at the corners of Lindsey's mouth.

"One gets used to travelling second class when one has done it all one's life." They had reached the train, and she selected a carriage at random. "I may see you at the other end. If not, have a good leave!"

When the train drew in at Glasgow Edna was nearer the barrier and she hurried on. Lindsey saw her once as she hailed a taxi in Gordon Street and was swept away to her destination.

The more humble bus took Lindsey to Shawlands, where she found Mrs. Birch coming home with her Friday afternoon's shopping.

"Hullo, Cousin Madge!" she greeted her, relieving her of the heavy basket. "I wondered if you'd be in when I arrived."

"In!" Madge Birch complained. "I've been out since two o'clock. I've been on my feet since half-past seven this morning, and as like as not I'll be on them till half-past seven tonight."

"You won't, you know," said Lindsey, "because you're going to sit down while I make the tea, and then we're going to the pictures."

"We'll see," said Madge, half mollified, yet reluctant to relinquish her complaint. "If it means walking any distance and then standing in a queue to get in, I'm not going."

"There won't be much of a queue on a Friday evening." Lindsey hesitated. "I'll be going out to dinner tomorrow, Madge. Norman's chief asked me."

"The Stewart Harvey man?" Madge's expression hovered between surprise and suspicion. "Really, you Hamiltons are close! I didn't know you knew him intimately."

"We only met recently. He seems to have been very kind to Norman."

"It appears so"—dryly. "Though you'll not get much out of Norman, either, if he doesn't want to discuss his affairs. I suppose you'll be wanting your friend in to a bite of supper tomorrow?"

Lindsey flushed.

"I don't know. I hadn't thought of that, really."

"Is he calling for you?"

"Yes."

"Then I expect he'll be bringing you home."

"I suppose so."

"I'll put up a sandwich or two and make some coffee, and you can please yourself about bringing him in. Norman will be here."

Although Lindsey suspected that curiosity was at the root of the suggestion, she was really grateful.

"I'll see what he says," she promised.

Several times before tea on the Saturday she had rejected and reconsidered the idea, and when Norman arrived a little before five o'clock she met him with a sigh of relief.

"Oh, Norrie, I wondered if you'd get home today! We expected you for lunch."

"We had a case." He took off his coat in the hall and she went on into the sitting-room where a fire burned cheerfully and the tea-table had been pulled into the centre of the semicircle of chairs surrounding it. "Stewart Harvey was still up to the eyes in it when I left."

The acuteness of her disappointment surprised Lindsey.

"He'll be working late?"

Norman smiled up at her as he settled himself in one of the armchairs.

"He's not cutting your date, if that's what you mean. He asked me to tell you that he might be a few minutes late and to explain. A doctor can't always make appointments and be sure that he's going to be able to keep them. He did a fair-sized operation this morning and I'll be taking over from him at six."

There had been a faint ring of pride in his voice, and a glow in his eyes that had banished, the haunting fear she had watched so helplessly at their last meeting.

"I know your program," he went on with a grin that was boyish and made him look like his old, light-hearted self again, "but I won't spill the beans. I believe he means it as a surprise."

"Then why did he tell you?"

"I'm not very sure how to take that one! Do you think me incapable of keeping a secret? Well, anyway, because he must let me know where he can be found if anything goes wrong with his patient." He took his teacup from her and reached for a scone, "Think twice before you marry a doctor, Lindy. Their lives are never ordered existences because they can never really get away from their work." He sat forward in his chair, his face half in shadow and half revealed by the light of the standard lamp in the corner behind him. "I've thought a great deal about research recently, Lindy, wondering if I'd be more good there than—just fretting around a clinic or even in a hospital."

Norman laughed.

"What does Mr. Stewart Harvey think?"

"I hardly think he considers me a future Jenner or a Lister," he said. "In fact, he told me quite bluntly not to talk rot. But"—more seriously—"he knows the sort of work I am doing now will get me down in the end—routine work, a bottle of medicine here, a prescribed treatment there. . . ."

Mrs. Birch came in with a plate of scones, and Norman's confidences ceased abruptly.

"I thought you liked them heated, Norrie." she said.

"Thanks, Madge. You pander to my frailties!" He stretched for a hot scone. "That is one childish affection I've never relinquished," he admitted, glancing at his watch as he spoke. "The old man's late, isn't he? He said he would be in at five."

"I don't think Dad should be asked to work on a Saturday afternoon," Lindsey said. "Normally, he would have retired by now and have settled down in a country cottage with a garden. Instead of that he's working twice as hard and almost twice as long."

51

Norman moved uneasily.

"I wish I could do something about it," he said. "I had it all planned. . . ."

Lindsey, avoiding Norman's eyes and their unhappy expression, changed the subject with quiet deliberation. Madge Birch was no respecter of anyone's feelings, and she hated the thought of Norman being hurt by anyone so unthinking.

He went out shortly before six, meeting his father on his way in, and Lindsey had only a few minutes for a word or two with the returned worker before she hurried off to change.

*   *   *   *

Richard Stewart Harvey was installed in an arm-chair in the sitting-room when she entered. He was talking to her father and she heard Norman's name mentioned as she came forward. Instantly he rose to his feet, holding out his hand.

"I am a little later than I said," he apologized," but I hope you will forgive me, and I see that you are ready."

She thought with simple pleasure that his quiet eyes appraised her, seeing another side of her out of uniform possibly, for the first time.

"Mr. Stewart Harvey and I have been talking about Norman," her father said, obviously delighted by this second meeting with his son's chief. "He believes his disability to be purely temporary, that something will come about to effect a cure. We all sincerely hope it will."

"Oh, Norman's improved immensely since he started to work again," declared Mrs. Birch, seeing no deeper than the surface. "He's still in the profession and surely one type of doctoring is much the same as another?"

Nobody sought to contradict her, but Lindsey knew that the tall young surgeon beside her understood her brother's problem perhaps better than any of them. They spoke for a few minutes longer and then took their leave.

"I won't keep her too late, sir," Stewart Harvey promised as they went out, and Lindsey saw her father smile, well pleased.

"I've ordered dinner at the Grosvenor," Stewart Harvey explained as they caught a bus on the main road. "Then—

I hope you will approve my choice!—I have booked seats for St. Andrew's Hall."

"The charity concert! How wonderful!" Lindsey exclaimed. "I didn't think there would be tickets available at such short notice."

"I have a friend at court!" he smiled; and suddenly Edna Halton's name leapt out at Lindsey, striking her with the force of a blow and dimming her happiness a little.

"Nurse Halton told me her father had helped to organize the concert," she said. "She is to be there tonight, I believe. I travelled over on the steamer with her yesterday."

"I know the Halton's quite well," he acknowledged. "We were near neighbors before they came to live in Glasgow."

"Oh? I rather thought they had always lived here, with Mr. Halton being a bailie."

Her companion smiled.

"Old Halton always did things both quickly and spectacularly. He farmed in Fife for many years before he became a grain merchant, and found it a much better paying proposition."

There had been no bitterness in his tone, but he had entirely given the lie to Edna's long and ancient lineage story, and Lindsey was left wondering why some girls chose to be so foolish.

"They've been very lucky to get so much talent for one concert," her companion went on. "It's for a splendid cause, of course, and I think you'll enjoy it. I see they have Beethoven's Symphony No. 6 on the program, and it's a special favorite of mine."

There was genuine love of music in his deep voice, and she wondered if he played any instrument. It was many days before she knew, and then the instrument he played was, somehow, not a surprise to her.

Their dinner was necessarily a rushed affair, but Lindsey thoroughly enjoyed it, revelling in the perfect appointment of the tables and the flowers and shaded lights that carried her far from her every-day life into a sort of fairyland, even though it might only be for this one brief evening in Richard Stewart Harvey's company.

During the meal he spoke quite frankly of Douglas.

"I have an idea that he may yet take an interest in the land," he said unexpectedly, over the sweet course. "It is in his blood, Miss Hamilton. We are farmers."

She looked up, sure that he had seen her surprise in her eyes.

"I am the second of three brothers," he added in explanation of his statement, "and my oldest brother turned his hand to the plough. I always feel that I was given the chance Stephen should have had in life, but he did not look at it that way. He was a farmer born and bred, and his heart was in the soil." His eyes clouded as he spoke. "He was killed two years ago in a fall from a silo in frosty weather while he was repairing wind damage." He paused for a moment, his eyes bent on his empty plate. "It has been a great blow to my father, more especially as it now seems that Craigmiles may pass out of Harvey hands."

"That is your home?" she asked, interested by this unexpected revelation of his background.

He nodded.

"It's on the Fife coast, a few miles from St. Andrews. It is a lovely countryside and I'd give anything I possess to keep Craigmiles in the family, but farming in Fife and consulting in Glasgow isn't an entirely practical solution for me."

"And you hope," she suggested, believing that she now saw the trend of his thoughts, "to induce Douglas to take it up?"

"Not induce. He'll never be forced. It must come about by his own desire. For over a year he was an agricultural student, but flying came first. It always has done." He bent over the table, looking directly into her thoughtful eyes. "But if there was the slightest show of interest in anything appertaining to the land on his part, you understand, to be aware of it would be most helpful to me."

"Yes, I see what you mean." Her brows drew together. "But, frankly, I can't truthfully say that I've noticed an interest in farming."

"Not even that show of interest in the tapestry picture the other afternoon?"

"You mean the field and the trees?" Her eyes brightened. "Of course, he was interested—for a moment or two. He said—he said it might almost be a real farm, and —yes, he *must* have been thinking of home!"

"I hope we are right," he said gravely. "At any rate, it's a line for us to work on, and I'm sure you are the right person to be with him at this time."

"Thank you," she returned simply, knowing that his compliment was not an idle one.

"I shall speak to Matron about this idea of mine when I am at St. Ronan's next week," he said, as they rose to leave. "I think she will agree with us that it is worth trying."

"Every avenue is worth exploring," Lindsey said. "I shall do all I can to help."

He had ordered a taxi and they sped along through the dark streets, with their strange starlight lighting effect, to St. Andrew's Hall, where the program was just about to begin. They slipped into their seats, unconscious that, two rows in front, a tall, dark-haired girl had turned to watch them coming down the aisle and that her eyes had narrowed perceptibly as she had turned back to busy herself with the contents of her program.

The overture to Rossini's *Barber of Seville* opened the program and, as always, Lindsey found herself entranced by the power and beauty of such music which she had come to love and know through her mother, who had been a pianist of exceptional ability. It was, therefore, to the performance of the celebrated solo pianist of the evening that she looked forward most. She had often wished to hear Ina Cargill play, and now her ambition was to be realized. The young pianist's first choice was Rachmaninoff's Concerto No. 3, and she came on to the platform, a young shy girl in white, looking almost a child, so slight was her build, her small oval face so flower-like, her whole manner so utterly free from ostentation.

When the applause was at its height Lindsey's companion bent over to her.

"I'd like you to meet Ina one day," he said. "Unfortunately, it isn't possible tonight because she has a supper engagement immediately after the concert."

"You know her well?" Lindsey asked.

"Very well indeed," he had just time to answer before the hush of expectation settled like a velvet mantle on the crowded hall.

Ina Cargill played with a power and sublime touch which lifted her performance into the realm of premier pianists, and she held her audience spellbound as the liquid notes fell from under her talented fingers. Lindsey watched them, fascinated, little realizing that these small, delicate hands would one day hold her whole world within their light grasp.

"She's marvellous—marvellous!" she whispered involuntarily in the silence which preceeded the first burst of enthusiastic applause from those around her. "I've always wanted to hear her play."

"Ina has excelled herself this evening," Harvey returned quietly. "This is what she has lived for for many years, but I knew it would come one day," he added with a warmth which proclaimed his deep admiration for the girl on the platform, who now stood shyly bowing her acknowledgment of the renewed thunder of applause.

It was a wonderful reception, and although the following item was Beethoven's Symphony No. 6, the lovely 'Pastoral' which was Lindsey's favorite, she could not quite banish the vision of the girl in the white frock who had looked shy and almost frightened by the tumultuous reception she had received.

She wanted to ask Richard Stewart Harvey more about her, how achievement had come to her so young, but they had little chance for conversation as they filed out along the crowded aisles at the end of the performance. In the entrance hall groups had formed to discuss the program, and in one of these stood Edna Halton in a flame-red dress and short white fur jacket, an arresting, brilliant figure among the more sedately dressed citizens of Glasgow in their fur coats and silk head-scarves who had gathered to hear a daughter of Scotland playing with a world-famous orchestra.

Edna recognized Stewart Harvey's tall figure immediately and, murmuring an excuse to her father, came swiftly across the intervening space.

"Hullo, Richard!" she greeted him, her dark eyes holding his. "I had no idea you were going to manage down tonight or I should have reserved you a seat with our party."

"Your father very kindly got me two tickets at the eleventh hour." He turned immediately to Lindsey. "You know Miss Hamilton, of course."

Edna favored Lindsey with a distant smile.

"Of course." She had endeavoured to force a certain amount of warmth into her voice, but the effort was a complete failure. "We work together. You must know that, Richard. But look here," she added with renewed zest, "you simply can't mean to go home yet. Why don't you join our party now? Daddy will be so disappointed that

56

you weren't with us all evening. Do come, and bring Lindsey with you."

The sudden change of tone confused Lindsey more than Edna's first frigid recognition had done, and she felt suddenly disconcerted and ridiculously shy when Richard Stewart Harvey turned to ask:

"Would you care to do that?"

"We're going straight home for supper, I believe," Edna said. "Do come along and join us, Lindsey. Richard should really have been one of our party, you know."

Even before Lindsey could reply, a booming voice sounded behind them and an elderly, portly gentleman with a very red countenance broke into their small circle.

"Hullo, Richard, my boy!" he greeted Stewart Harvey genially. "What did you think of our little show? Not too bad, eh?" He surveyed the thinning crowd with a satisfied beam. "Should bring in a nice penny, shouldn't it? Ina Cargill was well received, wasn't she?"

"She has a great measure of talent," Richard said quietly.

"Daddy," Edna broke in, introducing Lindsey, "this is one of our nurses from St. Ronan's. We travelled as far as Wemyss Bay together, but I hadn't the slightest idea we'd meet here."

Lindsey found her hand engulfed in a large, hard palm and firm fingers gripping close.

"Very nice, too. Glad to get out of the old uniform for an hour or two, eh?" He glanced over Lindsey's head to his waiting party nearer the door and firmly shepherded her towards the other group. "Of course, you'll come along with us now. We're going out to Pollokshields for a bite to eat to wind up a splendid evening."

Separated from her escort for the moment, Lindsey could not very well protest, since Richard Harvey might even want to 'wind up' the evening in the company of his friends rather than accept her offer of coffee and sandwiches at Fotheringay Road, yet, somehow, even as she gave rein to such thoughts, she wondered. He had seemed eager enough to talk to Norman and her father on the two occasions when they had met, but these people were his friends—friends, it seemed, of long standing.

She found him standing by her side as they awaited their taxi.

"I hope you don't mind," he said almost ruefully. "We seem to have been roped in for this very suddenly."

57

"Come along, Lindsey—and you, Richard," Edna called from the curb where she stood with one slim foot on the running-board of her father's taxi. "You'd better share with us. There's not going to be enough to go round otherwise."

Lindsey found herself in the back seat beside Bailie Halton, who made room for her with a good deal of wheezing and much laughing comment on his own obesity

"I don't think there's even room for another slim one on this side, Edna," he said as his daughter got in.

"Richard can sit beside me on the chairs," Edna returned quickly. "It's not the first time we've been deprived of the back seat in a taxi because you need the lot, Daddy!"

The taxi moved away, and Lindsey, sitting in her corner overshadowed by the bulk of her unexpected host, felt that she was being whirled too swiftly away from a scene of perfect happiness to one in which she must inevitably feel odd-man-out. His friends seemed determined to take possession of the young surgeon, and Edna had already succeeded in making her feel dispossessed.

The taxi slowed and drew up before a massive, pillared doorway which stood out from the shadowy bulk of a big, square house set in a shrub-filled garden a little way back from the main road.

"Here we are!" Edna exclaimed unnecessarily. "We're almost last in, so I hope the others have had the sense to go into the dining-room and help themselves. You needn't stand on ceremony, anyway, Richard," she added. "You know your way about."

Stewart Harvey put his hand under Lindsey's elbow to guide her inside, and she had the impression of a dim, lofty hall and thick rich carpets underfoot and a soft-voiced man-servant leading the way to a brightly lit room full of chattering people who were all evidently 'helping themselves' as Edna had hoped they would. A buffet supper had been spread on the long table and ample liquid refreshment adorned the sideboard, to which Bailie Halton gravitated as steel to a magnet. Richard Harvey drew Lindsey aside.

"I'm sorry about this," he said. "I didn't really intend our evening to end this way, but the Halton's are old friends and the old man simply won't take a refusal. He's not a bad sort, really, and he does all this sort of thing mainly to please his daughters." He glanced at his watch. "We needn't stay long. When do you want to be home?"

"About twelve, I think. I didn't say I would be late. They know we have gone to the concert." She hesitated and then added swiftly: "But if you want to stay . . ."

He smiled down at her.

"We'll make our adieux in half an hour, shall we?"

Edna Halton monopolized him quite unashamedly for that half-hour, protesting strongly when he said they must go. He was firm, however, and she left his side to descend upon Lindsey, announcing that she would go with her to get her coat.

"Quite a change from life at St. Ronan's," she remarked almost pleasantly as they crossed the deserted hall to a cloakroom on its far side, "but we'll be back there on Monday. My dear," she added confidentially, "Richard tells me that he expects you to make quite a success of Douglas' case. It's rather a compliment for you, you know. We've all been wondering why he took you up."

For a moment Lindsey found nothing to say. Although it was what she had told herself many times—that Richard Stewart Harvey's interests and kindness was merely professional—to hear the same conviction voiced by Edna Halton sent the sensitive color into her cheeks while a wave of disappointment went flooding through her heart. The thought of Richard discussing her in this way with Edna hurt her more than she would have believed.

"I appreciate the compliment, of course," she said briefly, "and I hope I shall justify Mr. Stewart Harvey's confidence in me."

Edna's mouth twisted into a little crooked smile as she tried to hide her chagrin at the fact that her barbed shaft had apparently not shot home.

"Don't tell me that your career means everything to you, Nurse!" she mocked. "You're not the type that would willingly accept the fate of 'Lefty' Collins, for instance, even with an M.B.E. thrown in and a staff sister's authority to take the place of a wedding ring."

"Sister Collins may not think of these other things. Perhaps she has lost them through no fault of her own, Edna. There may be some closed chapter in her life—a tragic love affair, even. We're best not to judge when we know so little of her private affairs."

She had steered the conversation away from the personal and she was determined to keep it so, succeeding as she followed Edna across the hall again because Richard Harvey came out of the dining-room at their approach.

"We've run it rather fine," he said, glancing at his watch, "but I think we should just manage to catch that last bus."

Lindsey took a hurried leave of their host, and they bade Edna good-night and hurried out into the darkness, which seemed more friendly than the brilliantly lit room behind them. For a few seconds her eyes, accustomed to the bright lights inside, refused to focus and she stood still.

"I must be down on my vitamins," she laughed. "I can't see a thing."

"All the vitamins in the world wouldn't help you to see under these conditions," he assured her, taking her arm in a firm grasp. "Let me help you. I know the way."

He guided her down a broad pathway out on to the pavement where she could see street lights at the end of the road, and they ran towards them in time to catch the bus which was just leaving the terminus.

When they reached Fotheringay Road he said:

"I should come in and explain to your people why we are so late."

Lindsey hesitated.

"You were invited to supper," she confessed, and then her sense of humor bubbled upwards. "So, if we have sandwiches for breakfast, Norman will have the satisfaction of being able to blame you!"

"Or the unfortunate fact that we were roped in by the Haltons! But, you know"—confidentally—"I believe I could do something to a sandwich even yet. There was so much talk of old Halton's end of the table that I didn't get a chance to eat."

A warm glow surrounded Lindsey's heart.

"Come on, then! I didn't eat much myself."

But not, she thought, because she had been talking, though all that was forgotten now.

The family were waiting for them, her father with the barest trace of anxiety in his eyes, Madge Birch with the indrawn line of her mouth showing her displeasure, and only relaxing very slowly under Stewart Harvey's smile when she realized that her preparations were not to be in vain, and Norman with a grin that was quite frankly amused, although he greeted his chief with his customary deference.

"Sorry to talk shop," he said, "but I'd better put your mind at rest about that case and let you enjoy your supper. She's as you left her—out of immediate danger and pro-gressing slowly. I still want to rave about the sulphanilamides, sir, though the new penicillen seems to have them all whacked." The light in his eyes died suddenly. "But I'm talking too much—how did you enjoy the concert, sir?"

"I thoroughly enjoyed it." Stewart Harvey glanced at Lindsey, who was helping Mrs. Birch with the coffee. "My only fear was that it might have been a rather selfish choice."

"Lindy would love it." James Hamilton assured him. "My wife was a fine pianist and we used to enjoy many an hour of good music in here when the children were younger."

"Do you play the piano, Miss Hamilton?" Stewart Harvey asked presently.

"I play a little, and, I'm now convinced, very indifferently, after hearing Ina Cargill's performance this evening. I admire that sort of talent so much."

"And Ina would admire your splendid physique, your ability to be a successful nurse, and I think, your patience."

"But surely it needs unlimited patience to become so great a pianist?"

"Ina is a genius, but she will tell you quite frankly that if she had patience, also, she would reach the heights some day."

"Your coffee, Mr. Harvey."

The conversation was becoming too involved for Madge, so she proceeded to take the centre of the stage, pressing refreshment of a material order upon their guest, and remarking genially upon the weather and the lack of any quantity of fish in the shops that week.

It was well after midnight before he left, and Lindsey heard her father inviting him to come again as she and Norman went to the door with him. Norman took down his coat.

"I'll come to the end of the road with you, sir."

"No need, Norman. I've not so far to travel, and it's a nice night for a walk. I'll drop in at the hospital as I pass, I think."

"I wondered if you'd care to. It would put your mind at rest about that case."

Stewart Harvey looked him squarely in the eyes.

"I'm not going for that reason. I have your assurance and that is good enough for me. It was that Marshall boy I was thinking about."

To Lindsey it seemed that Norman's gratitude for his faith in him quivered in the air like some tangible thing and happy tears were very near the surface of her own eyes as she wished him good night and tried to thank him.

"I've enjoyed it all so much," she said simply as his fingers closed over hers.

"So have I. You'll come some other time, Lindsey?"

She nodded happily, scarcely aware that he had used her Christian name, yet conscious of a little thrill of sheer joy as their eyes met in the starlight.

2

Lindsey went on duty on the Monday afternoon to find her patient restless, even, she thought, a little sulky.

"Well, did you have a good time?" he asked.

"Lovely, thanks. It was so good of your brother to ask me out."

His eyes sharpened as he turned in his chair.

"Rick took you out?"

She nodded.

"Probably to make up for your bad behavior on the last afternoon he was here!"—lightly.

"When was that? You've been away a devil of a long time."

"Only for forty-eight hours and a travelling allowance," she reminded him, picking up several American magazines from the floor beside his chair. "It seemed short enough to me."

"Naturally, when you were enjoying yourself so much. Where did Rick take you?"

"To the concert at St. Andrew's Hall."

"And probably you wanted to dance."

"No I enjoyed it very much. Ina Cargill was the soloist, and your brother tells me you know her very well."

There was no immediate reply, and she looked up from her task to surprise a strange expression struggling with displeasure in his dark face.

"We are very old friends and near neighbors. Did you meet Ina?"

"No. She had a supper engagement and we went on to the Haltons'."

"I've no time for Edna Halton. Neither, I thought, had Rick."

A deep color stained Lindsey's cheeks, and she was instantly aware that he had noticed it.

"Did you suspect an affair?" he asked with a twist of his mouth that was not a smile. "That may be Edna's idea, but I don't think it's Rick's, though why I should go out of my way to assure you of the fact, I don't know."

He picked up a magazine, glaring at it as she turned away, and Lindsey left him to his preoccupation while she went to attend to other tasks, although she sought him out an hour later, noting his glance of surprise as he saw her outdoor attire.

"Where are you going?"

"We're short of milk, and if I don't go across to the farm for some, you'll have no tea."

"That wouldn't worry me overmuch. The walk to the farm would, though."

"I am not even suggesting that you should come, though it's quite a nice afternoon for a walk through the estate."

"I've never had any desire to go to the farm"—aggressively.

"And I've never had the time, but I suppose I shall find my way all right. You'll be quite comfortable till I get back, won't you?"

"I suppose I'll have to be. I survived the week-end, didn't I?"

"Marvellously well—even without much chance of airing your supreme gift of irony. I hear Matron attended you personally."

"The woman fascinates me. I daren't say 'no' to her!"

He rose to his feet, while Lindsey said lightly, deliberately misconstruing his last remark:

"That's what makes for good matrons—the iron hand in the velvet glove."

He laughed and it sounded almost like a chuckle.

"Lindy! you do me good! Or mustn't I call you 'Lindy'?"

"Not in Matron's hearing. *She* might find it easy to say 'no' to *you*."

"How far is it to the farm and shall I need a coat?" he asked.

"About two miles, if we go by the shore, and certainly you'll have a coat. Hold the milk-can while I go and get one for you."

She felt almost gay as she ran along the corridor. She had jerked him out of that dreadful apathy, even although it might only be for the time being. This was what Richard wanted, and she would have this much at least to report to him on his return.

Douglas carried the milk-can for her, swinging it with the abandonment of a small boy as they went along the narrow pathway above the rocks where the tide swirled in, spreading and eddying in the deep gullies.

Once Lindsey lost her footing, slipping from the rocky foundation of the pathway on to soggy ground. Douglas Harvey caught her by the arm, pulling her to safety.

"You're all right," he assured her roughly, but when Lindsey had recovered her breath she found that he had not released her.

His hand was still fastened securely just above her wrist where her cloak had blown back, and almost reluctantly she met his eyes. There was something in them which she could not quite define—determination, perhaps, struggling with that casual, cynical bitterness which he had worn as a mask for so long.

"Lindy," he said deliberately, "you're very sweet," and that was all, but it left her strangely shaken. She must never let there be any complications of that kind, because once, right at the beginning, Richard Stewart Harvey had let her understand that he frowned upon the personal approach.

"Well, shall we push on? The cows are sure to be milked by now. They are all gathered in."

His tone had been light, but there was no gainsaying the tension in the atmosphere; no denying that the personal note had broadened and deepened into a quivering chord.

When they reached the outbuildings of the farm he grew silent although Lindsey noticed that it was not a moody silence this time. His eyes ranged over the well-drained fields to the pastureland and back to the lime-washed outbuildings in their model setting, with the tractors gleaming brightly in the sun and lending a gay touch of scarlet to the scene, and then they wandered to the moorland held at bay by the grey stone dykes and the farmhouse itself nestling peacefully among the hills, and it seemed that his mind was busy with thoughts that went deep into the past.

"It's—familiar, somehow."

She knew then that he was thinking of home, and she walked beside him silently, not speaking until they came into the stack-yard and he slowed his pace, still with that thoughtful, half-reluctant look in his eyes.

A white-barred gate lay across their path, and he opened it for her though he did not follow her through.

"I'll wait here."

She let him have his way, going on to the house for the milk. And Douglas Harvey watched her go, his dark face clouded, his eyes sombre. Why had he let her bring him here? It meant nothing to him, this small, compact farm with its stubble fields already undergoing cleaning. . . . There had been corn in the field across which he looked, and the high tide of harvest had passed, though there still remained the breath of the eternal miracle of man's endeavour and nature's blessing. Even as he listened he could hear the hum of the thresher coming down the wind like the breath of memory, a whisper from the past. He had been a kid then, driving horses out, big Clydesdales with their heavy tread and dark, friendly eyes, but now the reaper was a machine driven by petrol, as a 'plane was driven. . . .

Impatiently he turned away. God! What madness was this? There was nothing for him—nothing in the land. His life was finished, torn ruthlessly from his grasp when a 'plane had dived out of control above a seaside town. . . .

He could have baled out with the rest. He closed his eyes against the recurring horror of that moment of indecision when the natural impulse of self-preservation had almost overwhelmed his will, and his teeth set and a cold sweat broke out on his brow as he relived the split second when a machine out of control had dived relentlessly earthwards.

It had the power to shake him still, and his jarred nerves throbbed through all the horror of the impact—and then silence.

His mind refused to turn to the bleakness of the new dawn, that arid land wherein he had wandered for so long, hearing only the words of his sentence: 'You will never fly again.'

"Are you all right? You look shaken—ill."

She was standing beside him, a slight figure in her uniform that merged now into the grey twilight, making her look more ethereal than ever, but she had caught him unaware, and he did not want her sympathy.

"Why fuss? I have walked two miles before now and I'm still alive to tell the tale."

She did not press her point, although she still lingered by the gate.

"The cows were being milked," she said. "There's something rather strange about the electric milker, I always think. It's not so picturesque."

"How like a woman!" There was derision in his voice, though he did not look at her. "It may interest you to know that it is speedier, cleaner, and much more satisfactory to the animals."

"Yes, I suppose so, and, after all, we are a model farm here. They were busy threshing, too, and there was that glorious smell of chaff everywhere. Don't you think autumn is the loveliest time of all the year in many respects?"

He grunted, making her no direct answer, and she was forced to turn with him as he took the shorter way back to St. Ronan's, the road that did not wind by the sea.

On the crest of the hill he halted, however, looking back, and she saw something like longing in his eyes, although his mouth still retained the hard, cynical twist that marred the whole fine contours of his handsome face.

"A man's a fool who lets himself be bound to the soil," he remarked truculently, plunging downwards over the rough moorland track, not even waiting to help her this time although the way was often deeply hidden in heath and bog-myrtle or altogether lost in spent bracken and soft moss.

There was a lightness to Lindy's step, however, as they came within the confines of the big house, because it seemed that she had achieved part, at least, of that which she had set out to do.

Yet the following day was almost to rob her of her new-found elation, for she came into her patients room at nine o'clock in the morning to find him sunk in deep depression, not troubling to speak or even to look at her.

After a blithe good-morning she left him alone to go into the library where she was indexing new books, but by lunch-time the mood of the morning had not changed. He seemed to avoid meeting her eyes with any directness, and she found herself wishing again that she had more experience to back up her judgment. She had reported the visit to the farm to Matron the evening before, and had been aware of the older woman's immediate interest, but all she had been told was to carry the experiment on as warily as possible. A show of interest in anything at all was, undoubtedly, a step in the right direction.

Though such a little step, Lindsey thought now. At this rate would she ever reach her goal?

Douglas Harvey's mood persisted until the end of the week, when, almost miraculously, he woke up on the Friday morning to glance out at a blue sky and green, rain-washed hills and ask tentatively:

"Are you going to be busy this morning, Lindy?"

"Not more so than usual on a Friday, Why?"

"I thought we might walk along the shore again."

"To the farm, you mean?"

His brow clouded.

"No, not to the farm."

"I'll be ready by eleven. It's a lovely morning."

" 'And the walk will do me good!' Don't let's forget the rest of the formula."

But this was a mood she knew and understood, and when she was free shortly after eleven o'clock she brought his coat and her own and led the way down towards the shore.

"There's a fascination about the sea that's hard to describe," he reflected as he made room for her beside him on the narrow path between the rocks. "It can be so many things, from a vast expanse of grey desert seen from the air, to the friendly, noisy thing it is on our east coast."

"And here?" Lindsey prompted, surprised by such thoughts, or perhaps more surprised that he should trouble to share them with her.

"It has a sadness which I sometimes feel repelling—your western sea with the sound of it whispering among rocks, treacherous so often, forbidding, and nearly always grey. It has a poignant sorrow about it, too, that is bound up in all Celtic legend." He laughed sharply. "That is what I have found here—the essential sorrow of your Western Isles."

"It has touched you deeply, Douglas."

"It depresses me"—trying to force the old irritation into his voice. "You'll probably not believe that, since I came here in this frame of mind."

Lindsey's thoughts were flowing swiftly into new and clearer channels.

"St. Ronan's isn't helping much at present, is it?" she asked.

He shrugged, but his restless movements were arrested as he stood before her on the pathway looking down into her eyes.

"Not much, but you have helped—tremendously."

"I'm glad, though if you really feel that you might be happier away from 'my western sea,' we must find out what can be done to bring about a change for you."

"What's the use? Moving me around won't make a great deal of difference until after the final operation."

She looked back at him, surprised.

"I didn't know there was to be another. I had no idea. . . ."

"That I'm due to be hacked about a bit more?" He laughed bitterly. "I thought you had had experience of the persistence of surgeons?"

"But, surely—your brother . . ."

"Oh, Rick believes it necessary, and I suppose it must be. Seemingly they've discovered further pressure on a brain area. I may even be my own broght self again after it's over," he added sceptically.

Lindsey turned to face him squarely.

"Douglas, why have you no faith?"

His laugh was curiously harsh.

"I had faith in my ability to fly. But what does that matter? Faith doesn't get you much out of life. When you're a hundred per cent fit you can go out and get what you want by sheer grit and will power, but what use has anyone for a crock?"

"When you speak like that," she told him firmly, "you make me impatient."

"Well"—his eyes challenged hers with a flickering light leaping in their dark depths—"would a girl marry someone like me, for instance?"

So, there was someone he cared for, Lindsey thought swiftly. Might not this be all the trouble—his inability to offer the woman of his choice that 'hundred per cent fitness' which he had held to be perfection.

"She might promise to wait for you, Douglas."

The flame in his eyes glowed deeper.

"If I thought that . . ."

"Why not try to believe it, even to take it for granted for a while? After the operation, if it is successful, you could ask her."

He turned sharply away.

"I can't face another operation," he said. "You've no idea what it means—the hope, and the knowledge that you've lost again, that the whole nerve-racking affair has left you just where you were."

She put a detaining hand on his sleeve to check what looked like headlong flight.

"If I could do anything to help, Douglas—anything at all . . ."

He wheeled round, facing her, not speaking, but somehow she knew the truth that his dry lips refused to utter, and the knowledge struck her with the force of a blow. She had performed her duty, giving him sympathy and understanding in plentiful measure and in the performing of it she had stormed the citadel of a lonely heart, laying upon herself the need to stand by him at this difficult hour.

"I'll need you, Lindy," he said, and because the confession had come straight from his heart, stripped now of all cynical pretence, there was only one way in which she could answer him.

"I'll be there, as long as you'll need me," she told him.

"It may be longer than you think," he said, but his voice was lighter, his dark eyes still holding that bright gleam as they walked on.

And it seemed to Lindsey that the sound of the sea was all about her, and it spoke now with a poignancy of sorrow that is the very language of heartbreak. Why should she feel thus? What she was doing was only what Stewart Harvey had hoped for—giving his brother back the will to live, the power to fight. But had he meant her to give it in this way? Once—how long ago it seemed!—he had said that they must avoid the personal touch. . . .

"I don't know what Rick's plans are," Douglas said. "He may intend to do the operation in Glasgow, and probably it would be more convenient that way."

There was even interest in his tone as he discussed the future now, she noticed, so that she could not wilfully take away this prop from him, the sustaining power of her presence and her faith.

"Lindy, if I pull through this, I'll promise you to make the effort of my life."

Why did her heart sink? Why couldn't she answer him in a tone as enthusiastic as his own?

"You will pull through," was all she could say.

"If you will help. There's something about you," he went on hurriedly, "a sort of quiet courage that brings out all the finer qualities in people. I've felt it dozens of times. Oh, I haven't meant to let it influence me. I fought against it at first, and I'm even half reluctant to relinquish the struggle now, but somehow, I know that you'll win in the end. Perhaps Rick felt that, too," he continued musingly. "Anyway, he has great faith in you."

"It—just happened that I was at hand. Most nurses would have done as much. It is our duty."

He caught her fingers in a firm grip.

"One day, Lindy, I hope I shall be able to make you confess that there was another reason for all this sympathy and understanding." His face changed, looking almost grey in the morning light. "One day when I have more right to speak to you like this."

A deep, sensitive color flooded her cheeks.

"Douglas," she protested, but his low laugh interrupted what she was going to say, the old mocking note in it again, though now it was mellowed by a fond tenderness.

" 'But, Douglas, I'm not in love with you!' You were going to say that, Lindy, weren't you? Heavens! I don't expect you to be in love with me after the way I've treated you since you came to nurse me, but I was on the defensive, and very nearly giving in altogther when you appeared on my dark horizon like the morning star. I'll never forget how you looked that first day with your little cap so stiff and correct just managing to keep its dignity on your dark curls and your cheerful refusal to take my bearishness seriously." He smiled reminiscently. "It didn't go down very well at first, I'll admit, but now I'm getting used to it." His fingers tightened their grip on her hand. "Just as you're going to get used to the idea of loving me one day —if everything goes the way Rick hopes."

"The way—Rick hopes?" she echoed, her lips trembling over the words.

"About the operation. He's staking all he's got on that, and I'm staking everything on you."

Swiftly, and before she could even guess at his intention, he had bent and kissed her on the lips, and, as she drew away, confused and surprised by his action, she became aware of a tall figure approaching them along the narrow path.

The whole world seemed to stand still for an instant as she recognized Richard Stewart Harvey, and knew that he must have seen the little incident as he had rounded the rocks, yet she was aware that he was making a supreme effort to hide his feelings.

"Good morning," he greeted them quietly. "Matron told me I should find you out here, and I haven't a great deal of time to spare. We'll be off again immediately after lunch."

"You've come down about the operation, I suppose?" Douglas asked. "Well, I've changed my mind about it. I'll go through with it. One other, more or less, won't hurt me," he had to add in defence of his former attitude of blunt non-compliance.

A light broke in the older man's eyes.

"Good boy!" he said with quiet enthusiasm. "I thought you would come round to our way of thinking sooner or later."

"Lindy brought me round," Douglas returned. "I want her to be there all the time. You'll see to that, won't you, Rick? It's a very small request."

Was it? Lindsey wondered as she awaited Stewart Harvey's reply. Was it?

For the barest perceptible second the young surgeon hesitated while an emotion which was difficult to define struggled in his eyes, and Lindsey took that hesitation and his ultimate answer as the most polite way out of a difficult situation.

"If Miss Hamilton can be spared from her duties here," he said, and she felt that he might have spoken thus had he been humoring a fretful child who had an embarrassing request in the presence of a stranger.

"You could arrange that," Douglas said with implicit confidence. "A transfer, even if it were only a temporary one, would do the trick, and I don't suppose Lindy's any more enamored of this backwater than I am."

"Nevertheless, your stay at St. Ronan's has done you quite a lot of good," his brother pointed out, "although now I believe a change might be a good thing." He walked between them back along the way he had come, saying as they neared the house. "What about a visit home, Doug?"

Lindsey was conscious of her patient's swift scrutiny.

"I'm not terribly keen about going to Fife. It's a long way, and I suppose you'll want me back in Glasgow for the operation?" he objected.

"Not for a week or two. I must have you completely fit first."

"I'll think it over. I don't like too many decisions thrust upon me in one morning."

"Take your time to consider it, but it would be worth while for so many reasons."

Was one of those reasons, Lindsey found herself wondering with over-sensitivity, that Douglas might be removed from her influence? Did he, seeing that kiss on the path above the rocks, believe that she was playing the romantic fool rather than the conscientious nurse, and was he disappointed because he had believed in her professional integrity?

He came into Douglas' room to say good-bye before he left, meeting her in the doorway with an armful of books.

"May I take those for you?" he asked.

"I was returning them to the library," she explained. "Douglas has read most of them."

He relieved her of her burden, standing aside so that she might lead the way along the wide, tiled corridor which ended in the library building. It was almost one o'clock and the occupants of the occupational wing were preparing for their midday meal so that the big, airy room was deserted.

He gave her the books and she stacked them on a table to sort out later while he stood reading over some of the titles with a thoughtful frown on his brow.

"Miss Hamilton," he said at last, "you told me some little while ago that you thought Douglas might find a new interest in farming, and Matron and I both accepted the idea as one that might prove fruitful in the future." He turned, facing her squarely. "You've worked wonders over this changed attitude to the final operation, and for the present I can only thank you for your supreme effort."

"It was nothing," Lindsey said haltingly. "Douglas is so very much worthwhile, and one would do anything to help."

"There's something else I must ask," he said, his eyes going beyond her with that remote look in them again, as if he were forcing himself away from some dominating train of thought to the need of the present. "I want you to use your influence further in suggesting that he might follow my advice and go home."

"I think he will do that in any case," she returned, suddenly confused because it seemed that he was openly acknowledging her power to sway this wayward brother of his where he himself had failed. "It was a new idea to him, coming rather suddenly on the heels of his other decision."

"And after all, that was the main point." He smiled a little. "I feel doubly convinced now that the operation is going to be a success."

"You want him to go home to Fife almost immediately?"

"I think it would be best."

"I don't really think you'll have much difficulty with him," Lindsey said as they left the library. "He has been speaking quite a lot about home these past few days."

"Once we get him there I believe it will be fairly plain sailing. The mild climate here was most suitable when I first brought him to St. Ronan's, but he should be able to stand the invigorating air of the east coast now and, I think, the inevitable sight of aircraft in flight. That, as a matter of fact, will be part of my experiment. St. Ronan's has served its purpose."

"I feel that I shall be leaving an experiment half-way," she admitted candidly, and was surprised when he replied almost brusquely:

"There will be no question of that."

Matron bore down upon them as they reached the hall, and Lindsey made her escape, going back to the library after lunch to replace her books and standing with the first one in her hand for a long time.

"Well?" asked Douglas, coming up behind her. "What task has that unscrupulous brother of mine placed in your willing hands this time? To see me safely to Fife?"

"He thinks you should go home for a while before the operation."

"And what do *you* think?"

"If he suggests such a move, it must be for the best reasons."

He smiled at that.

"What other answer could I expect from a conscientious member of the nursing profession! The Big Chief Surgeon is always right."

"Undoubtedly, on this occasion."

"And you won't even condescend to admit that you'll miss me?"

"That's beside the point. You know that you ought to go." She turned to him impulsively. "Douglas, don't make it difficult for him. He has so much on his mind just now, so many calls on his time, but first of all, there's you. You mean more to him than anything else, and this final operation will be a big one. It may even mean all or nothing, so don't prejudice your chances beforehand just for a whim, perhaps even a selfish whim, my dear."

Her earnestness, the deep conviction in voice and eyes, moved him out of his perverse mood, sobering him, although there was still a flicker of suspicion in his eyes as he asked:

"Are you doing all this for Rick or for me?"

"For you both. I know how much it means to Rick, and how much it is going to mean to you—afterwards."

"I don't give a damn about 'afterwards,' it's now I'm concerned with. Why do you want to banish me to weeks of loneliness without you?"

"You'll be going home, Douglas."

A shadow crossed his eyes.

"I swore I'd never go back there."

"The skies are full of 'planes," she said softly. "I know."

"I suppose I'll have to face it sometime, so why not now," he reflected after a pause. "You can tell Rick when he comes down again that I'll go."

"Why not write to him?" she suggested. "It would give him time to make the necessary arrangements and you could travel back with him."

"You seem inordinately eager to be rid of me."

"I refuse to answer that, but you know that you are only marking time here, Douglas. Take this chance, and if it *is* an experiment, believe that it might be a successful one—for all our sakes."

He shrugged.

"How can I possibly argue further? You shall have your way, but do you sincerely believe that you can pass on faith in a miracle?"

"This isn't a thousand-to-one chance you are facing, Douglas," she reminded him steadily. "There will be no need for a miracle in that respect, but you must have a certain amount of faith in the future and what it can still hold for you."

He looked at her for a long moment without answering, the mocking gleam utterly gone from his eyes, and in its place a vague, questioning light.

"Perhaps there's something in what you say," he remarked at last. "This faith of yours carries conviction, Lindy, but you'll have to bear the torch for me for a while longer."

"I'll do all I can for you, Douglas," she said, and when he had ambled slowly from the room she stood rigid by the window where he had left her, the book she held clasped tightly against her breast while she thought that, if she had this to give, she must give it freely.

CHAPTER THREE

I

THE BROTHERS LEFT St. Ronan's on a windy afternoon a week later. Lindsey stood on the steps of the old house waving Douglas good-bye, conscious of an emptiness of heart such as she had never before known as her eyes clung to the tall, broad-shouldered figure sitting upright by her former patient's side.

"Well," remarked Matron, "there goes a difficult but peculiarly lovable patient. I sincerely hope the experiment will prove a success, but I doubt whether moving him so swiftly to the east coast is entirely wise. We'll hear, of course, how the case goes when Mr. Stewart Harvey comes down again."

It seemed, however, in the weeks which followed that they were never going to hear of Douglas Harvey again. Richard, it was revealed, had gone to London on an important case, and it was eventually through Norman that Lindsey heard of his return. They were busy, her brother wrote, 'up to the eyes in work,' and he was being given more important jobs to do, work with sterner responsibilities, and she guessed by the tone of his letter that Richad Stewart Harvey still had Norman's interests at heart.

Of Douglas she heard nothing, and so she thought that he might even be regretting his amorous advances in the surroundings of his old home.

It was with surprise, therefore, that she saw Richard standing at the entrance to the conservatory one afternoon about three weeks later, his bulk seeming to fill up the doorway and shut out most of the grey light of a rain-marred day. She had been on an errand to the home farm and came in shaking the rain from her cap, and he waited until she had taken off her coat and hung it up before he spoke.

"I see you have another patient in the old room. More amenable to reason that Douglas, I hope?"

She smiled.

"We have difficult days, but he's progressing."

"Enough to be able to do without the services of a special nurse?"

"I think so. Matron was very pleased with him last week, and he has even shown an improvement since."

It was a wholly professional conversation, yet she felt as if it were leading to something more personal.

"That's fine, because I intend to ask for you for a while." He sat down on an arm of the chair nearest her, one long leg swinging idly. Then, almost abruptly, he continued: "Douglas has been slipping back, and he is asking for you."

"Oh, I'm so sorry! I hope the change hasn't done him any harm."

"I don't think so. It doesn't seem to be a physical condition at all." His eyes were grave and thoughtful as they rested on her face. "At the moment he is being 'difficult' again, and I firmly believe that only you will be able to handle the situation this time. At least, that is my opinion, and I think I'd like to try the course." He hesitated for a second, going on with the determination of a man who has suddenly made up his mind over an issue that has long perplexed him. "Norman tells me that you are due some leave—fourteen days, he thought. It would mean sacrificing that, of course, at least for a week or two, and I doubt whether I have any real right to ask you to do this for us."

"Why not? You have done so much for us." She flushed a little, hurrying on before he had time to reply: "Couldn't I take my leave and help out with Douglas? It would simplify matters at this end, wouldn't it? Official sanction, and all that sort of thing."

"It would considerably, but . . ."

"Don't hesitate to ask this of me, please," she begged. "Norman could have assured you that it would be all right."

He smiled as though he had already been assured of the fact by her brother before he came to St. Ronan's.

"I had to ask you. It will mean going to Fife, you know, but if you are willing to sacrifice your holiday, we will do our best to make up for it. Craigmiles is near the coast, south of St. Andrews, and I think we could make you comfortable and—happy."

He appeared to hesitate over the last word, and she said steadily:

"I'm sure I should be happy. It's good of you to ask me to your home. I thought at first that you were bringing Douglas to Glasgow."

"There can be no question of operating while he remains in this condition." he returned, his lips tightening a little. "You will see for yourself when you meet him again." He got off his perch on the arm of the chair, straightening his broad shoulders. "I'd like you to come to Fife as soon as possible," he said. "Would it be rushing you to suggest next week-end?"

"Provided you can persuade Matron to put my leave forward a week," she answered, conscious of her heart beating rather wildly at the prospect and feeling sure that he must notice the heightened color in her cheeks.

"I'll see what I can do." He was holding out his hand with that mixture of professional aloofness and friendliness which had baffled her so completely at their last meeting. "Will you go ahead with your plans? I shall take you through, of course. It's a tiresome journey by train."

Strangely enough, it was the thought of that prospective journey in his company which occupied most of her thoughts for the next week, almost to the exclusion of the work on hand. She knew that she was looking forward to it, and yet, perversely, she dreaded it.

Travelling from St. Ronan's on the Friday afternoon, she was surprised to find Norman meeting the train at Glasgow. He whisked her away to have a meal after the briefest of greetings. When they were settled at their table in the restaurant he had chosen she saw that her first impression of suppressed excitement was more than ever evident, and she asked eagerly:

"Well, what is it? Don't keep anything back."

"It's nothing very much," he said, but he bent nearer across the table to say it and his eyes were very bright. "It's just that the lie of the land is better all round, I guess. Stewart Harvey's swell, Lindy! He's had me on two operations with him this week—big ones, where one slip would have meant finis."

78

"And you've come through the test?"

"Well, I haven't let him down."

"Norrie, this is the best news I've had for a bit! Do you think, in time . . .?"

"Don't jump to conclusions. I'm still just assisting, but assisting a man like Harvey means quite a lot."

"Are you still nervous?"

"A little."

"It will pass, Norrie."

"I wish I could think so."

"You must believe so."

He looked at her whimsically.

"You have a lot of faith in me! You also appear to think that Stewart Harvey can work miracles."

"He is a very clever surgeon and he, also, appears to have faith in you, otherwise I don't think he would ever have allowed you to assist him."

"True. My one hope—in fact, it's a fervent prayer these days—is that I'll never let him down, though sometimes I wonder what would happen should he ever ask too much of me."

"I don't think he ever will, Norrie. You must trust him to know."

"He thinks a lot of you, Lindy." He considered her thoughtfully as the waitress brought the second course. "There's—nothing definite between you and the other brother, is there?"

Lindsey flushed.

"Nothing. I am going to their home mostly in my professional capacity."

"Is it going to swallow up all your leave?"

"Most of it, I'm afraid." She flashed him a smile. "Don't look so disappointed, and don't try to tell me you haven't a date during the next fortnight apart from your sister!"

"I was holding up dates so that we might do a show or two together. I had Molly Nicholl at the theatre last week, by the way. Harvey and I were on a case over at the Alexandra, but I expect you've heard all about it."

"No. Molly hasn't written this week, probably because she knew I'd be coming up today. I must 'phone her, though I don't suppose we'll even have time for a coffee. Mr. Harvey wants to travel by the one-o'clock train tomorrow afternoon."

"*Mr. Harvey?* Haven't you reached the Christian-names stage yet?" teased Norman, cutting into his portion of cheese with exaggerated preoccupation. "He calls you Lindsey in unguarded moments when we happen to be discussing you."

A swift, tell-tale color stained Lindsey's cheeks, but she said quickly:

"I thought men never discussed women."

"Oh, they do occasionally—in weaker moments! Rick thinks you're a splendid nurse."

Her color subsided, leaving her rather paler than before.

"Well, I hope I won't let him down," she said.

"You won't." He offered her a cigarette, lighting it for her as he said: "You've never let anyone down in your life, Lindy, and I believe you would even go to the length of sacrificing your own happiness if you believed the cause justified it."

She made no reply to that, but as they drove southwards over the river she looked out of the bus window at the grey waters of the Clyde and wondered what had made Norman suggest such a thing. There was no question of her sacrificing anything for the Harvey's, though it seemed that she was giving up her leave to accommodate them.

She met Richard the following afternoon in Queen Street Station as they had arranged, finding him standing near the bookstall with a new book and several newspapers under his arm, prepared for the journey which he had described as tiresome.

"I think we had better get along to the train," he suggested. "It is generally fairly full these days."

When he had installed her in a corner of a first-class compartment he went to the window to look out for Norman.

"He thought he might get along to see us off," he explained, "but I left him in the laboratory doing some blood tests, so he's probably forgotten all about trains and even about time!"

"He'll probably turn up at the last minute in his lab. coat and a scarf, with an unpaid taxi-driver chasing him along the platform!" Lindsey laughed, realizing with a little thrill of pleasure how easy it was to be gay in his presence this morning.

Her brother ran along the platform three minutes before the train was due to leave, thrusting a packet of sweets through the open window into her hands. He gripped Harvey's outstretched hand. "Have a good time sir, and don't worry over any of your cases. I promise to 'phone you if anything goes wrong."

"I hope there won't be anything. I've been looking forward to this week-end for quite a while. Well, it looks as if we're off." Richard stepped back from the window to make way for Lindsey.

"I'll write as soon as I arrive," she promised. "Take care of Dad till I get back."

The train gathered speed, and the slim, upright figure on the platform was lost to view as they rounded the first curve. She sank back in her corner, and Richard passed the book he had been carrying across to her.

"I hope you haven't read this. I thought you would like it."

She read the title, but she did not open it at once and he made no attempt to unfold the newspapers he had retained.

"You'll have to take us very much as you find us at Craigmiles," he observed presently. "We're short-handed, of course, like most farms these days, but we never did stand much on ceremony. My mother died when Douglas was born and my father has carried on alone ever since. We've had a housekeeper for twenty years." He smiled a little. "Mrs. Creighton is an institution at Craigmiles now and we depend upon her for most things."

"You don't get home very often?" she asked.

"Not very often. This is the first week-end I have managed for about three months."

"It will be a new experience for me," Lindsey confessed. "I've never spent a holiday on the east coast, and I've always wanted to visit St. Andrews. You said your home was quite near there, didn't you?"

"You can walk down in less than an hour. If you are fond of walking, we have much to offer you in Fife, and always there is the sea and the hills of Angus and, beyond them, the Grampians."

For a moment or two he lapsed into thought, and she saw his glance ranging over the green fields which slipped past them to the gentle slopes of the Campsies, knowing that he was thinking of other hills, the blue silhouette of the Sidlaws, perhaps, or the sterner, more distant Grampians.

They spoke of St. Andrews, of its colleges and ancient tradition, most of the way until they were nearing the Forth Bridge and she had to stand up with childish enthusiasm to look out at the giant girders and down at the blue Firth far below while he bent over to explain each point of interest to her with a pleasure that appeared to match her own.

"This is perhaps the most trying part of the whole journey," he observed as the hollow sound of the bridge faded and the train ran smoothly through wooded countryside once more. "We're so near and yet so far, because the railway winds round by the coast here.

"I can sympathize with you," she said, knowing him impatient to be home, "but for me it is a first experience, and I have all the pleasure of seeing well-known names materialize."

He smiled at that, sensing how she felt, and they shared some of Norman's sweets while he told her that they would probably be met at Anstruther.

At Thornton Junction Lindsey stepped out of the train to be met by the breath of a wind from the sea, the North Sea, from which breezes came in keen and invigorating, whipping the color into pale cheeks, riotously bracing, shouting a welcome.

"You'll feel a difference just at first," her companion said. "Are you quite warm enough? We have a few minutes to wait for the other train."

A train for the north came in at another platform and they stood watching it idly. It was very full: golfers; men in uniform going on leave; women with children and stacks of luggage, and over and through it all the cheerful Fifeshire drawl as a porter gave a friendly direction or offered advice in his inimitable way.

"Strange how an hour or two's journey can confront one with an accent that seems almost foreign!" Lindsey observed. "I love it, though. There's a lilt to it, and everybody seems so pleasant."

"No use being otherwise." he observed as their train drew slowly in. "We're going to stop at dozens of places along the coast, but at least there will be the sea."

It was a clear day and he pointed out landmarks to her: the Bass Rock, dark against the distant Lothian coastline; a convoy of little ships passing down the Firth below Inchkeith; Berwick Law, and nearer, the Isle of May lying peacefully on the green water. Then, almost before she had realized it, they were at Anstruther and he was helping her out on to the platform where Douglas stood waiting to meet them.

"Hullo!" he greeted Lindsey, "so you've come? Under what sort of pressure?"

"None," she returned cheerfully. "I wanted a holiday, and your brother very kindly offered me one after my own heart."

"I see." He marched her off towards a waiting car with not much more than a nod of recognition for Richard. "We'll all have to crowd into the front, I'm afraid. The back is full of fertilizer and rations."

And so Lindsey Hamilton drove to Craigmiles, seated between the brothers, two men who were to play their separate parts in her life, and even at this early stage the vague shadow of events to come seemed to lie across their way. Amid the beauty of that new and lovely countryside, with its wide vistas of sea and rolling hills, she experienced a breath of misgiving as cold as the breath of the wind which swept in from the east.

Douglas looked much as he had done when he had left St. Ronan's, and only her experienced eye could have detected the signs of change, the scarcely visible proof of that 'difficult' mood of which his brother had complained. He seemed in his element as he drove the car along the narrow country roads, asking her about St. Ronan's and Matron and the nurses, and what sort of patient she had been given when he had been 'snatched from her clutches.'

Presently he swung the car into a side road and they drove more slowly along a little-used track where low, bare-branched hedges on either side afforded an uninterrupted view of the fields beyond. Rich red soil lay open to sun and wind and hardy sheep grazed on the low hills.

The warmth had not gone entirely from the sun when they breasted a hill and Richard commanded his brother to draw the car up. The hoary towers of St. Andrews stood dimly against the northern skyline, bathed in light. The old town on its rocky plateau overlooking the sunlit bay seemed to have gathered all the peace of the world into that one spot, guarding it jealously, and Lindsey felt it deeply, longing to go there right away to wander along its quiet streets imbibing some of its tranquillity. Seen thus at a distance for the first time, with slanting rays of sunlight throwing the turrets of the cathedral into bold relief against the pale opal sky, she thought of it suddenly as the Mecca of all happiness, and wondered what it would be like to go there, with Richard.

"When you've gazed enough," remarked Douglas, "we might get on. I told the Admirable Creighton that we'd be back for tea."

"Yes, of course." Richard appeared to rouse himself from thoughts that were far removed from tea or even the remainder of the journey home. "We haven't far to go now, but I thought Miss Hamilton would like to get that first view of St. Andrews. It is one of the most effective presentations of the old city I know, seen against the backcloth of the Angus hills in sunlight."

To this Douglas made no reply, giving all his attention to the art of passing a farm cart on the narrow road while he hailed the elderly carter in familiar terms. Lindsey had eyes for nothing but the scene before her, for Craigmiles had come into view and the old steading was almost as arresting a picture as St. Andrews itself.

It stood on a rise overlooking the sea, sheltered from the north wind by a group of ancient yews, a lovely old house of mellowed stone flushed by the dying tints of Virginia creeper and made gay by scarlet blinds at the many windows. About it, but in their way, apart, stood the rougher outbuildings, byres and barns and stabling, and the long, high-roofed sheds that housed the hay harvest of the summer just gone. There was richness in the look of it and the deep knowledge of nature's blessing amply bestowed on man's endeavour.

The road over which they drove ended in the stack-yard, and a flurry of pigeons rose and flew low over their heads to the cote in the barn wall as Douglas drew up the car, saying laconically as he did so:

"Well, here we are, Lindy. You've a whole fortnight to get 'browned off' in, so make the most of it!"

She smiled, realizing instinctively that it was not his reaction to life at Craigmiles which had brought about the change in him. It might even be some battle within himself, she mused, as Richard helped her down and an elderly lady in a lavender-grey knitted costume and white apron opened the door to them.

It was Richard who led Lindsey forward.

"This is Mrs. Creighton," he introduced them, while Lindsey was aware of a pair of brown eyes, as bright and interested as a bird's, scrutinizing her eagerly. The round, weather-beaten face broke into a smile of instant approval and Jean Creighton, housekeeper and counsellor, said in her quiet voice:

"I hope that long journey hasn't tired you, Miss Hamilton. Come away in and we'll get your things up to your room and then we'll have a wee cup o'tea." She turned to the young surgeon, addressing him with maternal concern as if he were still the schoolboy she had cared for in those far-off days when she had first come to the farm by the sea: "You've been working too hard, Rick. This holiday is long overdue. You'll go in to your father right away? He's been waiting to see you this past hour."

"You'll be all right with Mrs. Creighton," Richard told Lindsey before he went off to obey the old housekeeper's command, while Douglas turned the car to run it round the gable-end of the house to the garage.

Jean Creighton led the way indoors across a low-ceilinged hall where black rafters matched the fine black oak of the broad stairway leading to the floor above. Brass shone and sparkled where a truant ray of sunlight penetrated through the arched stone window on the half-landing, the depth of which testified to the substantial construction of the old house.

They mounted the stairway, coming out on a circular landing from which several doors opened, but Mrs. Creighton turned along a corridor to the right, pausing before a recessed door at its far end.

"Mr. Richard wanted you to have this room, Miss," she explained. "It faces the sea and the Kinkell Braes and there's always the sun on them in the morning."

Lindsey found herself walking into the room as if into some little sanctuary. He had given this thought to her, and something in the mere fact sent every pulse in her body racing madly until she told herself that it was indeed madness and turned to look about her.

The room was simply furnished with a low divan bed against one wall and a flounced skirt on the dressing-table to match the sprigged muslin curtains which hung at the high window facing the sea and the distant Braes. It was, she thought, vastly attractive and so much in keepink with the old house and its surroundings.

"If you'll just come down when you've had a wash," Mrs. Creighton suggested, "I'll be at the foot of the stairs. I must run and see to the tea."

Lindsey washed in the small bathroom on the other side of the corridor, changing into a grey woolen suit with a gay coral belt and necklace to match, which had been one of Norman's presents to her.

Mrs. Creighton was waiting at the foot of the stairs when she went down ten minutes later, and she led the way to a room at the front of the house where a fire burned cheerfully in a red-brick fireplace and big red-leather chairs testified to a man's taste in furnishings which was austerely comfortable and, again, satisfying to her sense of its fitness at Craigmiles.

Douglas detached himself from the trio round the hearth and came towards her, drawing her hand within his arm as they crossed the room together, and Lindsey was aware of Richard standing between a white-haired old man, whom she knew must be the farmer, and a small, dark girl whose eyes were frankly quizzical as they met her own.

"This," said Douglas airily, "is Ina Cargill," and Lindsey knew as he spoke that Ina's eyes were upon her hand drawn so familiarly through his arm, and she recognized the effort which the young pianist made to say with so much sincerity:

"I'm glad you've come, Miss Hamilton. Rick thinks it will do Douglas so much good to have you here."

"And what Rick thinks goes with everyone," said Douglas, but without rancour, and then he turned to the elderly man. "Dad, this is Lindsey Hamilton."

"Come away in to the heat, my dear," Gavin Harvey invited making room for her beside him. "You'll excuse me not getting up, won't you? I've been tied to my chair these past few weeks with rheumatism, and even Rick doesn't seem to have a cure for me."

"If I knew of a complete cure for rheumatism, my name would be made," his son told him. "But you're not doing so badly, Dad, with the treatment you've had."

"No, I can't grumble, I really can't grumble." The old man's eyes still lingered on Lindsey's face, liking what he saw there, but presently they moved to his younger son's and then to Ina Cargill's with a strange questioning expression in their depths, as if some feature of the relationship between these young people, two of whom were already very dear to his heart, puzzled him.

"What sort of journey did you have?" Ina asked, addressing Richard. "The trains were packed last weekend and I came through with the luggage!"

"We managed not so badly," Richard replied. "I warned Miss Hamilton beforehand, though, that it was a trying journey, but she seems to have survived it."

"I didn't feel it a bit long," confessed Lindsey. "I've been very keen to come to Fife for a long time, and it was so interesting, especially on the way over the Forth. It may seem queer to you who live here, but I had never seen the Forth Bridge until I came across it this afternoon. Pictures of it don't give one a very accurate idea of its size and magnificence."

"I think we take these sort of things rather too much for granted," Ina said. "I suppose the radio and the airplane have done that for us."

Lindsey saw Douglas stiffen at the mention of 'planes, and was aware of Richard watching him intently.

"I think perhaps Mrs. Creighton will have a meal ready for us," he said abruptly. "Have you people had tea?"

"No, we waited for you, of course." His father glanced towards the door and, almost as if at some signal, it opened and the housekeeper wheeled in a large tea-trolley.

Ina helped to guide it towards the farmer's chair.

"Move the dog, Rick," she commanded. "He's had priority rights at the fire all afternoon, so I think it should be about our turn now."

"Come along, old fellow," Richard coaxed the reluctant pup. "Really, you know, it isn't at all good for you this coddling in the house."

His voice was softly persuasive, as Lindsey had so often heard it when he had been dealing with a difficult patient in the old Alexandra days, and the collie rose to lick his hand before it crept slowly behind the farmer's chair.

"Doug.'s spoiling that dog," the old man said. "We'll never train her to the sheep now."

"Won't we?" Douglas asked, a light that was almost interest breaking in his sombre eyes. "You just wait and see. She's one of old Bess' pups, isn't she? Well, I bet I can lift a prize with her at the trials in a year's time, provided I'm left alone with her."

His father and Richard exchanged glances.

"If she's got half Bess' qualities," the farmer said, "she shouldn't disappoint you."

Mrs. Creighton brought in the tea, and Lindsey noticed that Ina rose quite naturally to help her set out cups and saucers and plates on the gate-legged table which Richard drew in to the fire.

"If it would have been easier for you in the other room, Jean," Gavin Harvey suggested, "I could have managed along easily enough."

"It's cosier here, and there was no real need to move you," Mrs. Creighton returned as she set a tureen of potatoes on the table and began to serve 'high tea,' that most welcoming of all Scottish meals. "I thought Rick and Miss Hamilton might be cold after that long journey, and they're sure to be hungry."

Lindsey confessed that she was ravenous, and certainly the unconventional meal and the homely way in which it was served made her feel eager to begin. Douglas placed the chairs, sitting down in the one next to hers, but refusing to eat anything but a slice of buttered toast and to drink a cup of tea which Ina poured out for him, valiantly trying to hide the concern in her dark eyes.

Richard, after one swift glance at his brother's empty plate, gave most of his attention to his father, asking about the farm, discussing the extra yield of the season just gone, and forecasting the next with complete knowledge of his subject, which rather surprised Lindsey, since he had worked so long in the city.

Although Douglas fired innumerable questions at her and generally kept the ball of conversation passing at their side of the table, she gained the impression that at least part of his interest lay in the other discussion. He seemed determined to take no open part in it, however, and presently he made the conversation general again by asking:

"How long are you home for, Rick?"

"Only a couple of days, I'm afraid," his brother replied. "I must be back in Glasgow by Tuesday morning, and that means travelling on Monday."

"You'll have time to show Miss Hamilton round a bit, though," the farmer suggested. "She'll want to see St. Andrews."

"Lindsey will have plenty of time for that," Douglas declared, "though, if she's very keen to see St. Andrews right away, we might walk down there tomorrow sometime." He glanced across to where Ina sat beside his brother. "How about you, Ina? Can you tear yourself away from Birkha' on a Sunday morning without causing a riot?"

"It would cause a minor earthquake, never mind a riot!" laughed Ina. "Can't you imagine Mother's consternation at such a suggestion when someone must be at the kirk, and someone in the byres, and someone at the kitchen fire?"

"We'd best make it the afternoon, in that case," Richard suggested. "If you're the 'someone at the kirk,' Ina, we may see you there."

Ina flushed.

"I hardly think I shall be, Rick. I'm more likely to be the 'someone in the byres.'"

"While Hattie presides in the kitchen? How is she, by the way? I thought she would have been with you this afternoon."

"She's much better," Ina returned, her eyes clouding as she thought of her younger sister who had come back to the old family home in such tragic circumstances. "You'll see a difference in her, Rick, and you are right about bringing her back for a while. She would never have picked up after Tommy's death if we hadn't managed to persuade her to leave the bungalow and come out to Birkha'."

Her gratitude for his advice shone in her eyes, while Lindsey thought how completely genuine and unaffected this girl was, knowing that she was going to like her and everything about Craigmiles.

"What time will you be wanting your dinner tomorrow, then?" asked Mrs. Creighton. "If you're going to St. Andrews, it had better be early."

"If you don't mind having it ready about one," Richard said. "I'd like Miss Hamilton to see as much of the old town as possible, so we'll have to set out round about two-ish."

"I'll manage that," Jean agreed, as Ina rose to go.

"I feel like the beggar folk, bolting as soon as I'm fed," she laughed, "but I must get back. Hattie has Jennifer to put to bed and she'll have done the afternoon milking, so I'll have to take over tonight in all fairness." She turned to Lindsey, her smile genuinely eager as she suggested: "You'll come over to Birkha' for some music while you're here, Miss Hamilton, won't you? We should really make it tomorrow evening so that Rick can join us."

Douglas said, "Yes, make it tomorrow. We'll need a rest after walking most of the way to St. Andrews and back."

"If you think the walk's going to be too much for you," his brother suggested, "we'll call it off till next week-end."

Douglas looked up sharply, almost the first direct look he had sent in Richard's direction since their meeting at the station.

"So you've made up your mind to come back next weekend? Aren't you busy, or are you just determined to keep me under observation?" he asked.

The remark appeared double-edged in some obscure way, and Lindsey felt suddenly uncomfortable, although Richard said lightly:

"You're still my patient, and I don't mean to take any risks with you."

"Well, I'd better go." Lindsey could detect some of her own discomfort in Ina's clear eyes. "I haven't a torch with me and I don't want to be too late on the road."

Richard moved towards the door.

"You can't go home alone. Let me see you safely home, Ina."

Ina accepted his escort gladly, although for a fraction of a second her eyes had rested on Douglas' bowed head where he had stooped to the fire to light a wooden spill for his father's pipe.

Richard and Ina went out, and a silence fell on the small circle round the fire. Presently Mrs. Creighton rose and began to collect the cups on to a tray.

"May I help?" Lindsey asked.

"You can carry some of them through to the kitchen, if you like," Jean agreed. "I've got help in the scullery, though, so you must come straight back and enjoy yourself."

"Had you met Ina before?" Mrs. Creighton asked as she put the bread back into its bin.

"We hadn't been introduced, but I had heard her play in Glasgow."

"Oh yes." It almost seemed as if Jean had recalled the fact of her young neighbor's popularity with difficulty. "We never think of her as Ina Cargill, the great pianist, here. She's aye been jist 'Miss Ina o' Birkha',' the quiet one o' the Cargill lassies. The other one—Hattie—might have been expected to do the spectacular thing, now, for she was aye the steerin' one when they were younger, but she just married unexpectedly an' settled down. Her happiness has been short lived, poor lass."

"Her husband was killed?"

"Lost at sea, like many another braw lad. He never saw the wee bairn after that first glimpse o' her in the Edinburgh nursing home."

"How sad. And now she has come back to live with her family?"

Mrs. Creighton nodded.

"I'm wonderin' how she will settle down after Edinburgh, though."

"All her life must have been uprooted—her happy life," Lindsey mused.

"Aunt Hattie was the gayest child I have ever seen. I don't think Ina ever expected happiness as Hattie did. It seemed to be her birthright." Jean sighed heavily.

Lindsey found herself telling her about Norman and all Richard Harvey had already done for her brother.

"Ay, he'd do that. Rick's always ready to help, and I've heard him speak of your brother. If it had been possible for them to have come away together, Rick would have invited him with you this week-end."

The statement sent a warm glow into Lindsey's heart because the fact that Richard had permitted Norman to deputize for him, if only for three days, was simple proof of the young surgeon's confidence.

"Norman would have loved it," she returned, "but he will be equally pleased about being left at the helm in Glasgow, I'm sure it's just a little more confidence he needs, Mrs. Creighton. I feel that he'll make good yet—with Mr. Stewart Harvey's help."

Jean Creighton gave her a swift glance, while something in her eyes seemed to clear a little.

"Rick's done well for himself," she said. I always knew he would, though, for he was the type to get to the top of the tree no matter what profession he had chosen, and he always wanted to be a doctor. His older brother was the farmer—took after the old man, and was never content, even as a laddie, unless he was handling a beast or riding on the hay wagon or away with the milk. Douglas, now —well, I don't know what to make o' Doug. these days."

"He's been badly smashed up, Mrs. Creighton, and all those operations must have caused him considerable mental strain into the bargain. He's been through far more than we'll ever be able to imagine."

"Ay, I know. Mr. Douglas would hae taken to farming in time like a duck to water. It's in his blood, and he wouldn't have been able to get away from it. He did well enough at the Agricultural College, though this flyin' notion o' his was always uppermost in his mind, I will admit."

"He'll come back to Craigmiles yet," Lindsey said with a certainty which carried conviction.

"Do you think so?"

"I'm almost sure of it, though we can't afford to rush things. He's quite evidently passing through a difficult phase just now, and the slightest suggestion of coercion would probably make him sheer off in the opposite direction."

"Mr. Richard said you understood his case, and you'll see him through this, won't you?" Mrs. Creighton's eyes were steady on Lindsey's. "It will mean such a lot to the master—to us all, in fact."

"I'll do my best," Lindsey heard herself promising, while inwardly she wondered what that best might yet demand of her.

2

The following afternoon at two o'clock they set out for St. Andrews, picking Ina up at a cross-roads about a mile from the farm.

They went down the shore path to the Kinkell Braes where nature ruled supreme, with no artificial adornments to mar the wild beauty of the scene, and Douglas excelled himself narrating the history of Kittock's Den and pointing out the Rock and Spindle and the more distant Maiden. He appeared to be exerting himself untiringly for Lindsey's benefit, and she was glad, if only because it seemed to be lifting him out of himself. Once or twice she glanced in Richard's direction as he walked quietly by Ina's side, but she could read nothing in his expression. Certainly, the polite, professional cloak had been cast aside, but it seemed to have been exchanged for a mask which hid his inner feelings even more effectively, and in some ways she felt glad that Douglas had annexed her.

They walked in by the East Sands, along the Scores, and halted at the Martyrs' Monument to 'stop and look again,' as Lindsey expressed it, and then Richard suggested that they should go a short way over the famous golf links.

"Not tired, are you?" he asked looking down at her as she stood for a moment by his side.

"Not one little bit!" Her heart was suddenly racing. "It's all wonderful, and I must say thank you for bringing me."

His eyes held hers for a moment while the soft wind from the sea blew round them, seeming to isolate them for a second in time that was infinitely precious.

"I didn't think we'd be allowed to walk across the courses, especially the old one," she remarked as they set out over the springy turf. "I imagined there would be all sorts of restrictions."

"It's a favorite walk, on a Sunday," he explained. "There is no Sunday golf. Tom Morris' famous 'If the gowfers dinna need a rest on Sawbath, the green dae,' still applies, it appears." He walked beside her, so close that she could almost feel his arm against her sleeve, and in sudden, inexplicable confusion she quickened her pace, stumbling over a thick tuft of coarse grass and falling before he could save her. A burning pain shot through her ankle, but she was able to bite back the cry which rose to her lips, saying shakily:

"I'm all right. It's nothing, really."

He helped her to her feet.

"Are you sure? What about your ankle? From the way you fell, I should think it might be damaged."

"It's nothing very much." She wondered if she dared put her weight on it, and was immediately conscious of his supporting arm going round her. "It was so foolish of me."

"Trying to get away?"

The quiet challenge surprised and confused her, so that she had nothing to say.

"There's a shelter a few yards back," he continued. "Let me help you there and you can sit down for a few minutes."

"Hullo!" said Douglas, coming up with Ina, "what's happened?" His face reflected quick concern. "Are you hurt, Lindy? Whatever did you do?"

"It's idiotic!" She tried to smile. "I tripped over a tuft of grass. Heaven knows what I would have done to myself if we had gone down on to the rocks at the Braes!"

"Any damage, Rick?"

"I'm wondering." They had reached the shelter, and Richard sat her in a corner, kneeling down to take her foot between two expert hands while his sensitive fingers felt for any sign of damage. "I thought so," he observed a second or two later when the slight pressure he applied made her bite her lip to suppress a sharp cry of pain. "You can't walk back like this."

"Oh, but I can try—I must try! It will soon be all right —if I rest a little."

"Don't talk foolishly." His voice was brisk but kind as he looked directly up at her. "You know as well as I do what this ankle will be like in an hour's time." He turned

93

to his brother. "Doug., you'll have to get a car from some-where. What about the Andersons'?"

"Let me take the bus back to Birkha' and get the Vaux-hall," Ina suggested. "It won't take more than half an hour." She glanced at her watch. "There's a bus due in a few minutes, and I could make it easily."

Richard accepted without any hesitation.

"Thanks, Ina. Go with her, Doug., will you?"

They set off at a run across the grass towards the town and Richard sat down beside Lindsey on the wooden bench.

"Birkha' is on the bus route," he explained as he took off her shoe and bound the injured foot with his hand-kerchief. "They shouldn't be long, I'm sorry this had to be the ending to your day."

"It's all my own stupid fault, and I don't really know how I managed it." She felt like weeping and being glad at the same time. "I've spoiled your afternoon, too. You were looking forward to the walk."

"Principally to show you round, and we managed to see quite a lot before this happened. You can always come again," he reminded her.

"I hope so, because it has all been as lovely as I expected it would be!"

He sat looking out over the green sward in front of them, watching the long sweep and dip of a gull on the wing, his lips rather tightly compressed, as if he restrained speech with the utmost difficulty, and then he said casually:

"This is going to upset your evening at Birkha', but we must have it at Craigmiles instead."

"I'm going to feel the complete nuisance."

He turned to face her.

"You mustn't feel that, Lindsey." Her name came out quite naturally and he did not even seem to notice that he had used it, at last. "We want to make you feel at home among us."

Her heart leapt and all her pulses went jangling madly at his quiet words, words she had never thought to hear from him, and suddenly this fair day which had ended in an accident grew even more fair as she realized that it was not yet ended.

"You've made me feel at home already," she told him impulsively. "Everyone has been so kind—your father and Mrs. Creighton, and Douglas and Ina. . . ."

A faint shadow crossed his face.

"Ina is one of the very best," he said briefly. "Once she is your friend she'll never go back on you, and that is one of the finest attributes on earth."

"I couldn't imagine there being anything small or petty about her," Lindsey said warmly.

"There isn't. She's as great as her music."

"I suppose I pictured her in a different setting before I came here. I had no idea her people were farmers."

"They weren't originally. David Cargill lost a lot of money in China and Malaya. He had been farming as a hobby, and that often takes more money than it brings in at first, but Ina has turned to it in earnest since his death, and she and her mother are working wonders at Birkha'. Mrs. Cargill is a very practical woman, and Ina's musical talent doesn't appear to be inherited in any way."

"It so seldom is," she returned thoughtfully. "So very few brilliant people seem to have brilliant children. I wonder if it is that they are so obsessed by their own talent in most cases that they haven't time to cultivate it in their offspring?"

"I don't think real talent needs cultivation—not in that sense. It will out, don't you think? Ina, for instance, played without a great deal of encouragement at first. As I remarked, her mother is an intensely practical woman, and I fancy she considered hours per day spent at a piano was so much wasted time."

"But now, of course, she appreciates it all."

"Naturally." He smiled faintly. "She even enjoys basking in all the reflected glory in such a straightforward and natural way that one can't take exception to it."

"You make me very eager to meet the remainder of the family," she told him.

"How is the foot now," he asked in the pause which followed.

"Swelling—as you predicted!"

"Even more so, I'm afraid. Can you put any weight on it at all?"

"I'll do my best." She made a wry little face. "It won't look very pretty tomorrow, will it?"

"Nor the day after, nor the one after that, I'm afraid. You'll have to stay put at Craigmiles now for at least a week."

"And I only came for two," she said, thinking for perhaps the first time since they had sat down just why she

95

had come to the farm and what was expected of her. "I'm not going to be much use in my nursing capacity with a swollen foot, though, am I?"

"Douglas doesn't need a nurse in that sense," he returned slowly. "It is the stimulus to his mind I am banking on mostly, and you possess the power to give that in abundant measure."

She said "Oh" rather faintly, relaxing against the hard back of the seat and sitting thus until she heard Ina's voice on the far side of the shelter.

"Where's the casualty? I've managed to bring along the ambulance, but I'm sorry we haven't thought of a stretcher! How are we going to manage, Rick?" she went on more seriously as she came round the green wooden partition, her eyes anxiously scanning Lindsey's pale face.

"I think it should be quite easy," he said getting to his feet. "Douglas and I can take most of her weight between us and we haven't far to go."

"The going will be soft enough and the car's parked over there on the roadway as near as possible to that green."

Douglas came up to ask:

"How are you now, Lindy? Feeling any better?"

"Much better, thanks. The rest has done me good, I think."

"Well, do we carry her?"—to Richard.

"I don't think there's any need. If we go slow and take most of her weight between us, we should manage as far as the car."

Richard helped Lindsey to her feet and she felt his arm go round her, felt him so close and knew that she was quivering at his touch, and then Douglas had thrust his hand through her arm on the other side in a possessive gesture that made her hold her breath and wonder where all this was going to lead. Nowhere for Richard, and perhaps somewhere disastrous for Douglas and herself?

It was slow going, but they covered the distance to the car at last, and she closed her eyes as she settled down in the back seat and Douglas drove swiftly away. Ina sat in front beside him, while Richard had taken the back seat beside her and sat watching her quietly after he had satisfied himself that the swollen foot was firmly supported on a pile of rugs.

Twenty minutes later he pointed out Birkha' to her, a big, grey sandstone house half-hidden in trees, with a central tower rising above its red-tiled roofs, which must have afforded a magnificent view of the whole rugged coast-line from Eden's mouth to the distant tip of Fife Ness.

Ten minutes later they reached Craigmiles to find Mrs. Creighton out in the yard waiting for them. Ina had telephoned from Birkha' and the old housekeeper was full of concern for her guest.

"Are you badly hurt, lassie?" she asked in her motherly way. "What were you doing that you fell?"

"Just walking over the Links," Douglas returned rather dryly. "These things happen occasionally, but Rick assures us that she's not too badly injured."

Richard was helping Lindsey from the car and when he noticed the sudden pallor of her face as she put even a small part of her weight on the injured ankle, he bent abruptly and took her in his arms, carrying her as if she had been a child across the cobbles of the yard into the house. Her arm was round his shoulders and she could see a little pulse beating under the smooth, tanned skin of his cheek, but his eyes were looking straight ahead and he carried her swiftly into the drawing-room where Jean Creighton had lit a fire.

It was a big, airy room with windows at both ends, one overlooking the sea, the other affording a view of the low hills, and one of the two ample chintz-covered settees had been spread with a cosy travelling-rug and drawn close to the fire.

"I've got her bedroom ready, too," Jean announced, "but I didn't know whether it would be serious enough for that. Ina said she didn't think so."

"She'll have to sit with her foot up, but I don't think it will be serious enough for bed," Richard said. "I'll want bandages, Mrs. Creighton, and plenty of water."

He took off his jacket and rolled up his sleeves.

"You should have your surgery coat, Rick," Ina laughed to cheer Lindsey. "Do the job properly, you know."

He smiled as he applied pads of cotton-wool to the hollows of the rapidly swelling ankle and bound them expertly in place, while Lindsey noticed that he had difficulty with the adhesive bandages, although he managed his point at last and looked satisfied.

"I thought it had swollen too much," he explained, "but I wanted the elastoplast on because you'll be able to use it sooner that way. I needn't tell you, of course, that you'll have to use it within an hour or so, and I know you'll persevere."

"And now here's a cup of tea," said Mrs. Creighton. "It'll put you right in no time."

"Jean expects miracles from tea. It's her panacea for all ills!"

It was Gavin Harvey who spoke from the doorway, leaning heavily on a shepherd's crook on one side and supported by Douglas on the other. "What have they been doing to you, lassie, to get you into this state?"

"It's what I've been doing to myself!" Lindsey smiled, feeling much better now that Richard's expert bandaging had eased the pain in her ankle. "It wouldn't appear so stupid if I hadn't tripped over a clump of grass!"

They laughed at that more easily, seeing that there had been no serious damage, and Ina helped Mrs. Creighton with the tea again, staying afterwards to play to them for an hour. Half-way through the evening, to Lindsey's surprise, Richard rose from his seat in the corner and crossed to the piano, where he brought a violin from its case. She saw Ina smile and nod her encouragement.

"What's it to be?" she asked when she came to the end of the *Rosenkavalier* waltz which Lindsey had requested. "You play for us so seldom, Rick, that this is a great treat."

"Let's have 'Tambourin Chinois,' lad," his father suggested, and the violin went under Richard's chin as Ina struck the first soft chords.

They played together for an hour while request followed request from the chairs round the fire and Lindsey watched Richard spellbound by this new discovery. She realized that he was a musician to his finger-tips as well as a surgeon, an artist who could have made his way as easily in the realms of music as in the world of medicine, and as she lay watching them it seemed that he and Ina played in perfect harmony of spirit.

At last, when he had put down his violin, he crossed the room to where she sat.

"I think you've had enough for one evening," he said quietly. "It's time you went to bed."

Mrs. Creighton hurried out to prepare a hot drink and Ina rose to make her departure.

"I'll run you across," Douglas offered unexpectedly, and Richard looked swiftly across the intervening space but Douglas refused to meet his brother's eyes.

"I hope you're not going to be shut up indoors too long, Lindy," Ina said in her friendly way as they shook hands. "It seems a shame that this should have happened on the first day of your holiday."

So, Ina had no idea that she was there to help Douglas in her professional capacity? What, then, did she think had brought her on this visit to Craigmiles? Unhappily she was forced to admit that Ina must think she had come on Douglas' special invitation as the girl he wanted his family to meet. And how could she tell her otherwise without seeming to probe deep into the secret places of a sensitive heart?

"I'll have to use the ankle somehow," she returned, "though how, at the moment, I feel far from sure!"

Richard looked in her direction, but he said nothing as Douglas followed Ina out. His keen eyes had noticed all the signs of strain, however, and he advised Mrs. Creighton to see his patient to bed immediately.

"Leave the hot drink to me," he suggested. "I'll see to it."

"I feel very useless in all this," remarked Gavin from his chair by the fire. "I should really be doing something to help."

"Rick's done everything," the housekeeper assured him, putting an arm round Lindsey's waist. "Can you put any weight on your foot at all, lass?"

"A little——"

"Try to persevere, Lindsey." It was Richard's voice, steady and encouraging behind them. "You must try to use it now or you're going to have a bad time later on."

She sank her teeth into her lower lip and took the first few steps towards the door, conscious of him following close behind should extra help be needed.

"Don't worry about leaning on me," Jean urged. "You're no weight, really. I could pick you up and carry you like a bairn."

"Which wouldn't be at all good for you with your palpitating heart," said Richard, watching Lindsey's apprehensive face as they negotiated the wide expanse of the hall and neared the foot of the staircase. "And now you can leave the rest to me."

Again he lifted Lindsey into his arms, carrying her up the stairs with the same ease as he had brought her indoors, only at the top his heart was beating more swiftly and the pressure of his arms did not immediately relax as he set her down.

"I'm going to be cruel enough to force you to make the remainder of the journey on foot," he told her unevenly.

She clung to his arm, strangely shaken.

"I'm afraid I'll still need your help."

"I know. Lean as hard as you like."

They moved slowly along the corridor and he opened the door of her room. It was bright with the glow of firelight and warmly intimate, and suddenly she was remembering that Jean Creighton had said he had chosen it for her himself. She wondered if he was remembering that fact now, but there was no sign of any such thought reflected in his face as he led her to the arm-chair beside the fire. Jean Creighton followed them, carrying her coat and handbag.

"I've brought up your things," she explained, "and I'll help you into bed."

Lindsey was wondering how she would ever be able to sleep, for the pain in her ankle had grown intense. She had really enjoyed the evening's music and was glad that she had been permitted such an intimate glance into Richard's home life. Relaxing between the cool sheets at last with a little sigh of relief, she smiled her thanks into Jean Creighton's concerned eyes.

"I had no right to make such a liability of myself," she whispered. "All this will be added work for you."

"You mustn't think of it that way. We only want to do all we can to ease your pain, and you'll soon be on your feet again. I'm very glad Rick was here, though, because I should have been worrying about you otherwise, but he's quite sure there's no serious damage done. I'll just see if he's got your drink ready, now, and then you can go off to sleep."

She scurried away downstairs and Lindsey lay back with her eyes closed, the throbbing pain in her ankle seeming to beat through her entire body until it reached her head where every nerve throbbed in unison. The quiet house only accentuated the beat of pain, and presently she heard the Birkha' car being driven away and gathering speed until the sound of it died in the quiet all about her.

"Will you drink this, Lindsey? It's something to let you sleep."

She had not heard him come in, and he was standing beside the bed when she opened her eyes. She tried to smile at him, but instead her eyes were full of tears, foolish, weak tears which came welling direct from some newly opened spring of emotion in her heart and had so quickly overflowed at the gentleness of his voice and the deep concern of his regard.

"That won't do," Richard chided softly. "You've been such a brick so far, you know."

She fought the tears, blinking them aside to smile at him.

"What sort of fool must you think me?"

"A very brave one, Lindsey."

"It—wasn't entirely the ankle." She stumbled over the confession. "I think—it must have been your music, too. . . ."

"I thought it would help—make you forget your hurt." He hesitated, looking swiftly away.

"Oh, it did help! But I had no idea you could play like that. Even that night at the concert in Glasgow you gave me no indication of your own talent."

"I play so seldom I must be rusty by now, but occasionally when I listen to Ina it brings it all out. It's a means of expression in its way, I suppose," he added thoughtfully. "A medium."

"For your thoughts, you mean?"

He nodded.

"Perhaps for thoughts that could not be expressed in any other way." He bent rather abruptly, holding out the glass he carried, and she saw that his mouth was suddenly tightly compressed. "Will you drink this now? I've given you a bromide so that you can get some sleep."

She lifted the glass to her lips, her heart beating unsteadily.

"Thank you," she said when she had drained its contents. "It should help."

"You won't read?" His hand was on the light-switch. "I wouldn't advise it."

"No, I don't feel that I could concentrate."

He switched off the light, leaving them in the warm glow of the dying fire that was soft and kindly and flung long shadows on to the low ceiling, his own among the others.

"Good-night, Lindsey."

"Good-night, Rick."

The minutes ticked away, but the drug seemed to be having little effect. She could not sleep, although the pain in her ankle was now reduced to a dull throbbing.

Sitting up, she stretched out, pulling aside the curtain which Jean Creighton had drawn across the window beside the bed, and a stream of pale moonlight filtered into the room. She leaned back against her pillows, contemplating it dreamily, seeing, after a while, the tall figure of the young surgeon as he had stood there less than half- an hour ago, friendly, smiling that grave smile of his, and her heart contracted with a pain that was new and bitter-sweet. She loved Richard Harvey. Rick!

And then it was as if a cold breath stole across her heart and she knew that there could be no such hope of fulfilment for her, now or ever, because he saw her as the courage by which his brother must live, Douglas' mainstay in the hour of his trial.

A sigh escaped her parted lips, a sigh for heartache and longing and hope that must surely die, and some-where out in the quiet garden it seemed to echo, so that she raised herself in the darkened room and looked out.

There was nothing to see but the moonlight and the shadows and the distant gleam of the silent sea, but she did not stir, held there, it seemed by the very stillness of the night until a shadow detached itself from the shadows beneath her window and a man strode silently under the trees.

She caught her breath as if to catch back the sigh, knowing that it was Richard who walked there alone, his head bowed as he faced a problem that was as great as her own.

CHAPTER FOUR

I

FOR THE REMAINDER of that week Lindsey was confined to the immediate precincts of the farm, hobbling about on two sticks at first, but later able to go a little farther afield, and always Douglas Harvey was her companion.

Richard had returned to Glasgow on the Monday afternoon, having satisfied himself that the sprain was taking the usual course of such injuries, and with his going Douglas had taken his place, seeing that she exercised while making sure that she did not overdo her efforts to walk, acting host with a charm and light-heartedness which had superceded his strange, restless mood of the past few weeks almost with the suddenness of a miracle. And not so very far under the surface, she could detect that compelling suggestion of possessiveness which had so disquieted her at St. Ronan's.

Now that she had acknowledged her love for Richard, even if it were only in her own heart, this possessiveness in his younger brother irked her, though she could not blame Douglas for it because such an attitude came natural to him, believing, as he did, that one day his affection might be returned.

Many times during that week she had thought to disillusion him, to let him see how hopeless his desire was, but something in this new boyishness locked the words back into her heart. The nurse in her knew so well what his reactions would be at this stage of his recovery, and Richard's faith in her to help complete the cure stood up to mock her. He wanted her help—he had asked for it quite straightforwardly—and she could not deny him.

Then began days of adventure for Lindsey when they drove through the heart of Fife, winding among green hills in the mellow light of autumn, between fields which had yielded their harvest, hearing everywhere the bleat of sheep as they cropped the lush grass and seeing field after field dotted with the familiar Black Angus cattle. Even the airplanes weaving ceaselessly in and out of the cloud-banks seemed remote and curiously meaningless on those lovely sun-filled days, although she realized that to Douglas they must be an ever-present reminder of all he had lost.

Slowly—so very slowly that it was barely perceptible in word or look—Douglas appeared to be turning back to the land, but she was too wise to remark openly on the change. He must come to it gradually: she knew that as surely as Richard did.

Twice they went to Birkha'. On the first occasion 'the ladies were out,' explained John Milne, who had charge of the Birkha' herd, but on their second visit Ina ran to meet them before they had drawn up at the front door.

"I've been coming over to see you all week," she explained to Lindsey, "but I've never seemed to find a minute. I was so glad to hear when I telephoned that your ankle was improving."

"I don't need to depend on my sticks now — see!" Lindsey demonstrated.

"Richard will be pleased." Ina flushed and hesitated, looking at Douglas, and then she added to Mr. Harvey who had come with them: "Do come in for a while, Mr. Harvey. Mother was just saying this morning that we haven't seen you over this way since seed-time."

"We've both been busy enough since the spring, Ina," Gavin answered, allowing Douglas to help him, and Lindsey saw again the gentle caress which was his look at Ina and the faint question in his eyes as they turned to his son.

Douglas seemed to be avoiding any direct look at Ina, and he walked into the house in a rather moody silence.

In the square, dim hall a tall girl was standing before the open hearth, one slim, daintily shod foot resting on the red-brick fender, a girl so unlike anything Lindsey had expected to find at Birkha' that she drew an involuntary breath of surprise.

"Lindsey, this is my sister, Hattie."

Hattie Wilson came forward, one small, white hand outstretched, a smile hovering in eyes that were strangely remote, as if this slim lovely creature in the simple black frock was only half aware of their presence.

"How are you, Miss Hamilton? I do hope the ankle is much better."

Conventional words, yet raised above the plane of convention by a deeply modulated voice that was instantly arresting and would be hard to forget, and suddenly Lindsey was thinking what a beautiful thing it would be to hear Hattie Wilson laugh. Almost instantly she knew that laughter—the rich, spontaneous laughter that was surely Hattie's birthright—had been frozen at the spring of her heart one sad day over two years ago.

"It's almost better now, I think, but I'm still very much ashamed of myself for causing all the stir," she found herself saying.

Hattie turned to shake hands with Douglas and the farmer, and Ina put a friendly hand through Lindsey's arm.

"Come and meet Mother," she invited. "She's baking in the kitchen, helped—or hindered!—by Jennifer."

"Jennifer is your niece, isn't she?"

Ina nodded.

"Douglas has christened her the 'Terror of Birkha',' but he secretly adores her! They have become even greater chums since he came back from St. Ronan's." They had left the hall and were half-way down a wide passage when Ina turned to face her companion. "Lindsey," she asked, deep emotion vibrating behind the quiet voice, "do you think this operation is the best thing for Douglas? He seems to dread it so."

"Rick wouldn't have suggested it if it hadn't been," Lindsey returned immediately.

"I know that, really, but you are a nurse—you have nursed Doug., Lindsey, and you probably know him better than any of us."

The envy in the quiet voice was a thing that Ina made no effort to hide and, curiously enough, it caused Lindsey no embarrassment.

"He'll pull through this all right, Ina," she said softly.

"With your help. We all feel that you can give him so much confidence, Lindsey."

With your help! The words seemed to reach out to her, clutching at her heart. Even Ina believed it inevitable that Douglas should turn to her in this hour of emergency when all his world looked black.

"You helped him so much at St. Roman's, Ina added

"He's come a long way since then," Lindsey said quietly. "Ina," she confessed as they walked on, "I believe he has already found compensation at Craigmiles, although he may not yet be quite ready to acknowledge the fact."

"You mean—on the land—compensation in farming?"

"Yes. I think the soil has claimed at least part of him —that part which has been lying dormant while he rode the air in the first flush of exaltation of his youth, and I think Rick believes—I certainly know he hopes—that it will prove the deeper, fuller life which he himself has found in his own work."

"Rick's wonderful," Ina said as they reached the kitchen door, and she paused with her fingers on the handle for a moment as she added: "Thank you for telling me about Doug., Lindy."

As the door opened a shrill treble voice was raised in song and a small girl with two fair plaits tied with blue ribbon stood on a three-legged stool at the table with her back towards them. The song ended somewhat abruptly.

"That's all of it I know, Gwan'ma. Mummy . . ."

Jennifer turned, twisting round on the stool, but it was not Mummy who stood in the doorway but Auntie Ina and a strange lady, from whom she retired in confusion round the table and behind 'Gwan'ma's' skirts.

"Well, Jennifer!" Ina laughed. "I thought you were going to tell Miss Hamilton how sorry you were about her sore ankle?"

There was no reply, although Jennifer ventured a second glance from her hiding-place which ended in a shy smile revealing two dimples in her rosy cheeks.

"So, this is Miss Hamilton?"

Ina's mother dusted floury hands on a towel and came across the red-tiled floor, Jennifer still clinging to her apron. Mrs. Daisy Cargill was a tall, spare woman in her late fifties, with an amazing fund of energy plain in every line of her agile body and in the springy step and practical handshake with which she greeted her visitor. A woman who had lived a sheltered life for over fifty years, she had met adversity when it came with a resolution and determination which had even surprised her family. She had 'turned her hand to the plough,' as she put it simply, and in so doing had discovered a new zest in life.

"You're busy," Lindsey said. "We should not have disturbed you."

"I'm never too busy for the folks at Craigmiles," Daisy Cargill declared. "If you'll wait till I get this cake into the oven, I'll come through with you," she added practically.

"Isn't it a cake for someone's birthday?" Ina remarked, not looking at the half-concealed Jennifer. "It's John Milne's, isn't it, Grandma? So it will have to have sixty candles on it."

"No," burst out the silent one, "it's for me! Old John's birthday's tomorrow, an' Gwan'ma said the cake won't be ready for then, so he'll have to have a dumplin' instead, 'cos, anyway, he likes a dumplin' better!"

"He's not much of a judge, then, my precious!" laughed Ina, taking her up in her arms to implant a kiss on the round, red cheek. "Do you think we might have a piece of John's dumpling if we traded a piece of your cake for it next week?"

"I's promised him some," returned Jennifer with dignity.

The fat legs wriggled and Ina set her down again, but Jennifer stood by the table this time, regarding the visitor with eyes that were twin blue lakes, eyes that were probably so like her dead father's as to wring Hattie Wilson's heart every time she looked into them.

"Are you coming to my party?" she asked solemnly.

"If I may. When is it, Jennifer?"

"On the tenth. I'll be four." The dimples appeared again, giving the small face a mischievously elfin look. "I'm going to get a pony."

"Who told you that?" demanded her grandmother as she lined a cake-tin with swift, decisive movements.

"Uncle Douglas Harvey," promptly replied Jennifer, meeting the raised grey eyebrows with a confident smile. "He knows 'bout one at Leven."

"Oh, does he indeed!" Somewhere behind the grave countenance laughter lurked, and Jennifer knew it. She clapped her floury little palms together in glee.

"Is he here?" she demanded of Ina. "Has he brought it?"

She ran off to see even before her aunt could assure her of Douglas' presence, and Lindsey saw Ina smile a little wistfully.

Mrs. Cargill conducted her over her big kitchen, of which she was very proud, and they passed on to the dairy where everything had been made ready for the afternoon milking.

"We've just time for some tea before Ina goes for her cows," she said, leading the way back to the hall where Hattie and the farmer sat deep in conversation.

"Jennifer has spirited Douglas away, probably to see the new rabbits," Jennifer's mother explained. Doug gives in to her much too easily, I'm afraid."

"You'd better call them in for tea," her mother said practically. "It's much more important than rabbits, and that child never seems to eat a substantial meal. She's up and away outside within five minutes of sitting down."

Hattie smiled, going out in search of the miscreant, while Ina appeared with the tea-tray which she set down beside her mother's chair. As Mrs. Cargill poured out, a gust of laughter heralded Jennifer's approach and she came into the room seated high on Douglas' shoulder, his dark hair ruffled by her clasping hands. Lindsey knew that she was seeing yet another side of her patient, a side which she recognized and liked—the man who could descend to a child's level and gain its confidence and understanding.

"Put me down now, Uncle Doug.," Jennifer said rather primly as they reached the group round the fire, " 'cos there's tea first before we go to milk the cows."

"Who brings them in?" Douglas asked with feined ignorance of farm ways.

"Aunt Ina an' me, an' we have old Judy to help. She barks a lot at the sheep, but she doesn't say a word to the cows."

"Probably that's because she knows discretion to be the better part of valor."

Jennifer regarded him with a puzzled frown.

"No, I 'spect it's because they are bigger than sheep an' have sharp horns," she concluded with all her garndmother's practical outlook.

"It works out the same way." Douglas set her down in the empty chair next to Ina, and as he straightened their eyes met and held.

"Are you coming to help with the milking, Doug?" Ina asked.

"I'd only cause trouble for you. The cows don't take kindly to amateurs."

"But you're not an amateur! At least, you could drive them in for us."

"Ask Lindy to help. She'll love it."

"Oh, please come, Uncle Doug!" Jennifer appealed. "We'll show you the poor ol' cow with the broken horn."

"With such an inducement, how could I possibly refuse!" Douglas smiled as he laid down his cup. "Do you lend a hand with the milking, Hattie?"

"Not if I can get out of it! I'm not very fond of cows, and I've a strong suspicion that the feeling is mutual."

Amid the general laughter, Jennifer urged Douglas towards the door. Lindsey sat still, not wishing to join them in the fields because she wanted to give Ina this short time, at least, alone with Douglas and the devoted Jennifer, who seemed to have divided her allegiance between them. Presently, however, Gavin Harvey rose.

"We'll have a look at your place and let you get on with the good work," he said to Daisy Cargill. "Do you make an evening journey with the milk?"

"Ten gallons to the station, that's all. Ina takes it down when she can, and when she has an engagement Hattie lends a hand, but she prefers to be in the house."

They walked round the house, ending at the byres where Ina and John Milne were busy milking.

Unconscious of their presence for these first few seconds, Douglas worked on, his thin face almost animated as he gave all his attention to the task.

"I've won my bet, Ina!" he called, his head still down on the cow's warm flank. "We're away past the mark, and old Peggy hasn't kicked the pail once—or me either, for that matter!"

His chuckle of amusement was almost gay, and Lindsey stood very still, realizing something that she had seemed to know instinctively. The past—Douglas' past and his inherited love for the soil was going to prove a big factor in his final cure, and today it was Ina Cargill who led him gently along that pathway to final freedom.

When the milking was done and the cans loaded on to the wagon, Ina climbed into the driver's seat and waved them good-bye.

"The Cargills are getting a marvellous yield from that small herd," Douglas mused as he drove home. "We could do with a few more head at Craigmiles, couldn't we?"

"More cattle means more work all round, my lad," his father reminded him." He was looking straight ahead, but Lindsey got the impression that he was fully aware of each changing expression on his son's face and the struggle going on within. "Every place is short-handed these days, Craigmiles with the rest, and I'm getting to be a bit of a passenger myself, I'm thinking. It's a problem, and I've a feeling Rick's worrying about it, too."

"He couldn't very well chuck his job and come home," Douglas said almost sullenly. "It's a man without a job you want. I suppose you both want to hang on to Craigmiles?"

"It has been in the family for five generations," his father said quietly.

The conversation ended there and they drove the remainder of the distance to the farm in silence, but there had been no mistaking the look in the younger man's eyes, the faint definite gleam of interest even although it was not, as yet, backed by the motive power of enthusiasm.

The following morning they drove to Cupar for provisions, and Douglas marched into the various shops with the big, marketing basket over his arm, while Lindsey followed, armed with Jean Creighton's shopping list. It was a small task she had been happy to perform, knowing that it was indeed a help, because she had felt a very decided hindrance at Craigmiles for the past week.

"We'll have a spot of lunch before we do any more," Douglas suggested shortly after twelve o'clock. "You've been on that foot of yours quite enough for one morning."

He guided her into an hotel where they were shown to a table and served immediately.

"Lindy," he said unexpectedly, the old half-note of pleading strong in his voice while his eyes searched hers, "Rick will be coming down again for the week-end—probably tomorrow—and I've a strong feeling that the sooner this operation is over and done with, the better. I've been thinking a lot and I seem to be marking time now, not going anywhere, and I must move one way or another. I know that now."

"The operation is the first step, Doug."

"Then, I guess I'd better take it right away." His eyes held hers compellingly over the white expanse of cloth. "You wouldn't be engaged to me?" he asked, and then, swiftly, before she could reply: "No, I don't really want that. It's a bit too much like forcing your decision and getting the answer I want out of pity."

"Oh, Doug.!" she said unsteadily, "if I could only give you the answer you want, but I can't, because, you see . . ."

Her voice failed her. How could she tell him, since there was nothing really to tell apart from the pitiful little fact that she, also sought love where it was not given.

"I'll ask you again when I've got more right," he said heavily, "but meanwhile, and so long as there's nobody else for you, Lindy, you'll stick by me in this, won't you?"

"Of course, I'll stick by you."

She made a movement to rise from the table, and he sought the waitress and paid their bill, following her out into the courtyard.

"We'll go round by Cameron and Grange," he suggested. "There's no need to hurry back. I haven't had you very much to myself all week, if you remember."

His tone was lighter now, as was his mood while they drove along the famous students' walk, and it was well after four o'clock when they arrived back at the farm. Douglas was forced to slow down to make room for a hired car, and he looked after it in surprise.

"Looks like we've got visitors," he remarked, frowning. "Rick isn't due till tomorrow."

Richard, however, was standing before the fire in the lounge when they went in, and Lindsey's eyes were drawn to his for a moment in which the whole world seemed to stand still before she turned to recognize his companion.

"Norman!"

"Surprise for you!" her brother smiled. "Rick insisted that I should come along, and I confess I came feeling worried about you, while here you are looking the picture of health and sound in wind and limb!"

"Not very sound in wind. You've taken my breath away!" She drew off her gloves. "When did you come, and how is Dad?"

"Off to Loch Awe for the week-end. There was a lot of fishing-tackle being examined last night, and he's going with Andy Stewart, so there may be a salmon in the bag on Monday morning!"

Richard excused himself to go in search of Douglas, and they were left alone.

"This is wonderful, Norrie!" Lindsey exclaimed. "I'm so glad you've come, and it will do you the world of good. The air's like wine here—rare wine."

"It has certainly sent a sparkle to your eyes, or was it just Rick's presence that made you glow when you came in?"

"Norman, please don't! There's nothing—nothing at all between Rick and me."

"Pity." He looked away from her hurt eyes. "I should have thought—but never mind! If you're happy here and having a good time, that's all that matters. How's the patient?"

"Improving. I think he means to speak to Rick about the operation this week-end. He'd like to get it over and done with now."

"He's very wise. It'll be a tricky job, but nothing to a man like Stewart Harvey." Norman crossed to the window, changing the subject abruptly. "They're a bit isolated here, aren't they?"

"Not when you come to live among them and realize how completely engrossing life on a farm can be. There isn't a minute of their day that isn't full, and nature offers a complete return for all-out effort."

"I suppose so. They're a great people, farmers, and old Harvey's a grand old man. I've just been smoking a pipe with him as he supervised some carting. He gets about amazingly well on these two sticks of his."

"He's having a good spell just now, but at times, Mrs. Creighton says, he is completely crippled."

The object of their conversation joined them at this juncture, and presently Douglas and Richard came in together. They looked as if they had been talking seriously, and Lindsey had the impression that Richard was very much preoccupied during the tea-hour and afterwards as they sat talking and smoking round the fire.

The farmer had his supper early, as was his custom, retiring after he had listened to the news bulletin.

"Anyone care for a stroll before we turn in?" Douglas suggested. "How about you, Lindy? Shall I get you a coat?"

"I'll run up for one," she said, rising, but when she came down to the hall again it was Richard who was waiting for her at the foot of the stairs.

"The others have gone on," he explained. "Are you sure you don't feel tired?"

Her heart leapt at the note of kindly concern in his voice. Tired? How could she feel tired before the prospect of at least part of a walk alone in his company?

They spoke very little as they walked along. The two in front were vague and shadowy figures in the distance, disappearing in the dark clump of a patch of trees to re-appear on the moonlit path again, always just far enough ahead to make their isolation complete. And suddenly Lindsey knew that Richard was deliberately seeking that isolation, and all her pulses quickened at the thought while she feared that her heart-beats must almost be heard in the quiet night.

They had reached the rocky headlands overlooking the sea before he spoke, and when he did his tone held all the steadiness born of long deliberation.

"Lindsey," he said, "Douglas has just told me that he is willing to go ahead with the operation at once, so in view of the fact that he has also asked you to marry him, wouldn't it be advisable to announce your engagement right away? I know it would help him to make the supreme effort he'll have to make if it is to be a complete success."

"He—we talked it over." She couldn't see his face clearly, even in the moonlight, because he had moved on and was walking slowly along the cliff where the wind now blew like a mocking breath of her love and the hopes she had cherished. "We don't think we should come to any definite understanding until after the operation."

She knew that her answer had surprised him, so much so that he halted on the path to look down at her, his face strangely grey in the pale light.

"You do care enough to stand by him, Lindsey?"

"Yes—oh yes."

She was trembling from head to foot, and suddenly his hands went out, taking her firmly by the shoulders.

"Lindsey," he said unevenly, "is there something standing in your way—something you might be able to tell me about?"

Struggling with the weak tears which threatened to betray her, she summoned all her courage to look into his eyes.

"There's nothing—nothing you can do but make Douglas happy."

The sob she had feared broke between her lips as she sought to free herself, but instantly his arms were round her and he was holding her close, as Norman might have held her, with infinite kindness and a world of brotherly protectiveness in his embrace.

"Don't fret, Lindy." His lips were very near her hair, her face hidden against the roughness of his coat. "I won't let anything happen to him. We've got to pull him through this for your sake and for mine."

She stood there while the seconds seemed to fly away into infinity, able to think of nothing but his nearness and the fact that she was in his arms. 'For your sake and for mine.' All this was tangled up with Douglas and his need of them; it wasn't reality, it was a strange, mad dream, but she was here with the sound of the sea in her ears, a sound that was like the heart's weeping, and the strength and comfort of his encircling arms was the sweetest and the bitterest thing she had ever known.

"Forgive me," she said, and he released her instantly. "I had no right to go to pieces like this." The desperation of deep despair made her tone seem almost cold. "You must think me a poor specimen of a nurse."

"I think you are the grandest person I know," he returned quietly, "and we'll pull this off together, Lindsey."

Together! She could not answer him because her heart was too full of the realization of what 'together' might have meant, but she knew that she would not fail him now. They walked on a little way and soon two dark figures came into sight over the cliff face, and Norman called out to them:

"We've been down on the shore. The tide's almost full and it's a picture, Lindy. Come and see."

Richard put a guiding hand under her elbow and they went forward together to meet the others. She thought that Douglas looked at her sharply when they came up, but he stood at her other side as they looked out over the sea, saying nothing, and his eyes seemed to hold the vision of the moonlit bay as her own eyes held it—sadly, wistfully.

Beyond the rocks at their feet the tide crept in over silvered sand, relentlessly, inch by inch, and the wind sighed and a sea-bird rose with a cry, winging its way inland, while Lindsey felt life and happiness slipping away from her like sand running between nerveless fingers.

With a little shiver she turned abruptly away.

"Cold?" asked Douglas.

"I shouldn't be, but perhaps—standing . . ."

He pulled her hand through his arm, holding it closely within his.

"We'll walk back more quickly than we came—give these two a run for their money!"

He appeared determined that they should walk back alone, and, indeed, there was no room for more than two abreast on the narrow path. Richard dropped behind with Norman, and her heart contracted with the thought that he had only sought her companionship on the outward journey because he wanted to make his request about Douglas.

If friendship, then, was all he had to give, she must accept it, because even friendship was something of him, and in the course of the next few weeks, at least, they would meet many times.

"Tomorrow," Richard suggested when they joined forces at the approach to the farm, "I think we should take Norman down for a game of golf. It's apparently his life's ambition to play over the Old Course."

"Would you like that, Lindy?" Douglas asked.

"I'd love it, though I'm no golfer."

"We'll see what we can do about you, providing you promise to keep your feet out of pot holes!" he laughed.

"It's a solemn promise!"

"We'd better 'phone one of the Cargill girls and make it a foursome." Richard suggested.

"Why not them both? Hattie gets out much too seldom, in my opinion." Douglas said.

"Will they both be able to get away together?" Richard asked.

"For a couple hours in the afternoon, I think. Anyway, we can always try our luck." Douglas decided.

The suggestion was left there, but in the morning Douglas came down to breakfast with all the symptoms of developing a cold, and Richard surveyed him keenly.

"Don't bother to get out your thermometer," Douglas said dryly. "I know I've run a temperature, and I feel like the devil, in fact."

"Which won't do if we're going to get ahead with the operation," Richard frowned. "I'm afraid it means a day in bed, Doug., old man."

"But, look here——"

"Doctor's orders! A day will avert all the trouble, and it's worth it, believe me. I'll fix up something for you that will put paid to it in an hour or two."

By lunch-time Douglas was safely in bed, and felt better for being there in spite of a morning's protest.

"Don't break up the golf tournament," he said. "Off you go, too, Lindy. I feel I'm going to sleep in spite of myself."

Lindsey hesitated.

"Let him sleep," Richard advised.

"Will he need anything before tea-time?" Mrs. Creighton asked on the doorstep.

"No, I wouldn't disturb him, if I were you. We'll be back by six," Richard decided.

"We'll go round by Birkha' and pick up the Cargill girls," he said when they were on the main road and only the tall chimneys of Craigmiles could be seen peering after them through the trees. "They were out when I 'phoned this morning, but Mrs. Cargill thought they would both like to come."

Ina, however, was not at home when they arrived; she had decided to go to Leven and hoped they would excuse her, and Lindsey found herself wondering if Ina had gone, seeking courage.

Hattie was dressed and ready for the afternoon's recreation. She stood just behind her mother in a brown tweed suit flecked with yellow and offset by the rich dark green of a hand-knitted sweater, dark green brogues and a matching suede hat. Her eyes looked less remote, as she stepped forward to meet them, and when Lindsey turned to introduce her brother she saw that Norman was looking directly at Hattie, utterly oblivious of anyone else in the whole mundane world.

"Hattie, this is my brother, Norman," Lindsey said. "He turned up unexpectedly with Richard last night."

"How do you do?"

Conventional words enough, but a faint flush had dyed Hattie's pale cheeks and she turned almost with relief as Jennifer flung herself against the short tweed skirt.

"Mummy, where are you going?"

"To play golf, darling, with Mr. Harvey."

"An' the new lady?"

"Yes, dear."

Jennifer nodded, but her bright eyes had gone beyond them seeking in vain.

"Where's Uncle Doug.?"

"He's not very well, Jennifer," Richard explained. "We've left him in bed."

The little face lost its brightness, but 'Oh!' was all Jennifer would permit herself. She made no attempt to enter the car, standing silently beside her grandmother and waving them off with a parting kiss blown from her hand in her mother's direction.

It seemed the most natural thing in the world that Norman should partner Hattie when they reached the course, while Lindsey and Richard played together.

"Mrs. Wilson and Rick are experts, I expect," Norman observed as they selected their clubs, "so that will even us up."

"I feel as if I should be on the putting-green with the old men and the children!" Lindsey laughed to cover that shy confusion which invariably claimed her when she was cast as Richard's partner in a game.

"You'll probably knock us all cold," he predicted.

"Not if you play golf as well as you do most things, Rick," said Hattie. "You have all the luck in the world, as well as being a bit of a genius."

"Don't make me nervous in order to add to your score! It's an underhand sort of trick, and, besides, it's most untrue. I'm not particularly lucky"—a shadow crossed Richard's eyes, but it was swept aside by a determined smile—"and no one likes to be persistently over-rated, you know."

"You won't dare play brilliantly after that!" Hattie smiled as she took her club to drive off. "This first green always makes me drive sideways or not at all! It's wicked of them to allow so many uncurtained windows to the Club-house!"

"I didn't think a row of windows would make you feel nervous!" Richard challenged, but Lindsey felt instinctively that Hattie's nervousness arose from a source far removed from the solid grey facade of the Royal and Ancient Club-

117

house behind them. She glanced at Norman swinging a driver idly on her other side, thinking that there surely must be such a thing as love at first sight. And before they had reached the seventh green she was heaving a sigh for Molly Nicholl and hoping that somewhere, some day, her old friend would find consolation and the happiness she deserved.

It was a gusty day, but dry and invigorating, a day when it seemed good to be alive, and she responded to a new feeling of freedom as she walked beside Richard, sharing his game and his thoughts, talking of books and plays and music, and gaining a further insight into his many-sided character.

Half-way round the course he suggested that they might rest a while.

"I don't want you to put too much strain on that ankle of yours, Lindsey," he explained. "You're going to have plenty of standing and plenty of running around to do during the next few weeks."

Norman had gone off with Hattie to see the view across the mouth of the Eden, and they were left alone.

"It seems more than a week ago since we were last here," he continued as they found seats on the wooden bench in a shelter beside the green. "I hope your accident didn't spoil the first week of your holiday."

"It added to it," she said. "I've had a complete rest, though I feel that I've been here on false pretences because, originally, I came to look after Douglas."

"You know he has improved during the past week. The change is most marked, but perhaps I see it more because I have not been here all the time. I—you're essential to him, Lindsey."

At least, for a moment, she thought, accepting the statement because it had been universally accepted by the Harvey's.

They spoke about St. Ronan's and her return there, but first of all there was the operation to be performed. Richard had secured her transfer to Glasgow for a few weeks, he told her, and then, in all probability, Douglas would be going back to St. Ronan's to recuperate.

"Unless," she said quietly, "he wants to come home."

An eager light showed plainly in his direct eyes.

"I wonder if I dare hope for that," he mused. "It isn't entirely a selfish wish, because it would be the very finest thing imaginable for him, but it would also settle a problem for us here at Craigmiles. I'm afraid my father isn't going to be able to carry on single-handed much longer."

"It would be a terrible wrench for your father to have to part with Craigmiles."

"It would break his heart, I think. He's never been quite the same man since my older brother was killed. They were such pals, and they lived and breathed farming, and were never happier than when planning ahead for a new season."

"Perhaps Douglas will one day fill his brother's place," Lindsey said, conscious once more of that steady conviction which was so strong in her that she felt she could assure him.

"I hope you are right." He sat for a moment in silence, swinging his putter, and presently he said: "This has been a glorious day; one I won't easily forget," and then, amusedly, as he glanced out over the bunkers to where Hattie and her companion stood in deep and isolated conversation: "I think it has been for Norman, too."

Lindsey smiled.

"It's so unlike Norman to go rushing in headlong!"

"Isn't all—attraction fairly headlong? You feel it or you don't right from the first moment of contact."

"I'm not sure. A while ago I thought not——"

She broke off, remembering so vividly the first time he had walked into the operating theatre at the Alexandra, coated and masked, with nothing visible but two grave, dark eyes which had compelled her attention and admiration from that moment onwards. No, she thought, it had not taken the instance of Hattie and Norman meeting to convince her that there was such a thing as love at first sight.

"I'm going off tomorrow," he said, brushing a piece of turf idly with his club. "I should have liked to stay longer, but I have an appointment in Aberdeen. Then, I must have Douglas back in Glasgow next week-end. Can you manage to travel with him, Lindsey?"

"Yes."

"I'll make all the necessary arrangements. I think my father may want to come through a day before we operate and stay till we have definite news for him. The Haltons have very kindly offered to put him up for a few days."

Lindsey remembered Edna Halton with a little inward stab of pain that was surely jealousy. Did Richard go there a lot while he was in Glasgow?

"I think your drive could be improved." He stood up to demonstrate. "You're swinging your body rather too far round, and I'd try this grip, if I were you."

His strong hands fastened over hers as she gripped her club and she looked down at the long fingers, fine and slender and capable and infinitely gentle, seeing them suddenly through tears. If only . . .

They played the remaining nine holes, walking back to the Clubhouse in time for tea. Hattie had promised to be back in time to take the afternoon milk to the station, however, so they could not linger, and they set out for Birkha' shortly after five.

"Want any assistance with the milk?" Norman asked as they approached the house, and Hattie smiled back at him as Jennifer ran out to meet the car.

"You would have to walk back to Craigmiles from the cross-roads," she warned.

"Someone once said golf was a good walk spoiled, so another one won't harm me," Norman returned. "Will it look badly at Craigmiles, Rick?" he asked.

"Not in the least. You're here to enjoy yourself, old man."

Norman got down, meeting Lindsey's eyes as he did so.

"You don't mind, Lindy, do you?"

"Not I! Mrs. Wilson will see you safely on the right road."

They heard him teasing Jennifer as they drove away, and Richard said:

"Have I started something there?"

"I think so. I've never seen Norman so interested in anyone before."

"And I've never seen Hattie so—awake for a long while, —not since Tom Wilson's death. She's too young to feel that life is over for her."

"She may feel that she has compensations." She spoke with sudden difficulty, her voice little more than a whisper. "The compensations of memory."

"Hattie isn't that type. I don't mean that her nature is shallow, but she just wasn't meant to live alone, and it's perhaps just as well for the world and future generations that we are not all made alike."

"She was passionately in love with her husband."

"I know"—quietly. "But Hattie will give it all again, and the second man won't lose by anything Ted Wilson had. I think she owes it to the child to marry again. Jennifer is going to be spoiled at Birkha' eventually. They say there's always a vulnerable spot in everyone's armor, and the vulnerable spot in Mrs. Cargill's practical armor is undoubtedly Jennifer. The child can do no wrong in her grandmother's eyes and she's beginning to sense it. It hasn't affected her yet, of course but I think Hattie sees the writing on the wall. A new home would mean new authority, although I don't suggest for one moment that Hattie would marry for that reason alone."

"I'd give anything to see Norman settled, but I know he won't marry until he has something concrete to offer a girl."

"It won't be so very long before he can be sure of that," he said. "I knew he wouldn't go under without a fight, and it just needs some little thing to encourage him and convince him that he has all his old skill at his finger-tips again. I don't really think he has lost his confidence; it has just been in abeyance."

"I hope so." They were nearing the farm, and in the dusk it looked like a shadowy ghost among the tall trees. "All his heart is in surgery, like your own, Richard."

He brought the car to a standstill in the cobbled yard, turning to help her down.

"Enjoyed your day?" he asked.

"More than I can ever say."

"I'm glad, Lindsey."

He walked with her to the back door, leaving her to make her way through the kitchen, and she found Mrs. Creighton making tea over the fire.

"I couldn't keep Douglas in bed when you hadn't made your appearance by five o'clock," she said," although Mr. Richard did say six. He's a terrible lad for working himself into a fury over trifles."

Lindsey flushed.

"Where is he, Mrs. Creighton?"

"In the lounge."

Lindsey went quickly through to the big room at the front of the house ,to find Douglas in slippers and dressing-gown staring moodily out of the window, which still remained uncurtained, although the firelight was strong in the room behind him. He swung round at the first sound of her foot-steps.

"Where have you been?"

"To St. Andrews. We played a round of golf."

"You came back alone with Rick. Where are the others?"

"Norman dropped off at Birkha' to help Hattie with the milk."

"And Ina?"

"Ina didn't come to St. Andrews with us. She had gone to Leven for the afternoon."

"And so you spent the afternoon in Rick's company after he had put me safely out of the way?"

"Douglas, don't be stupid. It's so foolish of you to be jealous."

He laughed sharply.

"Is that the emotion? It's a damned prickly sensation, anyway, and I'm convinced that I ought to have made you stay here and act nurse."

"I offered to."

"And Rick nipped that in the bud, too, didn't he?"

"So that you would sleep." She was trying hard to be patient, praying that she might be able to deal with the situation before Richard came in. "You know he has only your interests at heart."

"I wonder."

"Doug, how could you possibly doubt it?"

"Outraged at once in his defence! Very pretty, my dear, but don't fall in love with Rick if you are wise. I told you you belonged to me, and I know that Rick's interest is mainly in his career. It always has been."

"You don't know that, Doug., so why should you say it!"

Her heart had made the protest, and she wondered what betrayal lay in her eyes as they met his, because his face was suddenly as pale as death and his eyes flamed as he looked down at her.

"Because I love you," he said abruptly, and into the silence which followed Richard walked with the look of a man who had come upon a lovers' quarrel and was intensely uncomfortable in consequence.

Mrs. Creighton, coming in with the tea-tray, saved the situation, and Richard turned with obvious relief to help her with the table.

It was well after seven o'clock before Norman put in an appearance.

"Enjoyed the walk?" Richard asked.

"Very much; and I have an invitation for us all to go over to tea tomorrow afternoon." He turned to the farmer. "Mrs. Cargill specially mentioned that she'd like to see you, sir."

"I'll take her over a boiling of decent potatoes," Gavin said with a grin. "We'll take the car, for there's that fertilizer she ordered to go over, too." He drew out the card table, eager to begin the game he loved. "How are we playing?"

"I'll stand out," Richard said, and they took their seats round the table, while he stood watching the first few games from behind Norman's chair.

At the end of the first rubber he took up a book from a side table, but it did not seem to hold his attention for long. A restlessness of spirit appeared to have taken possession of him, and presently he got up and wandered from the room.

Lindsey, her ears sharp for his every movement, heard him playing the piano softly in the room across the hall, but soon the music ceased, and a few minutes later the outside door closed gently.

It was over an hour before the bark of a dog heralded his return and, since their game had come to an end, she went out to help Mrs. Creighton with the supper.

In the hall she met Richard face to face. He had walked through rain, and his coat and cap were sodden, but it was the look in his eyes which held her speechless. He looked defeated, and the cast of infinite weariness lay over his whole face, so that her heart seemed to turn over in her breast as a cold fear claimed her.

"Richard," she managed at last, crossing swiftly to his side, "you're not well. Can I get you something?"

He smiled, discarding the sodden cap and sweeping the dark hair back from his wet forehead with fingers that shook a little.

"I'm all right. You mustn't worry about me, Lindy."

The smile had chased that look from his eyes and he appeared normal again, but she could not forget the little incident, thinking of it as a curtain raised for a moment upon a man's innermost soul.

The following week passed swiftly for everyone at Craigmiles. There were preparations to be made and last-minute arrangements about the work on the farm so that Gavin Harvey could follow them to Glasgow almost immediately. Lindsey gave most of her time to Douglas because it became obvious, as the day of his departure drew nearer, that his nervousness was increasing.

"Somehow I never felt this way about the other ops," he confessed. "I guess it must be because I have so much more to lose now."

Lindsey was aware that this nervousness was precisely what Richard was trying to fight against, and she did everything within her power to mitigate the effect of it. She could not present his patient to him a nervous wreck, and gradually some of her sane reasoning reached Douglas, seeming to lift his spirit a little.

On the Friday, shortly after lunch, they left Craigmiles to drive to Thornton Junction, and there found Ina and Hattie Cargill waiting to see them off. Jennifer was with them, and Douglas made a great fuss of the child to hide feelings which Lindsey guessed must be running high. He did not look at Ina until the train steamed in, and then he shook hands with Hattie and turned towards her.

"Wishing me luck, Ina?"

"With all my heart."

And her heart was in her eyes. Swiftly Lindsey looked away, but not before she had seen the expression on Douglas' flushed face. He knows that she loves him, was her sudden thought. Ina couldn't quite manage to hide that from him today.

They got into an empty first-class carriage and soon the train was drawing away from the platform, leaving the two girls and Jennifer behind.

"Come back soon, Uncle Doug.!"

These last audible words in the childs high-pitched, pleading little voice echoed in Lindsey's ears for the remainder of the journey, while Douglas seemed strangely preoccupied with his own thoughts, so that she did not disturb him until he said, as they approached Queen Street:

"I didn't expect to be coming back with you, Lindy. I wonder if Rick will meet us."

"I expect so."

Strange how difficult it was going to be to meet him, in spite of her heart's eagerness, Lindsey thought. That last evening at Craigmiles lingered in her memory and the look in his eyes which had been like defeat. What had he sought to conquer, knowing as he did so, that it was too great for him? She could find no answer, and as she saw him waiting for them at the barrier, knew instinctively that he had not succeeded in the interval.

"I have a taxi waiting," he said. "I think it would be better if we went straight out to the nursing home."

"Not even one night's pleasure?" Douglas asked without any great enthusiasm for such things. "How like you, Rick!"

"I've had to arrange everything for Monday morning, Doug.," his brother returned patiently while he helped Lindsey into the taxi. "I shall be going south at the end of the week."

Lindsey glanced up sharply, but he was looking straight ahead as they drove down the incline into George Square.

"What about Lindy?" asked Douglas.

"I thought she might like to go home for the week-end, or part of it, at least. She'll have a room in the nursing home, of course. The Matron is a very old friend of mine and she has been most helpful in every respect."

They drove to Park Circus, drawing up before the dim portals of a massive, stone-built mansion-house, where the very spirit of peace and quiet dwelt in the shade of a spreading plain overlooking the more shadowy outlines of the trees in the park across the road.

Douglas was shown immediately to his room, and he came downstairs again as Lindsey was being introduced to the Matron, a small, pleasant-faced woman with kindly, bird-like eyes and fine, capable hands, which she kept clasped together in front of her over a gold lorgnette.

"Your brother will be very comfortable here, Mr. Stewart Harvey," she assured Richard. "If you would care to dine with us this evening, I should be very pleased."

"Thank you." Richard turned to Lindsey. "I'll see you home first, Lindsey," he suggested.

"Eight o'clock, then," the little woman smiled, greatly pleased.

Douglas accompanied them to the door. He looked tired, and Lindsey was glad that Richard had insisted that he should rest because he would need to conserve every ounce of strength for Monday morning.

Douglas maintained a sort of feverish brightness during the Sunday evening, which Richard and Norman spent with them, and even on the Monday morning, while Lindsey helped to prepare him for the theatre, his spirits appeared amazingly high, although she realized that it was a final effort. In no way would he ever be able to face this tension again. It had taken all his will-power to come thus far.

At ten o'clock he walked, outwardly calm, to the ante-room where Norman was waiting to administer the first anaesthetic, and Lindsey, glancing at her brother, saw him look in turn at the door. Was Richard already in the theatre? Norman's eyes were restless, and after greeting Douglas he went swiftly outside.

What had gone wrong? It was ten o'clock, and Richard was normally the soul of punctuality. It had always irked him if an operation didn't go on to time, because he considered waiting was a bad thing for the patient.

"Nurse, will you come, please?" Matron asked at the door.

"Where are you going, Lindy?" Douglas murmured.

"For something I've forgotten. I won't be a minute, Doug."

Outside Norman was standing at the door of the room across the corridor, and behind him she could see Richard's tall figure strangely hunched up as he stood beside the table in the centre of the floor. There was a third man in the room, and instantly she recognized Doctor Baer, the little Austrian from the clinic.

It was a second's recognition, for her eyes had gone beyond both her brother and the Austrian to Richard, seeing the white, set mask of his face and the empty, coat sleeve which hung down dejectedly over a heavily bandaged arm set in an improvised sling.

"Rick, you've been hurt!"

Her lips uttered the words while her heart cried: Doug.! Doug.! What's going to happen to you now—now that Rick can't operate?'

Richard saw the question in her eyes and answered her instantly:

"We won't keep him waiting. Doctor Baer will give the anaesthetic right away."

"But, Rick, you can't possibly operate. You've had a hell of a shaking and, besides, your arm . . ." Norman protested.

Richard straightened, his eyes calm and compelling on his.

"You're going to do this job, Norman," he said. "You *can* do it. We've been over it a dozen times, and you had a practical demonstration last Thursday. It's perfectly straightforward and I'll be at your elbow all the time. There's nothing to it that you don't know, and you're the only man I'd trust to pull me out of this hole."

He had spoken rapidly, as if determined that Norman should have no time to weigh the pros and cons of the situation, no time to feel that he could not rise to the occasion, and all the while his eyes had been cool and steady on the younger man's, compelling him.

For what seemed an interminable space in time Norman stood like a man carved in stone, his body rigid, tensed with the very thought of all that had been asked of him, and Lindsey's heart contracted as she saw doubt chase the first bewilderment from his eyes.

"You can do it," Richard repeated in the same level tone. "I wouldn't ask anyone else. You're a surgeon, Norman."

Lindsey's fingers dug into the palms of her hands. She saw small beads of moisture form on her brother's brow, although his eyes had never once wavered from Richard's steady gaze, and presently he squared his shoulders in a gesture which she had not seen for years, and which brought back memories of his student days when he had felt a certain nervousness before examinations.

"All right, Rick," he said as quietly as his friend had spoken; but she knew the inner struggle which had taken place, and her heart beat heavily, thumping against her breast with the slow persistence of fear.

Richard turned to her, looking at her kindly.

"You'll be all right, Lindsey?"

"Of course." Her eyes clung to his as Norman turned away. "Thank you—for all this."

He smiled, but said nothing.

"How did it happen—your arm?" she asked.

"I very foolishly travelled by taxi. I was busy on another case up to the last minute, and I hadn't my own car. We were in a collision with a lorry at Charing Cross."

"And your arm has been attended to?"

"Very efficiently."

"Is it serious?"

"A torn muscle or two. It will mend."

"Rick, I'm so sorry it had to happen today of all days. Douglas"—she swallowed hard—"will it affect him?"

"It may do if he knows anything about it." He was looking at her now as he had looked at Norman a few minutes before. "That's where you come in, Lindsey. You're going to reassure him, and Baer will give the first anaesthetic at once. Douglas need never know who did the operation."

"He may ask for you."

"I'll go in at the right moment."

"But your arm . . ."

"He won't see that. Do you think you can manage your end, Lindsey?"

She smiled wanly.

"I must, since you and Norman have tackled your's so magnificently."

"Good girl! I've had a word with Matron and she sees no reason why there should be any trouble with Douglas. What was he like when you left him just now?"

"Waiting to see you, but not really impatient. He's behaving very well."

"He's made the effort. We can't fail him now." He left her to walk over to where Norman stood. "My instruments are all ready, and by the time you've scrubbed up I'll be with you. Good luck, old man."

Norman gripped the proffered hand. There was no outward evidence of strain about either of them, no hint of the emotions which must be surging very near the surface, no sign of the anxiety in their hearts. They were surgeons, cool, clear-headed, practical in an emergency, and Lindsey watched them turn to the door with the decisive movements of men who now see only the task ahead, the sacred task of saving a human life.

Richard stepped aside to let her walk before them, and although her nervousness and fear of her own frailty increased at every step, she entered the anteroom briskly,

128

her face wiped free of any emotion, the steady light of purpose clear in her eyes.

Doctor Baer had already set up his apparatus in the theatre itself, and he was standing at the sink in the outer room waiting for his summons. Douglas' eyes interrogated her sharply.

"Hasn't Rick put in an appearance yet?" he asked, gnawing his lower lip with a hint of the nervousness he was doing his best to conquer. "He said ten-thirty."

"It's just that now, and he's here." Her fingers fastened on his pulse, coolly deliberate. "He's scrubbing up, but he'll be with us in a second or two." She bent over him reassuringly, feeling as though she were speaking to a child and conscious of a fiercely protective love stirring within her, although she knew that she had no right to be thinking of Douglas as anything but 'the patient' while the operation lasted. That was part-and-parcel of her training, but somehow, this was life, not just another operation. It concerned them all so closely: Richard, Norman, Douglas, and herself. They were all caught up in this titanic drama of living. "Doctor Baer is giving the anaesthetic, and we'd like you to be ready for Richard when he comes."

His fingers fastened on her hand.

"Don't go, Lindy."

"I'll be with you every minute of the time." Her eyes sought the door. "You'll be all right, Doug. Richard's here."

Her voice had strengthened audibly on these last two words because Richard's very presence carried its own abundant measure of assurance as she saw him entering behind Norman clad in his surgeon's gown, his arm, which must have been paining him intensely in that position, down by his side to give an appearance of normality.

Before Baer had adjusted the mask over his brother's face he was by Douglas' side.

"All right, old man, everything's set. Just leave it all to me."

Lindsey could hear Douglas inhaling vigorously and then came the short, jerky breaths as consciousness ebbed, the uncontrollable desire to fight against oblivion, and then oblivion itself. In the silence of the little room she imagined that she could even hear the ticking of her watch, and then Richard said quietly:

"You can wheel him in now."

He went on ahead, taking up his place beside Norman, and Lindsey stood behind her brother watching as he made an injection to combat shock trying to beat out of her mind the feeling that they were standing at a strange cross-roads in their lives.

Richard spoke quietly, his steady voice the only sound in the big, bare room, and the quality of supreme confidence in it passed swiftly round the table. Lindsey was aware of the little Austrian's eyes glued to his face in mute admiration as he gave the signal to begin, and then she was thinking of Norman, daring to look his way for an instant as he made the first incision.

"Clamp, please."

"Swab, please."

Norman's voice was calm and precise, and she knew, as she complied with his requests, that there was no need now to fear his ability to carry this thing through. Whatever feelings were surging within him there was no evidence of them in the lean, brown face, and the slim, sensitive hands moved about their task with a deliberation born of renewed confidence.

The minutes slipped away into half an hour, and the heat from the great shadowless lamp began to make itself felt. Richard's voice was still cool, but he spoke at longer intervals, so that she realized with a wild surge of joy that he had now no need to forestall her brother's thoughts before they were translated into action.

At the end of the first hour the bone grafting was done, and it seemed that it was the first time Norman had paused at all. It was then that his eyes met Richard's for a second, and a look passed between them that she felt she had no right to see. Richard's confidence had not been in vain.

Anxiously she watched Doctor Baer as the minutes passed, for they were now at the most critical stage of the operation. The little anaesthetist bent over the patient with renewed care, so that only the top of his white cap and a pair of bushy, grey eyebrows were to be seen from where she stood. He nodded his head reassuringly from time to time, though once the grey brows drew sharply together and her heart seemed to stand still as she waited with her hands clasped tightly round the drum of swabs like a drowning man's round a floating spar.

"All right again." Doctor Baer announced.

Norman began to suture up and her heart jerked on, stiflingly close to her throat. Douglas had come through so far. She watched as the slim hands put in the last stitch. Norman clipped it methodically, no sign of the strain under which he had worked about him even yet. He turned at last to lay down his scissors on the instrument tray and she heard Richard's voice across the table:

"A splendid job, Hamilton. Thank you."

Matron passed her, packing hot-water bottles round the blanket, and she was conscious of the little Austrian still at the head of the table, but for a moment she could not move.

"The pulse, it ees thin, but steady," Doctor Baer told Matron as he began to gather his apparatus together. "Yes," he added after a reflective pause, "indeed a splendid job!"

Pride and thankfulness and renewed hope were surging into Lindsey's heart in a great tide, yet she forced her mind to the routine tasks of the theatre, knowing that Matron would let her go as soon as she could be spared. Douglas was wheeled away, and she helped a small pale-faced nurse to tidy up.

"It was wonderful," the girl whispered, too awed to raise her voice even now. "He's a brilliant surgeon."

My brother! Lindsey thought, and she wanted to shout Norman's name from the housetops, but over and above pride was thankfulness for Richard, for this thing he had done, for his faith and assurance and the chance to prove them justified. They owed all that to him: Norman's return from oblivion, for she knew that it meant just that.

And they had given so little in return. The thought smote her as she wondered if she had been given the chance to make some return and had let it slip from between her fingers. Richard himself had suggested that she might announce her engagement to Douglas before the operation rather than afterwards.

Afterwards? That meant now, for they knew that Douglas would live.

131

The little nurse was carrying bowls to the sterilizer.

"Miss Hamilton, isn't the surgeon some relation of yours?"

"My brother."

The pale-blue eyes opened wide.

"Really? How proud you must be. He did the job at a moment's notice, too, Matron says. She's rather worried about Mr. Stewart Harvey's arm."

The color drained slowly from Lindsey's face.

"Yes," she said almost to herself, "he must have been in dreadful pain all that time, but Rick would put it behind him because he had to be there. He gave us the confidence we all needed."

Matron came in, smiling reassuringly.

"Will you go down to Mr. Harvey's room now? Thank you for tidying up here, Nurse. I'm hopelessly short of staff, and I've actually been washing this morning."

"If there's anything I can do?" Lindsey offered.

"You'll have a full-time job looking after your patient for the next few days. It was a wonderful operation, and your brother is certainly to be congratulated, stepping into the breach like that."

Lindsey wondered if the little woman knew just how great had been Norman's ordeal, how much he had overcome, and how far-reaching would be the result. She took off her white coat and went swiftly from the room, almost running along the thickly carpeted corridor, but before she had reached Douglas' bedroom door Norman was standing in her path. He looked pale in the strong morning light which flooded through the window just above them; but in his eyes there was a gleam that was beyond satisfaction, and above pride in achievement, the bright glow which she had seen dimmed there so many months ago, the light of life itself to this man who was, first and foremost, a surgeon.

"Norman!" she whispered, and then she could say no more, but she clasped his hands tightly in hers, and the tears which welled in her eyes were tears of joy and thankfulness.

"Richard is waiting to see you," he said gently, "but don't let him talk too much. He ought to be resting."

"He was magnificent," she said. "Have you looked at his arm, Norrie?"

132

"Not yet, but it's sure to be paining him. He won't rest till he has satisfied himself that Douglas is all right."

"He can't sit up for hours. That will be my job."

"You'll have to convince him that," he smiled. "Perhaps you can."

"I'll go and try, anyway. Is he with Douglas now?"

"Yes." Norman paused, seemingly hesitating over something he wanted to say. "Lindy, don't make any hasty decision. This—isn't the time."

She left him, wondering vaguely what he had meant, and it was many days before she recalled his words, realizing that they had been almost in the nature of a warning.

Her fingers closed over the handle of Douglas' bedroom door; she stood for a moment to collect her scattered thoughts before she went in to Richard.

The curtains were drawn across the windows and in the faint green light she saw him standing beside his brother's bed, his sensitive fingers closed over Douglas' wrist.

"Any change?"

He shook his head.

"He won't be out of immediate danger for the next thirty-six hours, at least," he said, laying the responseless hand back on the coverlet, "but there's no reason why we should fear a relapse now. He'll have every care and—you'll want to be with him, of course."

"Of course."

Her answer had been a mere whisper as her eyes left the pale face on the pillow and met his, seeing the shadow of untold weariness in their depths, while a wave of swift, protective love surged up from her heart.

3

Douglas regained consciousness in a room where dim green shafts of light pierced the grey haze he had been struggling with for an immeasurable length of time, his thoughts steadying and blurring again and a sensation of being not wholly part of the world wrapping him round.

A door opened somewhere beyond the foot of his bed, but he was too near to the edge of oblivion to turn his head towards the sound, and not until a shadow fell across his face did he realize that someone was standing beside him, cool fingers sought his wrist.

"All right, Matron?" Someone asked unsteadily.

"All right, my dear. His pulse is thin, but quite steady."

The first had been Lindy's voice. Lindy! He thought that he might have been able to call her name, but his lips had moved without sound.

"It's been a wonderful job. Have you had your supper, dear? We don't want you to go down for lack of food, and you don't seem to have eaten much all day," the other voice said.

"I'm all right, really, Matron, and if you don't mind, I'd like to sit up just a little longer. There's no word of Mr. Stewart Harvey?"

"None yet, dear." The deeper voice had receded, as if its owner had moved away towards the door. "It has all been very unfortunate, and how he managed to stand all that time in the theatre, I really don't know. He must have been in terrible pain."

The woman was talking about Rick, surely. Douglas tried to rouse himself, and his first feeble attempt at movement brought the shadow over his face again.

"Lindy, where are you?" he asked, groping vaguely.

"Here—beside you."

He had wanted to ask her something, what, he could not remember now. It was stupid to have forgotten so easily, and it had seemed so important. . . . He wanted her to marry him, of course, but that was to be in the future, and it was the present he was concerned with, yet his mind simply refused to concentrate.

"I—don't go away, will you?"

"No." Her voice was as comforting as Jean Creighton's had been when they were children. "Just go to sleep, Doug. It will do you so much good."

He remembered about Rick—something he should ask.

"Where's Rick?"

"Resting."

Her voice had seemed all tangled up in a sob, and he forced himself to open his eyes. She was sitting in a winged arm-chair drawn up to the bed, and there was a shaded light on a small table behind her, throwing her white cap and slim shoulders into sharp relief, and there were shadows about her face. Swiftly she knelt beside the bed.

"Douglas," she whispered, "you're all right. You're going to get well."

He smiled crookedly.

"Rick—never does anything by half, does he? He said he'd make a whole man of me in spite of all I believed to the contrary. It'll take time, I suppose?"

"Not very long." There was something at the back of her eyes he couldn't quite understand, a shadow that lurked there even when she smiled, but a problem even in the simplest form was beyond his powers of concentration at the moment, and the heavy lids closed over his eyes again. "Try to sleep, Doug.," she urged gently.

It was half an hour later before Lindsey stirred from her position in the winged chair and bent over the bed with a sigh of relief. Her patient had relaxed into a natural sleep, and his breathing was deep and regular. In the thirty-six hours since she had helped to carry him along the corridor from the operating theatre she had slept for less than eight, but any feeling of weariness had gone completely from her. She had watched beside his bed for the greater part of that time, relieved for a brief spell by Matron or the little nurse who had first brought her the news of Richard.

"Isn't it awful, Nurse? Poor Mr. Stewart Harvey has collapsed and they say there's slight internal haemorrage. . . ."

Lindsey had heard no more. The whole room had blurred before her eyes, as the world rocked under her.

It was Matron who had given her a more detailed and less dramatized version of Richard's injuries. It appeared that he must have been flung violently against the partition of the taxi and had sustained some damage to his chest. There was possibly a fractured rib and they were hoping that it had not pierced a lung. . . .

The explanation had sounded meagre in the extreme, and she was told that she could not go to him.

"He's on the floor above, in my own suite of rooms," the little woman had explained. "Your brother is with him, of course, and we're having an X-ray taken as quickly as possible. It may just be a case for manipulation. I sincerely hope it is nothing more serious."

'I sincerely hope . . .' How cold that had sounded, yet Lindsey knew that Matron's concern was almost as great as her own.

Then had come the period of waiting, and at last the plate, showing how near the splintered bone lay to the lung and the miracle that had kept them apart by a hair's-breadth. She was waiting now to see Norman almost for the first time in all these thirty-six hours, which had seemed like a lifetime.

Quietly she tiptoed from Douglas' room, switching off the light as she went out, so that only the faint glow from the fire flickered across the ceiling, casting long shadows on the wall as she closed the door on one anxiety, and turned to face another that shook her to the very foundation of her being.

She realized now how little fear had really been in her while Douglas' life hung in the balance because Richard had been a hand to sustain her, but now it was as if some bright light had been suddenly extinguished, and she stood in the dark alone. If Richard should die. . . .

Remembering him as he had stood in the theatre so short time ago, her heart refused to accept the fact that she might never see him again, but her feet took her to where Norman was waiting in Matron's sitting-room with the swiftness of fear. She reached the door, seeing that it stood ajar, and for one blind moment she could not find the courage to go in. Then she went forward to find her brother stretched out in an arm-chair before the fire, a tray of sandwiches and coffee at his elbow.

"Norman!"

He jumped to his feet, crossing the room in two swift strides to lead her swiftly inside.

"Norman——?"

Her lips were too dry to do more than utter his name again, but in the depths of her eyes he could see all her wordless agony of soul.

"Chin up, Lindy, old girl!" he said to hide his own anxiety. "He's holding his own. I'm not going to let Rick give us the slip."

"Then—it is pneumonia?" She had forced her lips to move. "I knew. Matron wouldn't say, but—I knew."

"We're fighting it, old girl. The Professor's here from Edinburgh, and he's the last word on lungs, you know. Rick was a pupil of his at one time, it seems, so he's not likely to let him go out without a fight any more than I am."

His voice was gruff with emotion, and suddenly he turned and took her into his arms. It was so much the gesture that had been Richard's that day at Craigmiles, the kindly, protective, brotherly embrace with which he had held her for these few infinitely precious moments against his breast. Tears that she had been fighting back for hours welled in her eyes and coursed silently down her pale cheeks.

Norman stood very still, conscious of her silent grief, and hoping that she might find some measure of relief in tears. The deadly tiredness with which he had struggled during the past twenty-four hours enveloped him again as he faced yet another situation which was far removed from every-day problems. Was Lindsey in love with Rick? He had always thought so, vaguely, at the back of his mind, but now he was almost sure. Why, then, had she almost become engaged to Douglas? He looked down at the ruffled hair crowned by the white coif which his encircling arm had crushed as he had held her close in that first instinctively protective embrace, and suddenly he was thinking how much she and Rick had done for him, and remembering a conversation he and Lindsey had had about responsibilities.

'You'd go to any length to repay a debt, Lindy.' His own voice sounded clearly in his ears. 'Even to the length of sacrifice,' and he remembered that she had not replied. She had just smiled.

His dark, finely marked brows were drawn closely together as he released her and drew a chair forward to the table.

"We're going to have some coffee and then I'll take you along to Rick."

"I couldn't eat, Norrie. I don't want anything." she refused.

"I think I must make it a condition, old girl." he insisted.

Meekly she took the cup he held out to her, drinking the black coffee obediently while she asked:

"Is Douglas out of the wood yet?"

"Completely, I should say."

"It was what he hoped for," she reflected, thinking of Richard. "If only Doug. would go back to Craigmiles now of his own free will, it would ease Rick's mind."

"And yours?"

"I only want—everything to go right for them both."

He stopped questioning her there, but he wondered if she was making everything 'go right' for his friend and benefactor.

"When may I see him?"

"Now, if you are ready." He looked at her keenly. "He may not be conscious, but you know about that."

"I won't make a fuss. It's good of you to let me see him."

He thought that the most pathetic thing she had said, and he drew her hand firmly through his arm in an oddly protective gesture as they mounted the stairs to the room where Richard lay. Lindsey's trained ears picked up the labored breathing even before her brother halted outside a heavy oak door at the end of the upstairs corridor, and although she knew that all the available medical skill of two cities was at their disposal, a cold fear clutched at her heart as she entered the room.

A bulky, familiar figure rose from the chair beside the fire and hobbled towards them. It was Gavin Harvey, and she recognized instantly the signs of strain that were already showing on his rugged face.

"This is a bad business," he said as they shook hands. "They're doing what they can for him, but that breathin' fair knocks the heart out o' me."

He clung to Lindsey's hand, as a child might have done, and he seemed to sense that she shared his anxiety to the fullest extent.

"We can't do anything but wait," she said heavily, her eyes following Norman's tall figure as he crossed towards the bed. "He's in the best hands in the country. We must remember that."

"Ay, I remember, and I've been prayin' in there for the aid o' a higher Hand, and in His infinite mercy to spare us Richard."

"We—mustn't lose him." Her voice failed her while tears burned against her eyelids. "Will you come downstairs and rest a little, Mr. Harvey? You've had a long journey."

"It's fine to know about Douglas." His tired eyes sought the bed again, and Lindsey's followed them imploringly, but she saw Norman shake his head and knew that it was no use even crossing to the bed because Richard would not know them. "I'll come down with you," he continued. "I don't want to be a bother to anybody, and if you'll just promise to let me know if there's any change, I'll rest a bit."

He moved to the door and Lindsey hesitated, knowing that she must go with him, this strangely forlorn figure of a man who sought sympathy and understanding from her almost instinctively, but her heart yearned for just one glimpse of Richard, and she knew that Norman understood as he motioned her towards the bed.

Softly she crossed the wide expanse of carpet and stood looking down at the shadowed face, Richard's face, yet so strangely drawn and unlike him, with the heavy eyelids closed against the world. For a second or two she stood immovable while the difficult tears of restrained grief fell silently in her heart. Slowly her hand went out to touch the slim fingers lying so unresponsively on the coverlet, and then she turned away to go back to his father.

"Will you come now, Mr. Harvey? Norman will be with him and he'll call us if—if we are needed."

As Norman had done with her less than half an hour ago, she tried to persuade the old farmer to eat, but he shook his head.

"I just couldn't manage anything, lass," he said. "Tell me about Douglas."

She tried to keep her mind on his younger son and the operation which had been such an outstanding success, although now all that seemed to be so far away in the past as to be nothing more than a memory.

"He came through splendidly, Mr. Harvey, and all he will need now is rest to make him strong and well again."

"I'm glad to hear that." He moved uneasily. "He was saying before he went away that he'd be thinkin o' settlin' down—marrying maybe, but that he couldn't be askin' a girl to tie herself to a lad without a future. He could have a fine future at Craigmiles."

She bent towards him.

"And I think, if we wait patiently a little longer, he will come to see that for himself, but we mustn't force him to any decision at this stage."

"But you think, maybe in time . . . ?" he suggested eagerly.

"I hope so, most sincerely."

"And—our sort of life would satisfy you?"

The question had been simply put, but there was no such simple answer, Lindsey realized. Married to Douglas,

139

would she be content to sever all her connections with the medical world, to put behind her the interests that had been her life for so long and around which her whole world had been built? Even before Richard had crossed her path, her mind and most of her time had been given to her work, and perhaps that had been why she had understood so completely Norman's crushing disappointment when his life's ambition had faded before his eyes, why she had known so surely what happiness and fulfilment would have come into her life if Richard had been able to offer her love as well as friendship.

Could she, then, marry Douglas and settle down at Craigmiles? She looked across at Gavin Harvey, knowing herself incapable of answering his question at that moment or for some time to come.

"If—you love a person," she said with difficulty, "you should be ready and willing to share his life whatever it is. I've never thought that environment mattered a great deal, but to share one person's thoughts—his ideals—to know and sympathize with his ambitions . . ."

Her voice dropped into silence, and presently Gavin said:

"I'm thinking you'll not make any mistake when it comes to the bit, lass, an' where your love is given it will be a grand thing for the right man."

She looked at him quickly and his eyes were clear and steady on hers.

"I hope I'll know the right thing to do," she answered, and the words echoed and re-echoed in her heart like a prayer.

4

For three days Richard lay unresponsive to their every effort, and in all that time Lindsey nursed Douglas with a mask of cheerfulness upon her face which belied the crushing anxiety in her heart.

Douglas, however, developed a restlessness which could not be overlooked when his constant requests for his brother's presence were met by one excuse after another, and it was Matron who finally suggested that he should be told something of the truth. She appealed directly to Norman, who was still supervising Douglas' case.

"I don't think it will harm him a great deal—not any more than the suspicion of something being kept back will. Yes," Norman decided, "I think you could tell him that Rick went down with pneumonia, though I wouldn't mention anything about the accident yet awhile." He glanced over Matron's head to where Lindsey was listlessly sipping her tea at the table. "Perhaps you'd tell him, Matron," he suggested. "I'm going to insist that this sister of mine gets some sleep."

Lindsey's eyes, deep-set in her pale face, met his as he crossed the room. She had heard very little of the conversation, and she looked up at him questioningly.

"An order for bed," he said.

"It's only eight o'clock, Norrie. I couldn't sleep even if I did go upstairs, and the Professor may have some news for us later."

"If it's anything that you have to hear, I'll call you. Meanwhile, I insist that you try to rest if you can't sleep."

"Nurse Binns will sit with Mr. Harvey until ten," Matron urged. "Do go up now, Nurse."

Lindsey rose to her feet.

"You'll call me, Norrie?" she asked as he led her to the door.

"I promised."

Slowly she went to her room. She was deadly tired, but she knew that she would not sleep, though she might close her eyes and try to rest.

She lay down on the bed fully dressed, drawing the eiderdown over her, but she could not relax. She found herself lying tensed, listening for the little noises of the house: the creak of a downstairs door; the distant striking of a clock; voices in the hall below, and once a step passing softly along the corridor outside. She counted the striking of the hour at nine and again at ten, and before the quarter chimes had rung out, her thoughts had drifted into a haze that was like dulled pain.

When conscious thought stirred in her again she knew that she had slept, the deep sleep of utter exhaustion that excludes dreams. She was cold and the house was very still, and suddenly her heart seemed to rise into her throat, fluttering like an imprisoned bird beating impotent wings against a cage. Fear! How quiet the house was, how still! Was there something ominous about that stillness?

The fluttering at her throat subsided into a dull, heavy beat. It must be after midnight. She switched on her bed-light and saw that it was almost half-past two, and she sat listening for the chimes of the half-hour from the clock in the hall, until she realized that they would not come. The chimes had been silenced.

Shivering, she reached for her dressing-gown and slipped it on over her uniform, taking up her torch to guide her along the corridor. The circle of light shone on the carpet, a little moving yellow pool, and she watched it as if fascinated, passing one closed door after another until she reached the end of the corridor.

"Lindy, is that you?"

The door before her lay ajar and she realized that it was the door of Douglas' room.

"Yes."

"Will you come a minute?"

She turned aside almost reluctantly.

"Yes, Doug.?"

He switched on the light above his bed, and their eyes met, and instantly she saw the shock in his.

"What is it? Is it Rick? Were you going to him, Lindy?"

She stared back at him for a full minute without replying, and then she nodded.

"I thought perhaps they would need me."

"We've both needed you," he said almost harshly. "And tonight it is Rick."

She stood on the threshold of his room, looking in at him, while footsteps came briskly along the corridor, and a light was switched on somewhere behind her. It was Norman.

"Lindsey," he said, "will you come? Rick's asking for you."

Following him along the dimly lit corridor, she felt as if she were moving in some strange dream, and even Norman's voice had the far-off quality associated with dreams when he said:

"Something appears to be on his mind—worrying him. It isn't the operation"—diffidently—"because he seems quite satisfied about that, but I think it concerns Douglas, and I have half a notion you might be able to satisfy him."

"In what way, Norrie?" It seemed that her heart was pounding close against her throat. "Do you mean about becoming engaged to Doug.?"

He turned, stooping a little to look into her eyes.

"Whatever you do," he said earnestly, "don't let gratitude enter into it. Go the way of your own heart."

The way of her heart! She sought for words, but could find none, and presently they had reached Richard's door and the wild beating of her heart was stilled, so that she walked into the presence of the man she loved as he had always known her in an emergency, cool, practical, efficient, with eyes that were level and steady on his own, when finally, she stood beside the bed looking down at him.

Experience had taught her to expect a change, but the thin, worn face on the pillow seemed scarcely Richard's; only the eyes were the same, meeting hers now with that quiet smile which she knew she would cherish for ever deep in her secret heart.

His voice was very weak when he spoke.

"Lindsey," he said, "how has Doug. come through? Does he view the world from any clearer standpoint?"

"It's—early to say, Rick. He knows the operation has been a success."

"I had no doubt about that." He looked past her to where Norman stood at the foot of the bed watching to terminate her visit at the first sign of strain in his patient. "Norman did a marvellous job. I knew"—his tired brain seemed to grope for adequate words to express his feelings—"I knew it would be a success, and that it would mark the turning-point for him, and I had hoped it would help Doug. to see things clearer, too. . . ."

She bent over the bed, taking one of the long, finely shaped hands in both her own.

"It will, Rick," she whispered. "You must believe it will."

He looked back at her intently, but she waited in vain for him to speak, and the light which had leapt to his eyes died slowly and he closed them, as if to blot out the vision of her.

"Go back to him, Lindsey," he said. "He needs you more than I do, I guess."

Not until she had left the dimly lit room behind did the full significance of his words penetrate into her numbed brain. 'He needs you more than I do.' He needs you, but I, also need you. Could that be true? Her heart-beats quickened and every pulse in her body began to throb to the echo of his words. Were they words of a confession which, but for his weak state, would never have been made, or were they but the vague impressions of a mind slipping back into semi-consciousness and unable to control impressions, however slight?

Her mind swerved this way and that, torn by cold reason and swayed by the dictates of her heart. If he needed her. . . . He had sent for her, and for one moment, as she had bent over his bed, he had looked like a man ready to cast off some great burden and confess in weakness what he would never have done in strength. Could she —dare she believe that he had stood aside because of Douglas' need of her?

CHAPTER FIVE

I

FOR THE NEXT few days Lindsey nursed Douglas through the daylight hours, seeing him growing gradually stronger and aware that Norman was more than pleased with his progress, although he could not say the same of Richard's. He had survived that night of crisis, but it would be some weeks before he was well again and able to go back to work.

"I hope I shall be able to persuade him to take a holiday," he confessed to Lindsey as they sat over a cup of coffee in the small study Matron had put at his disposal when the specialists had handed over both patients to his care. "He hasn't taken a decent holiday in years. A week-end here and a day there—never any time for real relaxation. He should go home to Fife when Douglas goes."

"Doug, hasn't promised to go yet," Lindsey reminded him.

"But he will."

"I think so. And Rick?" she asked uncertainly.

"I must make it my job to persuade him when he is strong enough to argue—perhaps even before then," Norman declared.

And so Christmas passed and the New Year, and in the first days of January Richard was able to leave his room and take tea with them in the study.

"You can bring Doug. down, too," Norman suggested. "He's been out of bed each morning this week, hasn't he?"

"He'll be glad to come down, I should think. He's been worrying about Rick." Lindsey told him.

She made her way to Douglas' room, walking slowly, her thoughts ranging uneasily over the past few weeks when she had been at a loss to understand Douglas and had sensed in him a strange reluctance to discuss anything very seriously. There had also been what amounted to reticence at the prospect of meeting his brother, although he had been genuinely anxious about Richard and had hoped for his speedy recovery as earnestly as any of them.

When she opened the bedroom door he was sitting in an arm-chair drawn up to the fire, a tartan rug wrapped securely about his knees, and she noticed that he had been re-reading the letters which had come for him that morning.

"Rick is coming along to the study for tea, Doug.," she explained. "Would you like to come? Norman thinks the change would be good for you."

For a moment he hesitated, and then he said:

"Is it a medical inspection, or merely a social call?"

"Why not call it a family party?"

"I'd like to." He caught her hand. "Lindy, about you and me. I guess I'm right on the road to recovery now, but I've still very little right to ask a girl to marry me. I've nothing to offer, I know, but maybe if I got a start at something . . . "

"Yes, Doug.?"

Her eyes were shining. Here was what they had been waiting for—the desire for a new start, the willingness to break away from the obsession for flying, the impulse to begin life anew.

"I'm not quite clear yet about what I want to do—what I can do—but I guess there must be something."

"Why not leave it all until you've had a chance to get properly well and strong first?" she suggested. "You'll have to be moved from here presently because they'll be needing the bed, and probably you'll go when Richard does. He'll be going home to Craigmiles, Doug. Wouldn't you care to go too? It would be company for you both."

"And you?" he asked. "What will you do?"

"I must go back to work. Probably I shall have to go back to St. Ronan's."

"Do you want to go back there?"

She met his eyes squarely.

"For the present, Doug."

"I don't suppose I can say anything after that. Will you stay here till we go to Fife?"

Her heart leapt at the inevitability of his tone.

"I may even travel through with you for the week-end. Your father very kindly asked Norman and I to come," she told him.

"When will Rick be able to travel?" he asked absently.

"Norman hopes by the end of next week."

"Well," he cast the rug aside, "I suppose we'd better get down to the tea-party."

She put an arm under his to steady him while she handed him his stick.

"It's quite like old times seeing you around in uniform again," he said as his finger tightened over hers, though he made no attempt to kiss her. "Thank God Rick pulled round all right. It was a near thing, wasn't it?"

"Very near." Her voice had sounded unsteady and she saw him look round at her, although there was no surprise in his eyes.

Norman had settled Richard in a chair beside the fire by the time they reached the study, and he was holding a spill to his pipe when they went in. To Lindsey it seemed that time stood suspended as she met Richard's eyes, and she wondered if he, too, was remembering those first moments of consciousness when his spirit had called to her in its weakness, confessing its need of her. He had passed all that now, the weakness and the confession, and she saw nothing in his face but the reflection of the old friendliness which had always been there.

"We were beginning to wonder if you had turned down the invitation altogether," he observed to Douglas. "But it's grand to see you on your feet again, old man. We've been waiting for you to make the tea, Lindsey," he added. "Neither Norman nor I have the courage."

Lindsey settled Douglas in the chair her brother had drawn up for him, conscious of hands that were not quite steady and a smile that was frozen on her lips. Richard had accepted her again as Douglas' chosen wife, had pushed aside or utterly forgotten his own need of her.

As she turned to her task of making the tea she wondered if there was anyway out of the maze in which they all appeared to be wandering so blindly, and suddenly she was thinking of Ina Cargill, conscious that Ina, also was part of this strange jig-saw of human emotions which would not piece itself into any very definite pattern.

"What's the truth about this operation of mine?" Douglas demanded suddenly. "It appears to be shrouded in mystery, and Rick's collapse seems to be part of it. I know it has been a brilliant success, so why all the hush-hush?"

Three pairs of eyes exchanged glances. It was Richard who finally spoke.

"You have Norman to thank for the job," he said quietly.

Douglas' eyes turned swiftly in Norman's direction and for a second or two he looked intently at the other man.

"I see," he said at last. "We all seem to be getting fairly deeply into each other's debt these days." He paused, glanced at Lindsey, and then added briefly: "Thanks, all the same, Hamilton. I'm deeply grateful, and now I suppose it's entirely up to myself."

"Entirely." Richard fixed him with steady eyes. "You can make what you like of your life now, Doug., on equal terms with the next fellow."

"I've yet to find something that will give me the incentive to put all I've got into the effort to reach the top."

"I thought you had found that," Richard said frowning.

"I mean work." Again Douglas glanced in Lindsey's direction. "Not the reason for wanting to make good."

"Don't try to cross all your bridges before you come to them, old man," Richard said kindly. "I guess things will sort themselves out more easily than you think."

His brother looked doubtful, though he said with a new humility that Lindsey, at least, was quick to notice:

"I guess I owe you all a devil of a lot I shall never be able to repay if I live to be a hundred. You seem to have written me a blank cheque, but I can't go on drawing on your generosity for ever."

"We don't intend to let you," Norman told him, going over to sit on the arm of his chair and offering him a cigarette. "We're hounding you out of here in a few days' time to make room for a more urgent case."

Douglas looked at Lindsey.

"And I'm going back to Fife. I suppose you wish that, Rick?"

148

"I want you to go where you feel you'll be happiest. If you think a few weeks at St. Ronan's first will do you more good, I can arrange to have you taken there."

"By Lindy?"

"She will have to report back for duty in any case."

There was a brief pause, and Lindsey watched Douglas' thin face flush and his brows draw swiftly together as he did battle with what appeared to be deeply conflicting thoughts.

"All right," he said at last. "I'll go home."

Norman crossed to a gramophone which stood between the two windows, glancing through the selection of records and putting one or two aside before he lifted the lid.

"Like some music?" he asked.

"It depends what you've got," Richard answered. "Matron's taste in music is somewhat alarming!"

"I've found half a dozen that are not so bad." Norman put on the first record and turned to switch on the standard lamp behind Lindsey's head. " 'Soft lights and sweet music.' What more could you ask?"

"Another cup of tea, if Lindsey can come down from the clouds to pour it out," said Douglas, dryly, and Lindsey came out of her reverie with a start, flushing sensitively because Norman's choice of a record had been Beethoven's Sixth Symphony and she had last heard it played when she had gone with Richard to St. Andrew's Hall that evening which seemed so far off now that the joy of friendship of it might have been theirs in another lifetime instead of just so many weeks ago.

She could not look his way lest he recognize the emotion in her eyes, but somehow, even across the width of the room, she knew that he, also was remembering.

The music filled the room in a great cadence of sound, tremulous now, then pouring out in the full volume of its beauty towards the final bars, and they sat listening in silence, even Douglas caught up in the spell of it, although it held no particular fascination of memory for him.

As Norman changed the record there was a soft tap on the door and a voice they all knew asked:

"May I come in?"

"It's Ina!" Douglas said.

Ina Cargill came into the room and there was a smile in her eyes that embraced them all, her very good friends,

149

but her glance went swiftly back to Douglas' pale face, where it had first rested, as she said:

"I stood outside for a moment to listen to your concert, because it meant that you were well, Doug. and you, Rick! I've wanted to come personally since I heard of your accident, but Mother has been in bed with 'flu and Jennifer developed a rash which looked suspiciously like measles at first and scared us all for a day or two until we discovered she had been eating berries out of the hedge and had actually hidden some away against the barren days of winter like the squirrel with his nuts!"

"The funny little beggar!" laughed Douglas. "I hope she hasn't come to any harm?"

"Not a bit! Mother's faith in the castor-oil bottle has been inherited by Hattie to a startling degree!"

"Poor Jennifer," Lindsey laughed. "She'll probably remember about forbidden berries for the rest of her life —and castor-oil!"

"How is your sister?" Norman asked as Lindsey rose to make fresh tea for their unexpected visitor. "She 'phoned several times to ask for Rick and Doug., but I never happened to be on the spot."

"Tough luck!" remarked Douglas with a grin. "Didn't you ever think of following up the call—just to be reassuring, you know!"

Norman gave him a dark look.

"I haven't your ingenuity, my lad," he returned, "but I dare say I'll learn."

Lindsey handed Ina her cup.

"We were prepared for another visitor," she explained. "We thought my father might drop in."

"What's the weather like on your side of the world?" Richard asked.

"Cold but dry," Ina returned. "Glasgow always makes me feel morbid because it's generally raining cats and dogs when I come through."

"You know that's a gross libel," Norman defended his native city as he put a fresh record on the gramophone. It was one he appeared to have selected with care, and after the first few bars Lindsey was aware that both Richard and Ina were listening intently.

"Isn't that one of your records, Ina?" Douglas asked presently.

"A very old one," Ina answered, flushing as the soft, clear notes stole through the quiet room. "It must have been made five or six years ago."

Her eyes met Richard's again and it was clear that they were both thinking of those care-free days of easy comradeship when that early record had been made before universal fame had claimed so much of her time or the conquest of the air had obsessed Douglas to the exclusion of all else, making him blind to some of the simpler things in life.

They heard the record through to the end in silence, and then Matron came in to summon Norman to the telephone, staying to be introduced to their visitor.

"Not *the* Ina Cargill!" she beamed, and on being assured that it was: "But this *is* a surprise, a very exciting surprise! I have several of your recordings, Miss Cargill, and I have heard you play in Edinburgh."

Ina who was still very shy of her fame, flushed and smiled and Lindsey saw Douglas looking at his old playmate with a puzzled expression in his eye, as if he couldn't quite come to accept Ina as the celebrity, thinking of her more often as the girl over at Birkha' who had been his boyhood companion, and who was so much part of the life at home that he had almost come to take her for granted.

They spoke of music and of Craigmiles and Birkha' until Norman returned.

"Time's up, Rick, I'm afraid," he announced, glancing at his watch. "The order is back to bed."

He put a hand under Richard's elbow to help him up, and Douglas, grinning in Ina's direction, said:

"Changed days for Rick, eh?—being at the receiving end of doctor's orders!"

"He takes it very well," Ina reflected.

"You've only about ten minutes of your own time left," Norman reminded him as he signalled to Lindsey to help with Richard, "so I'd make the most of it, if I were you."

They walked slowly along the corridor, Richard leaning on his stick with Lindsey supporting him lightly on the other side, and at the head of the stairs Norman left them to put in another telephone call to Edinburgh. They continued alone, silently at first, and then Richard said:

151

"I'm glad you were able to influence Doug. about coming home, Lindsey. I don't think anyone else could have done it in such a short time."

"I don't know whether I influenced him or not," she said. "Doug.'s changing in so many ways."

He turned to look at her.

"What do you mean?"

"I mean that he's lost most of the old bitterness and that dreadful cynicism has gone. His outlook on life is altogether brighter and he's grasping things much more quickly, things he didn't want to see in the past when he was so full of despair about his condition."

"I gathered most of that this afternoon," he spoke almost abruptly. "I'm glad we are going home together, because I shall be properly on my feet in a few days, and fully able to look after him. You'll come, of course, Lindsey—at least for the week-end?"

There was friendly welcome in his tone, but that was all. No eagerness, no personal note. He wanted her there because of Douglas.

"Of course," she said, adding nothing more because they had reached his bedroom and Matron had come up behind them to see her patient comfortably settled for the night.

When Lindsey went back towards the study she found her brother waiting for her at the head of the stairs and immediately recognized a new, half suppressed excitement about him.

"Lindy, just a sec. I've something to tell you."

"Yes?" She scanned his handsome features eagerly. "What is it, Norrie? A new job?"

"The best sort in the world!" She could see his eyes shining in the dim light. "Assistant to Rick. He asked me this afternoon before you came downstairs with Douglas, and I could scarcely believe that he meant it at first, because it's a chance in a million, a chance most other men would give ten years of their lives to get anywhere near! It means that I can't turn back now, Lindy. I've got to go on—for Rick. He's the swellest guy I know." He paused looking at her half-apologetically after that unaccustomed effusion. "Well, aren't you pleased?"

"Pleased! It isn't the word, Norrie! He had done so much for us already, but this—this . . . It puts us more heavily in his debt than ever," she added in a whisper.

"I don't think Rick would wish you to look at things like that," Norman said quietly. "He's not the sort to want repayment in kind, but I think I can repay him by working as I've never worked before, by never once slipping up and by justifying his faith in me to the end of my days."

There were tears suspiciously near the surface of her eyes as she replied:

"I know you will, Norrie. We all will."

And then she had gone, running swiftly along the corridor to her own room for five minutes in which to compose thoughts that were the most difficult and conflicting she had ever known before she rejoined the others in the study downstairs.

2

The hired car drove slowly along the narrow cart-road to Craigmiles, and the breath of the sea came to Lindsey as she sat in the back seat between Douglas and her brother, a breath like the whisper of something out of the past that was strangely sad, yet bitterly sweet. The last time she stood by that grey North Sea Richard had been by her side and he had held her close against him for a moment, although it had been only in the way of friendship and sympathy. Again it had been for Douglas, just as he had asked her to come to Craigmiles this time—for Douglas.

"We'll soon be there now, Doug."

He turned from the front seat beside the driver to smile at his brother and their eyes met.

"Tired, Lindsey?"

"A little. We were up very early this morning."

"You can go to bed immediately after dinner."

"Beginning to give orders again?" Douglas queried, but without rancour. "Sure sign of a complete cure, Rick!"

"I shall certainly have to take you in hand," Richard replied. "Who gave you permission to lie awake into the small hours of the morning, reading?"

"Someone's been up early at Park Circus, surely," his brother retorted. "Could have been Matron? Lindy, of course, has just admitted to it! Did your informer tell you what I was reading, by the way?"

153

"No. Does it matter?"

"Not very much. I thought it might give you a mild shock, though."

"Well, let's have it."

"An old text-book."

Richard frowned.

"On flying?"

"No—on agriculture. I wondered what should be going on around here in January."

There was a deep silence in the car, and Lindsey's eyes followed the direction of Richard's out over the fields of Craigmiles which his ancestors had tilled for generations, meeting good and bad in the seasons with the fortitude which comes of close contact with nature.

"I'm glad, Doug.," he said quietly at last.

They were running into the stack-yard and round the end of the house, where Gavin Harvey stood waiting in the failing afternoon light to meet them, with Jean Creighton close behind him, so eager to embrace Douglas that she looked almost impatient as the old man clapped his younger son on the back and said huskily:

"You're back, laddie, and this is a happy day for Craigmiles."

And Douglas looked almost embarrassed as he returned:

"It's good to be back."

"We've asked Hattie and Ina over for a bite at dinnertime," Gavin explained, when they had settled to a cup of tea round the fire. "Just a wee sort of family reunion, you know. The girls have been very good while you've been away, coming over to cheer us up and bringing 'phone messages and the like."

"Will they walk over?" Richard asked.

"I expect so." Gavin glanced up at the clock. "There's time yet, if one of you would like to go to meet them."

Richard rose to his feet.

"I'll go over. They'll keep to the road in the dark." He glanced across at Norman. "Care to come along?"

"I'm with you." Norman rose eagerly. "I won't be two shakes getting my coat."

Lindsey had to smile at his eagerness. Norman made no pretence of hiding his desire to see Hattie Wilson again at the very first opportunity.

The two girls were just leaving Birkha' when the car appeared in the drive.

"I was quite looking forward to the walk," Hattie remarked. "I've been sitting indoors all day sewing for Jennifer."

"Then, lets walk," suggested Norman. "We can leave Rick and Ina to take charge of the car and we'll still be over in time for dinner. I feel stiff enough myself after sitting in that train all afternoon."

Richard helped Ina in beside him, smiling slightly as they drove away.

"Norman has got a new lease of life, I think," he mused contentedly.

The two left behind on the narrow road glanced at each other a little uncertainly and then they laughed.

"What will Rick think of you?" Hattie demanded.

"Very much of the truth, I suppose—that I wanted to speak to you alone."

She looked away without answering that, but her heightened color betrayed the fact that she could not pretend to misunderstand his meaning.

"Hattie," he said, "it's early in our—friendship to speak of such things, but I know I shall feel no different after we have known each other for years. It's sort of inevitagle that we *will* know each other years hence," he added with that spontaneous boyishness which endeared him to all his friends. "I think you know that, too."

She smiled faintly, neither denying nor confirming his statement.

"I've had a marvellous piece of luck," he went on, "something I never imagined would come my way in a hundred years. You remember me telling you how gloomy the future looked that day on the links at St. Andrews, and how you said that something would turn up to compensate me for the loss of surgery?" He drew a deep breath. "Well, there doesn't need to be any compensation. Rick has seen to that twice over, I guess."

Her interest brought her to a halt and she stood, lips slightly parted, eyes wide and enthusiastic on his.

"Mr. Harvey told us you did the operation," she said. "It was splendid of Rick to give you that chance, and splendid of you to take it."

"You don't know how I felt, Hattie. It's something I'll never be able to explain, even to you. It was all my life as I had longed to live it on the one hand and on the other

—nothing. But Doug.'s life seemed to stand between me and what I wanted. Dare I take a chance with a human life for what I saw then as a selfish motive? And then Rick put it to me this way: You can do it; I can't. The operation had to be done. I was doing him a service, he said, and he had every confidence in me. How *could* I fail after that?"

"You just couldn't, and—oh! I'm glad you took your chance, Norman!"

"Rick's done even more than that for me," he continued quietly. "Last week he offered me the position as his assistant."

"How wonderful! I'm not really surprised, though, because he's talked such a lot about you—he believes you are a coming man,—but, all the same, he has given you a great chance." She smiled very sweetly. "Lindsey must be feeling very proud of you; but let me be the first outsider to congratulate you."

She held out her hand and he crushed it in his.

"Outsider? Hattie, you know you'll never be that! I love you my dear. And one day, if you can answer me in the way I want you to, I'll promise you that you'll never regret it."

Tears were very near the surface of Hattie Wilson's eyes as she looked steadily back at him.

"I wish I could answer you now," she said, "but that wouldn't be fair. I never dreamed that—that you cared for me like this, Norman. We have met so recently, yet I'll confess that doesn't seem to matter. But I want to be sure." She clung to his strong fingers. "Oh, forgive me, but I must say it! I don't want to feel that this—this attraction is just the aftermath of loneliness."

"My dear, I know exactly how you must feel about it," he said gently. "I've sprung it all on you rather suddenly, probably because I was so full of enthusiasm over my new job, but you'll forgive me, won't you, Hattie, and take as long as you need to think it over? I won't rush you, and I won't change."

She drew in a breath that was like a sigh, and he drew her hand through his arm, marching her off in the direction of Craigmiles, where she sat through the cheerful dinner-party in such a detached state that Lindsey guessed at once that Norman had asked her some all-important question which she was finding it difficult to answer.

"It's a lovely night," Norman remarked when Ina rose to go at last. "I'll walk back with you."

"May I come?" Lindsey asked. "Richard and Douglas are going to be banished upstairs, I expect."

"Certainly—after such a journey; but I think the walk would do you good," her brother replied.

"I admire your energy," Douglas remarked. "Birkha' and back would just about finish me, tonight!"

"It's a grand evening," the farmer observed wistfully. "I would fain walk across myself, if I could."

They set out, Norman and Ina walking on a little way ahead along the moonlit road while Hattie chatted to Lindsey about Jennifer. Half-way to the main road, however, she paused, and the silence between them was suddenly fraught with deeper things. At last Hattie said quietly:

"I'm wondering about happiness, Lindsey—if one can recapture all the glow and the ecstasy one once knew."

"With—someone else, you mean?"

Hattie nodded.

"Norman has asked me to marry him."

"If you love a person," Lindsey told her with utter conviction, "you are sure that you can have these things, whether it is for the first or the second time."

"Then, you don't believe there can be any happiness in a marriage without love?"

"No."

Lindsey's voice had been quiet and steady, and she knew that she had answered a question of her own which had been troubling her mind for many weeks past. There could be no happiness in a marriage without love, for happiness in marriage meant so many things—giving and taking, being patient and willing to see the other's point of view, being humorous and kind, and love alone could be the keystone of all these things.

"I know I'm the impulsive type," Hattie said presently, "but I want to be absolutely sure of my feelings in this before I give Norman my answer. I know it's a queer thing to say, but people marry recklessly the first time—they're in love and that's all that matters, they think; but even after you've been married to the ideal person you realize how many little pitfalls there can be and how—impossible your marriage would be if love wasn't

157

deeply rooted. Then you want to be sure, for the other person's sake as well as your own."

"Norman will wait for your decision," Lindsey said, putting a friendly hand on her arm, "and I'm sure it will be the right one, Hattie."

"He's got such a future before him, and it's absolutely thrilling to know he's going to work with Rick. I wouldn't fall down on him in that respect, Lindy. I'd take an interest in his career and do my best to be worthy of him, and I'll be perfectly honest and admit that town life appeals to me much more than the country does." She gave a little sigh. "That's what I'm trying to get quite clear: whether it's the chance of escape I'm grasping at or my second chance of happiness."

"I think you'll find quite soon that it isn't just a chance of escape," Lindsey said thoughtfully, "because, you see, I don't think you are really unhappy at Birkha'."

"Unhappy? Good gracious, no! It's lonely, of course, but I've got Jennifer and Mums and Ina most of the time. We're a happy family."

Lindsey walked on, thinking that Hattie had answered her own question very much as she herself had done, although in another form. It was not escape which she sought; and Hattie's words lingered in her ears long after they had said good-night at the gates of Birkha' and were walking back towards Craigmiles and the sea. 'I'll take an interest in his career and do my best to be worthy of him. . . .' A little ache of loneliness found her heart as she repeated them, because that was the way she felt about Richard.

"I've asked Hattie to marry me," Norman confided as they approached the farm, "but she hasn't been able to give me her answer. Maybe I should have hung on a bit longer to give her time to get used to the idea."

"You can still do that," Lindsey suggested.

"Yes, I guess so. I'm not usually such an impatient beggar."

"I suppose it's difficult to be patient when you're in love."

"If you're *sure* you're in love," he supplemented. "Then you don't see any need for hesitation."

"You must think of Hattie's point of view, too," she urged gently. "She was very much in love with her husband, and she's the kind of person who will want to make sure that she can give you the same sort of affection. It will be worth waiting for when it comes, Norrie."

"You seem convinced that it will come."

"I think so. She's not exactly unsure, she's just making sure."

He gave her arm an affectionate squeeze.

"Happy?" she asked, and he replied instantly: "Extremely," and then after a pause: "I wish I saw you as happy."

"You mustn't worry about me," she tried to say lightly; but she knew that he was thinking of Richard, and had long since guessed the reason for her unhappiness.

As they came into the stack-yard a faint beam of light broke the dark arch of the doorway, and they heard Jean Creighton's voice, gently chiding:

"Are you two men-folks going to stay out there a' night? You've had time to smoke your way through a dozen 'last pipes'!"

The door closed again and Richard's deep laugh sounded in the darkness.

"I expect we'd better go in, Dad."

Lindsey could see the little shower of sparks fly up as he knocked out the contents of his pipe against the wall, and suddenly the whole night was full of the simple beauty of homely things, full of starlight and warm, bantering conversation, and the sigh of the wind and the distant sound of the sea, and full of her love for him.

Norman greeted the farmer, offering the old man a cigarette from his case; but Lindsey stood back in the shadows and presently Richard crossed to her side.

"You should be in bed," she told him.

"Not much use going to bed when you can't sleep." His voice was almost whimsical, but she thought that he was crushing down some strong emotion. "Did you enjoy your walk?"

"Very much."

It was almost laughable to be talking to him like this when her whole heart was crying out that she loved him.

"Doug. went to bed an hour ago most obediently." He was very close in the darkness. "He's been talking a lot about farming, Lindsey—asking questions about this and that, and the old man's elated. He feels sure he will settle down and run Craigmiles and be contented here."

"He will," she answered. "I feel sure of that now."

"And you, Lindsey?" She could just see his eyes in the dim light, faintly questioning. "Will you be content here?"

It seemed that she was held in a spell, the spell of his personality. Which way did he want her to answer?

"I don't know," she said desperately. "I don't know."

Her queer little inarticulate reply dropped into the silence of the night, leaving her with a vague impression of disappointment.

"Richard," she said, her voice low-pitched and unsteady, "will you arrange for my return to St. Ronan's?"

"Immediately?"

"Yes."

"You are really due back on Monday."

"Then, I must go."

"You're sure of this, Lindsey?"

"Quite sure."

He said nothing more, walking with her into the house to break the news of her early departure to Mrs. Creighton.

"And here was me thinkin' that we'd have you for a week or two!" observed Jean, obviously disappointed. "Must you be in such a big hurry?"

"I've been away from work for quite a long while," Lindsey pointed out, "and the people at St. Ronan's will be thinking I have deserted ship."

"But Mister Richard needed you," said Jean, and evidently to her simple heart that was all that mattered.

Douglas heard the news of her departure the following morning when he came down to breakfast later than usual, and after they had finished, he sought Lindsey out in the lounge where she was sitting alone reading a book.

"What's all this nonsense about going back to St. Ronan's tomorrow?" he demanded with a touch of his old irritability. "You know you can't."

"I must go back sometime, Doug."

"Not if we need you here."

"Rick has given his consent."

"The devil he has! When?"

"Last night."

"Were you out with him last night?"

"I met him at the door when Norman and I came back from Birkha'. He was smoking a last pipe with your father."

"And discussing the prodigal, no doubt?"

"They naturally hope you will settle here, Doug."

"I'll not be forced into it!"—with a flash of the old temper. "I'll make my own decisions."

"I know you will. That's why I'm asking you to let me make mine and go back to St. Ronan's for a while."

"To make up your mind whether you can marry me or not?"

She did not answer him, and he said:

"I don't see why you have to go," but he broke off as their eyes met. "Oh, well, I suppose I have no real right to stop you."

"No, Doug."

"All the same"—doggedly—"I don't mean to let you go as easily as all that, and I don't mean to take 'no' for an answer when the time comes."

She did not reply because she could not, and presently he said:

"We're going over to Birkha' this afternoon. You'll have time to come, won't you?"

"I'm not leaving until the early morning train tomorrow."

They drove to Birkha', Lindsey sitting between Norman and Richard, with Douglas driving at a rather reckless speed.

Ina was out at the front door, having seen their approach from an upstairs window, and presently she was joined by Mrs. Cargill and Jennifer.

"Mummy's got a dre'ful cold," Jennifer informed them solemnly in her grandmother's most severe tone. "That's what comes of flying about at night without a hat!"

Douglas laughed, but said he was sorry about the cold, and Norman asked:

"Is she in bed?"

"Oh, no, she's in the sitting-room with a book. Ina's in the middle of milking," Mrs. Cargill added. "Will you go down to the byres or come in for a rest and a cup of tea first?"

"We'll look Ina up, I think," Richard suggested, seeing that Norman had already disappeared in the direction of the sitting-room and Hattie.

"An' I'll show you the new kittens, Uncle Doug.!" breathed Jennifer excitedly. "There's four all black, an' a black-an-white one like Tibby! They're all curled up and they've got their eyes shut. They came this morning. I could give you one," she added reflectively, "if Mrs. Creighton says you can have it."

"I'm sure she'll have no objection, seeing that they're Tibby's," Douglas assured her, "and one cat more or less at Craigmiles won't make much difference."

"Last time Tibby had kittens they all disappeared." Jennifer's voice was plaintive, and then she frowned. "That's the naughty elves up in Bruce's wood, I 'spect," she added in a lowered tone. "They're always taking things."

"Like the Lying-About fairies?" Douglas laughed.

"Oh, no,"—in a serious little voice—"*they* only take things that are left lying about. That's 'cos you're untidy, an' if you don't want the Lying-About fairies to get the things you like most, you put them away safely at night."

"Carefully out of reach," Douglas mused, while his glance rested on Lindsey for a moment and then went swiftly to his brother's set profile. "There's a lot to be said for it, Jenny, when one comes to think of it."

Jennifer studied him in silence, and they moved off towards the byres where Ina had just finished the afternoon milking. She looked up, flushing with pleasure as she saw her visitors, and her eyes held Douglas' glance for a moment as she said:

"I'm so glad you've come—though I wondered if tomorrow would have been more convenient for you," she added.

"Lindsey is going back to St. Ronan's tomorrow," Douglas informed her. "We can't persuade her to stay."

"It isn't a case of persuasion," Lindsey said. "I must start work."

"I'm sorry," Ina returned, and then looked across the small circle to where Richard stood by the door. "You'll be staying a while, though, Rick?"

"For a week or two," Richard agreed.

"Uncle Doug.," Jennifer demanded, "come and see the kittens!" She tugged at his hand, impatient to show her treasures. "Soon it will be time for them to go to bed."

"Since they appear to sleep all day, that seems hardly necessary," Douglas observed, flinging a sharp glance at his brother, who stood beside Lindsey. "Aren't you going to invite Uncle Rick to the inspection?"

Jennifer looked shyly at the taller man, awed a little by the unexpected suggestion.

"He could come if he liked——"

Richard smiled.

"May I? I'd like to very much, Jennifer."

They went round the end of the big building and Lindsey and Ina were left alone in the failing light inside, with the warm smell of cattle and new milk around them and the clanking of pails in the dairy beyond as the coolers were started—all familiar noises, seeming only to accentuate the silence between them. At last, Ina broke it to say:

"You were expected to stay at Craigmiles, Lindy."

"I know, but I've told them I can't." Lindsey turned almost desperately in the half-light, seeking understanding from this girl who loved Douglas Harvey yet who had not grudged her her friendship. "Oh, Ina, it's so difficult to know just what to do!"

"You mean because you don't love Doug. sufficiently?" Ina put the question as straightforwardly as she did most things. "Is that it, Lindy?"

"I'm sorry for him."

"And he's in love with you! It's a tangle, isn't it?" the quiet voice went on, making no effort to include her own hopeless love in the statement. "But running away won't straighten it out, Lindy. Must you go tomorrow?"

"I feel that I must."

"Does Rick agree?"

"Yes."

There seemed nothing more to be said, but after they had joined Richard and the others Lindsey wondered why Ina had asked so pointedly if he agreed to her speedy return to St. Ronan's.

Before she left Craigmiles on the Monday morning, Norman sought her out alone for a few minutes. He had offered to travel through to Glasgow with her, but, since he had another day's holiday to take, she would not hear of it.

"Lindy," he said as they stood waiting for the car, "I know Douglas has asked you to marry him, but don't be forced into a decision so quickly. He's not the type to go completely to pieces because of a girl's refusal—not now that he's cured. Before his operation the situation was different, and, somehow, I'm glad you've decided to go back to St. Ronan's. It's easier to think clearly at a distance because we see things in their true perspective."

Before Lindsey could reply Richard had joined them, pulling on his gloves.

"Everybody ready?" he asked.

"Except Doug. He was here a minute ago."

"He's probably round at the stables getting the car." Richard glanced at his watch. "We haven't a great deal of time."

The arrival of the car was heralded by the churn of wheels on the gravel of the drive, and Douglas made his appearance determined, it seemed, to supervise Lindsey's departure as part of his own personal responsibility.

The farmer and Jean Creighton came out to wish her good-bye; and they covered the distance to the Junction in record time. The train was standing at the platform when they arrived, and their good-byes were necessarily hurried.

"I'll be seeing you in Glasgow, soon," said Norman.

"Cheerio, Lindy!" Douglas added, bending swiftly and deliberately to kiss her on the cheek.

Looking up, confused and startled by the little possessive gesture, Lindsey met Richard's eyes.

"Good-bye, Lindsey," he said.

3

"Hammy," was Sheena Smith's agonized greeting when they met," why didn't you stay away while the going was good? We can't even breathe here any more, and as for 'special' nurses and 'special' cases, they just don't exist!"

"What happened to Matron?"

"They made her an M.B.E. and moved her to fields and pastures new on the strength of all she had achieved here."

"But surely it won't all go for nothing—all the good work that has been put in on the occupational side?"

Sheena made a wry face.

"Search me! The new Lady in the office is purely surgical in all her leanings, and she thinks occupational an amazing waste of time and money—the country's money."

"Surely the consultants—Stewart Harvey and the others —will have some say in the matter?" Lindsey protested.

"Dare they interfere a great deal?" Sheena smiled. "How is the brother, anyway? Are you engaged yet?"

Lindsey shook her head, angry that a wave of deep color should have spread so swiftly across her cheeks.

"No."

"He's slow, isn't he? Or is it you? I often wondered if you really cared for him."

"Douglas had a rough deal, Smithy."

"I know, but one doesn't exactly marry a person because one is steeped in pity for him. Goodness, I'd have been married a dozen times if that were the case!"

"And been locked up for bigamy by now!" Lindsey tried to laugh lightly.

"It would be almost better than being here! Edna Halton's got out, by the way. She wangled her transfer back to Glasgow a week ago, and gave it out that Stewart Harvey did the trick for her, but you know what Edna is. Even Alicia doesn't believe her, and, of course, Alicia is jumping mad!"

"Perhaps Rick did manage the transfer," Lindsey said slowly, speaking almost to herself. "They were friends— long ago. But he's been too ill . . ."

"Yes, we know all about that. Edna's family kept her posted with the latest bulletins. It must have cost her old man a bit in telephone calls every day."

"He was very ill," Lindsey said, back in the agony of those days when Richard's life had hung in the balance. "I was in the nursing home at the time."

Sheena's eyes opened wider.

"You don't say? By Jove? Halton didn't come across with that bit of news. I wonder if she knew?"

"I—it wasn't important. I didn't even nurse him." Unconsciously there had been regret in her tone; she had been denied that one service, the sort of service she could have given Richard freely and with what utter happiness. "Don't mention it here, Smithy. It's all over now and— forgotten."

"Do you think he'll come back here? There's been a complete reshuffle of staff."

"I don't know. He'll be recuperating in Fife for at least three weeks, and then—I don't know."

It was said rather desperately, and Sheena favored her friend with a shrewd glance. If Lindsey had seen next to nothing of Richard Stewart Harvey in the nursing home, at least she had nursed his brother, and there were rumors that her own brother had operated on young Harvey, so that it seemed quite a family affair.

"Well, I guess we can only hope for a visiting surgeon with the strength of character and personality of Stewart Harvey," she observed.

It seemed, however, in the weeks which followed, that St. Ronan's was not to be favored by Richard's intervention. Lindsey was taken from occupational and put on the general ward, where she nursed sprightly young officers with displaced cartilages until her work became a vague routine of days spent in an atmosphere of careless banter, with always that ever-present ache at her heart and the thought of Richard never far from her mind. St. Ronan's was full of memories of him. She could never forget him here—nor anywhere.

And then leave! It came unexpectedly, but evidently her full period away from St. Ronan's had been counted as duty, and she was informed that she was due, at least, forty-eight hours.

Telephoning to Norman at the clinic, she arranged to catch the early morning steamer, and he was waiting at the station, when the boat-train arrived at Glasgow, to take her to lunch. Instantly she saw all the signs of elation about him, the springy step, the light in his eyes, even the new suit.

"There must be some good news," she teased.

"Aren't sisters the most personal of creatures!" he observed to the Glasgow buildings in general as they passed out of the station into Gordon Street. "But not a scrap of news do you get till we are well settled before a white tablecloth!"

"I hope there will be something on it!" She took his arm. "Because I'm quite hungry, but I refuse to wait for your news. Has Hattie promised to marry you?"

"Not a word, I told you!"

"I don't think I need an answer. My dear boy, you're going about simply shouting the news! One look at your face——"

"Part of one's professional training, my clever sister, is not to register emotion, to develop a poker face for all occasions."

"Then, all I can say is that you're being most unprofessional at this very moment. You *are* to be married, aren't you?"

He smiled down at her and nodded.

"Norrie!" She gave his arm a delightful squeeze. "This is grand! When?"

"We haven't fixed the details yet. I'm leaving all that to Hattie."

"But there must be a few details."

"Only that we're to be married in Fife."

"In Fife?" She echoed his words almost with dismay. Fate seemed to be forcing her back to Craigmiles, or, at least, to Birkha'. But it was Norman's happiness that really mattered. "I'm so glad, though I didn't think she'd take long to make up her mind."

He laughed softly.

"Strangely enough, it was practically made up that Sunday before you left. A cold in the head is a queer adjunct to romance, I'll admit, but Hattie felt very sorry for herself that afternoon and I guess I caught her in the right mood."

"Don't let her hear you say that! She thought it all out most conscientiously," Lindsey told him.

They reached the restaurant he had chosen, and found a table in a corner.

"Jennifer's a great kid," he continued reminiscently. "I suppose I'll still have to play second fiddle to 'Uncle Doug.' for a bit, but I think I'll make the grade in time."

"How is Doug.?" Lindsey asked.

"Very fit." There was a pause in which he consulted the menu with the elderly waiter. "He's going all out on farming, by the way, and Ina's helping him all she can. In fact, he's more often at Birkha' than at Craigmiles these days, and he's even beginning to dictate to Ina."

"I knew she would help him. Norman, you know that Ina's very fond of Doug.?"

"Anyone with half an eye could see that, and since he's come round to her way of thinking about farming, there's no reason why he shouldn't come to it in the other way, too."

"You think he may?"—with a queer little catch in her throat.

"Would it solve all your problems?"

"The greatest one."

He bent over the table, covering her hand with strong, warm fingers.

"Lindy," he said, "don't do it. Don't sacrifice your life's happiness for a whim."

She smiled across the table at him because she could not tell him why she had all but promised to marry Douglas Harvey, and very soon she had changed the subject and they were talking about their father and some plans Norman had for his future.

"Rick wants me to live in at Kenningmount after we're married," he explained. "The nursing home has been enlarged and he needs a resident doctor."

"I've always wanted to see Kenningmount," Lindsey confessed, although the expressed desire was accompanied with acute heartache. "Rick has put so much of his time into his nursing home."

"It is him. It's out of town, too, and ideal for the special post-operative treatment he gives, although it's not too far away from the hub of things and I'd always be in touch at the clinic. The grounds will be splendid for Jennifer, and Hattie will still be near enough town."

"What were you going to say about Dad?"

"It was a suggestion." Norman put down his coffee-cup, tracing little patterns on the tablecloth with the handle of his spoon. "The Birch Tree has decided to transfer her affections to those relations of hers at Dunbar and is going into the boarding-house business with them, I gather, but I don't want you to think I'm breaking up the home, Lindy. I thought Dad would be better with us than getting a stranger in at Fotheringay Road. He'll be retiring soon and there's a big garden at Kenningmount where he could be very happy, I guess. He's not the type that could sit idle for long and I think a garden would be his salvation. It's up to you, though. If you don't like the idea of making your home with Hattie and me while you're on leave, we'll reconsider the whole business."

"You mustn't consider me at all," she said quickly. "What does Hattie say?"

"She's all for it. She was through here last week-end and met Dad and they got on like a house on fire. They even talked furniture, and I was able to assure them that there will be room for all Hattie's stuff and most of what we have at Fotheringay Road. The Lodge House at Kenningmount is a big, rambling place about half a mile across the park from the main building."

"And—if Rick ever marries?" she asked with self-inflicted cruelty.

"It wouldn't suit him to be so far out of town. A place on the Great Western Road would be his choice, I should think."

Had Richard discussed such an eventuality, she wondered wretchedly. Had he made up his mind so far ahead and had it any connection with Edna Halton's transfer to Glasgow which Smithy declared had been 'wangled'?

The swift flash of jealousy died in her, however, as she thought of him. There was nothing hidden about Richard, and he would have told them frankly had he made such plans. They had lived too close to each other during these past few weeks for him to have excluded her from his confidence in that direction, and Edna had not even visited him. As a friend he would surely have told her of his forthcoming marriage.

"Of course, there's always the possibility that you'll get married at an early date yourself," Norman suggested.

"Ten minutes ago you were advising me not to get married."

"To the wrong man."

She looked away from his frankly searching eyes.

"Need we discuss marriage? I have my career, and it has always meant a great deal in my life."

"Coupled with marriage to the right man, it could mean everything."

He hesitated as he saw the tears which his words had brought to the surface of her expressive eyes.

"I know," she whispered. "Don't you think that — I know."

"I'm sorry," he said, meaning it with all his heart, "but sometimes I find it difficult to understand you, Lindy."

"Don't try just now," she said, rising and forcing a smile. "Dad will be expecting us home."

They spent a quiet weekend at Fotheringay Road, and Lindsey went back to St. Ronan's convinced that her father would be truly happy at Kenningmount, and once more she was forced to acknowledge that it would be by Richard's kindness that his future had been so pleasantly assured.

For three long weeks she tried to bury her persistent heartache in her work, performing her duties conscientiously by day and studying in the evenings so that the sleep of utter exhaustion might claim her at night.

And then one day she saw Richard walking down the ward with Matron following behind him, a fixed smile on her face while the flame of suppressed anger burned in her blue eyes. He walked slowly, going from bed to bed to speak to the men, and to Lindsey it seemed that the weary months had rolled back and they were at the Alexandra again, for this was how she had first seen him, the grave, thoughtful surgeon with that air of distinction about him that singled him out from other men.

She had an hour off duty immediately after lunch, and with a strange little feeling of panic in her heart she made her way into the grounds, walking swiftly along the path which led down to the shore. Escape? Perhaps, because she could not face Richard and remain calm and self-possessed.

"Lindsey!"

She had reached the end of the path where it went down among the rocks and grass on to the shingle when the sound of his voice arrested her and she turned to find him standing just above her.

"I walked across the moor," he explained. "I was hoping I would meet you out here."

For a moment she could not answer as she looked back at him, unable to tell what he was thinking because his face was a grave mask with only the eyes smiling a little.

"I—had an hour off duty and it was such a lovely day that I had to come out," she explained breathlessly.

"Shall we walk on a little way?" he suggested, glancing at his wrist-watch. "I have half an hour yet before I need leave for the pier."

They walked beside the sea and the sun came out and danced recklessly on the little rippling waves, while behind them lambs called to their mothers on the hill and the voice and breath of spring was everywhere, isolating them there on the lonely strip of shingle.

She broke the silence, asking the conventional questions that would be expected of her.

"How did you leave your father—and Doug.?"

"Both very fit. I think we've almost gained our objective, Lindsey, where Doug. is concerned. He's a changed

170

person these days, so changed that just describing it wouldn't convey one half of it. You must see for yourself."

"I can imagine it. Norman says that Ina has helped him tremendously, and I'm so glad, Rick."

He halted in front of her, bringing her hurried little walk to an end close above the sea.

"Lindsey, I want you to go back to Craigmiles. You'll be going to Fife for Norman's wedding, of course, but I'd like you to go even before then, if you can."

She knew by his tone that he would not be there, but she could not go.

"Rick," she said, "I can't go back. I'm failing you all most miserably—I've failed you, and you have done so much for Norman . . ."

He moved, catching her by the shoulders, and beneath them the waves lapped round the jutting rocks, repeating, repeating, 'I have failed you!' 'I have failed you'!"

At last she looked at him, and for one breathless moment it seemed that he was about to take her into his arms, no longer in the way of sympathy, as he had done that day on the rocky headland beyond Craigmiles, but as a man might take the woman who means everything in the world to him, and then suddenly she saw his mouth harden and a pulse beating strongly beneath the tanned skin high in his cheek.

"You must go to Fife," he said. "This thing is between Douglas and you just now."

She stood very still feeling as if some great tide had swept over her, and as it ebbed she felt revitalized and curiously undaunted.

"I'll go," she said quietly, "but it won't be till the wedding, Richard. I can't possibly get leave before then."

"I am going to London," he told her, "but I shall be back to stand by Norman. They expect to be married at Easter, I think."

"It was good of you to suggest Kenningmount," she said as they walked slowly back towards the hospital.

"It was convenient for Norman," he agreed. I'm setting up house myself, as a matter of fact. My army work takes a good deal of my time, but I also have a growing practice, and I feel that it is time I had a home. I've been lucky enough to find a grand old house on the Great

Western Road which was thoroughly modernized a year ago. The owner is an old colleague of mine who is retiring to his home in the Highlands, and I may also get first chance of some very fine period furniture into the bargain."

He had spoken in a strangely detached voice, and she was glad that he did not look round at her because she knew that all her efforts to conceal her heartache had been in vain in that first moment of his confession. He was making a home. He was going to be married. There could be no other reason, and she had been fool enough to will herself into discounting all the rumors, the pointers to such an event, reasoning that he would have told her in the way of friendship, at least.

Well, now he had told her, and he had forgotten her to such an extent that he could walk silently by her side, thinking of the future, planning the home he would make with someone else.

She was relieved—almost glad—when they reached the old grey house and were received into its shadow.

"I'm on duty at four o'clock," she said hastily. "You'll forgive me if I run away now, Rick. I don't suppose I shall see you again till we meet for the wedding."

"No, I think not."

His smile hovered between perplexity and regret.

"Until then," she said, "good-bye."

He took her hand, holding it very gently.

"I'd like to travel through with you, Lindsey," he said unexpectedly, "but I think it would be better if you went alone."

Why? she thought a dozen times after he had gone. Why? Did it matter if she had just one hour out of all those empty years stretching ahead? She knew now that she could not marry Douglas, whatever happened, and probably the strength of her conviction had been carried to Richard as they had stood there so close in the pale sunshine, with the sound of waves all about them and the coolness of spray against their cheeks. The same coldness lay in her heart now, and a numbness of despair took hold of her spirit so that even her work failed to hold her interest and the days passed as in some vague, unhappy dream.

Douglas wrote once in all that time, an affectionate but brief epistle which confirmed Norman's description of his life at Craigmiles these days. She took almost a week to answer it, but even then she could not bring herself to write her definite refusal of him. 'This thing is between Douglas and you,' Richard had said. He expected her to go to Fife, and she knew that she would go.

The invitation to Hattie's wedding came in an informal little note from the bride, which was followed by one from Ina including a few details. It was to be a simple ceremony in the church in St. Andrews where the Cargills of Birkha' had worshipped for four generations, and Ina was to be her sister's bridesmaid.

"It's to be such a quiet affair that she's only having one attendant," Ina wrote, "otherwise she would have asked you, Lindsey, but we know you will understand. We do so want you to be there, though. . . ."

Yes, they all wanted her there, even Richard! The painful swelling in her heart was almost more than she could bear as she folded the invitation into her writing-case, to be answered in the morning. They all wanted her. They were hedging her round with love and kindness and consideration, making her one of them, yet only in the secret places of her heart would the cost be known when she met Richard Harvey again, perhaps to hear him announce the details of his own happiness and forthcoming marriage. She could not think clearly of Edna Halton; it seemed strange that Richard and a girl of her type should have anything in common, yet she knew that jealousy was dead in her. There was nothing left but the aching pain of regret, the knowledge that life and all it could hold was beyond her grasp.

The day before they were to travel to Fife she arrived in Glasgow to find Norman waiting for her at the station.

"Lindy," he asked excitedly, "will you come out to Kenningmount with me right away? I've a call to make at the home and I'd like you to give the Lodge the once-over just to make sure that I've got everything the way Hattie would like it. She's been through, of course, but Dad has sent some of our stuff over since then, and you know what I'm like about a house."

"I've had years of experience," she admitted, as he led her out to a grey car standing in the carriage-way.

"It's Richard's, he explained. "We're using it between us just now."

"Then, he's back from London?"

"Got in this morning. He's gone over to see about his own place this afternoon. The old chap who owns it is offering him first selection before the auctioneers go in, and he's rather keen to take the chance. You were hot stuff on old furniture at one time, weren't you?" he went on as he opened the car door to let her in. "I told Rick he ought to consult you, but I think he knows quite a bit about it himself."

She sat in the car staring blankly in front of her, knowing that she was answering his animated conversation, yet quite unconscious of making sense out of it as her mind whirled round the events of the next forty-eight hours. Richard in Glasgow; Richard buying furniture with a knowledge of and love for old period stuff as great as her own; Norman taking her over the home that Richard had made possible for them; Hattie and Norman married—and afterwards at Craigmiles. And then the journey home, the journey into emptiness, with perhaps even the added torture of travelling back as far as Glasgow with Richard.

"What are the arrangements about Dad?" she asked.

"He's sprung one on us in that respect! He's coming back to a holiday—a fortnight's fishing on Loch Awe! It's more than Hattie and I will get for our honeymoon, but I think the old man's real idea was to let us get settled in at Kenningmount before he moved over. Not that we'd mind a bit having him right away. The house is big enough for us all, and Mrs. Cargill will be bringing Jennifer through almost immediately after we get back."

"Already-made home, Norman," she said, unable to keep the slightly unsteady note from her voice or the wistfulness of longing out of her eyes. "Where are you going for your honeymoon?"

"Now, look here, this isn't exactly *the* most unconventional wedding on earth! You don't seriously expect me to answer that question, do you?" he protested, laughing.

"No; perhaps I shouldn't have asked. How far is it out to Kenningmount?"

"We're half-way there now. We go out along the Maryhill Road. You'll like it, Lindy, and everything's beginning to look very fresh and green." He hesitated, almost self-consciously. "That's why Hattie chose Easter for the

174

wedding, because it's sort of a new beginning, a revival of the first freshness of things. I had no idea she thought that way. . . ."

He drifted off into happy musings.

"Gosh! I've been lucky," he observed presently as the houses on either side began to give place to wooded parkland. "I'd never have dreamed that I'd get back on to my feet like this inside a year, far less thought about anyone like Hattie, and it's all been thanks to Rick Harvey! There's nothing in this world I wouldn't do for Rick."

She knew that he glanced down at her, and then his eyes were back on the road as he turned the car in between two stone pillars, and she forced her mind to take in the details of her surroundings, knowing that she would come here often in the future to witness someone else's happiness, the sort of happiness and the sort of life she had dreamed of, yet she thought it without bitterness and without envy. Hattie and Norman deserved every bit of it because they had both walked so quietly, so unflinchingly, through the valley of the shadow.

"That's the nursing home over there among the trees." Norman pointed to where a square, grey sandstone mansion stood on a raised terrace of brilliant green turf gilded over with bright daffodils and gem-studded with purple crocuses beneath the shrubs. "We've got a little stream down at the Lodge and there's a pool where I can put in a few goldfish for Jennifer. I guess she'd like that, and Douglas has persuaded Hattie to let him give her a pony."

It was the first time he had mentioned Douglas since they had met, and a frown appeared in two deep furrows between his brows. It cleared, however, as they came in sight of a low, one-storeyed building rising against a background of newly budded trees, a house with long, french windows along the entire frontage and a sundial set in a paved terrace which stepped down to a shallow stream.

Lindsey, so susceptible to first impressions, drew in a deep breath of delight. She could picture the Lodge steeped in summer sunshine with Hattie sewing on the terrace; she could hear a little girl's shrill laughter and see Jennifer, her short pig-tails flying, riding 'Uncle Doug.'s pony recklessly along the stretch of grass sward on the far bank; she could see golden fish in a brown pool with sun shadows shimmering among the floating plants, and Norman striding eagerly across the distance between the nursing home and the Lodge; she could see happiness and contentment and love in every line of the old house and, shaken beyond all power of resistance, she pictured Richard's pale grey coupe drawn up on the red gravel before the front door, Richard welcomed as the originator of it all, the friend whose life was their life, whose interests were theirs.

The car slowed up before the door and Norman produced a key.

"I didn't know there was such a strange feeling about letting oneself into one's own house," he confessed, helping her out. "I suppose it's part of the primitive joy of possession."

Or the simple joy of love, Lindsey thought.

"Here we are!" He stepped aside as the heavy outer door swung back to reveal a white, glass-panelled vestibule door which stood ajar. "On you go in."

They went through the house, room by room, and she made suggestions about some of their own furniture until Norman opened a door at the end of a narrow hall.

"We thought of putting Dad in here," he suggested. "There are two rooms, and Hattie thought he could use one as a sort of study if he wanted some of his old cronies in for a yarn about the fish that got away!"

They entered a large, sunny room with long, leaded windows leading out into a lovely garden, and Norman stepped quickly across the bare floor to open them wide.

"It's a garden after his own heart," he said. "It's been neglected a little, but that will be all to the good, I expect. Can you see him happy here, Lindy?"

"Happy! Has he seen it?" Her eyes were shining with enthusiasm, with just a suspicion of tears behind it all because, as they stood there in silence for a minute or two, she knew that they were both thinking of the mother who had obtained such a fund of simple pleasure from half a dozen rose bushes in the back-green of a Glasgow tenement flat.

"He didn't want the two rooms at first. He said one would be enough, and he began pottering around in the garden in the rain!" He closed the window and turned to a door in the adjoining wall. "We'll make this his bedroom. It has a window looking out on to the garden, too," he explained.

Finally, they stood in the hall looking through the open doorway of the living-room, where a gleam of sunlight slanted in across the polished surround to pick up the gay colors in the Mirzapore carpet.

"It's not so bad," Norman reflected with pride, "and we can add to it as we go along. Before you go, though, come and see Jennifer's nursery."

The big room was tucked away in the sunniest corner of the house, and already Hattie had furnished the walls with some delightful wood-cuts and a few good, colored paintings of animals.

"It's lovely, Norrie!" Lindsey exclaimed. "She'll be such a happy little girl here."

"I hope so. I'll do all I can to make her that." He slipped a key from his key-ring. "I'd better give you this now, Lindy, in case it's forgotten later. It's decent of you to come out and make the place look welcoming for Hattie."

Richard's car was standing in the sunshine at the foot of the steps and she stood looking at it, remembering that somewhere on the outskirts of the city Richard, also, had been viewing old furniture and the house that he would one day make his home.

The evening was spent quietly at Fotheringay Road.

"No bachelor parties these days?" her father asked Norman as they sat talking round the fire. "Are they a thing of the past?"

"Pretty nearly. I never did see much sense in getting hilarious on one's last bachelor evening." Norman pulled contentedly at his pipe. "This suits me much better."

They spoke a good deal about Kenningmount, and Lindsey could see that the idea appealed to her father immensely, although there was a certain natural regret in him at leaving Fotheringay Road where most of his happy married life had been spent.

In the morning he was first up, and Lindsey came through from her bedroom to find him bending over a treasured case of flies and spinners which was to go by carrier to Loch Awe. He was dressed for the wedding, and she felt a glow of pride as she appraised him, realizing how distinguished he looked with his white head and fine, patrician features.

Norman had ordered a taxi, and they arrived at the station in good time. The early trains were busy, though not too full, and they found seats easily enough.

"Can you imagine the excitement at Birkha' this morning?" Lindsey smiled. "I suppose cows have to be milked and cattle fed even although it is Hattie's wedding-day."

"I think the most excited one will be the wee lass," her father observed. "Bairns are always excited over a wedding."

Lindsey looked away out of the window, seeing the drab platform through a mist of tears.

"Look! there's Rick!"

Norman bent over her, fumbling with the window-strap, and the tall man striding along the platform turned and saw him, pleasurable recognition lighting his grave face.

"Hullo, Norman!" Richard opened the door from the outside. "Hullo, everyone! How are you, Mr. Hamilton? Feeling up to all the excitement?"

"It won't kill me, and Norman seems to be weathering the storm so far. How do you feel?"

"Much more nervous than I look, I expect; but I've got the ring quite safely and I'll try not to let our blushing groom down!"

"You know, I never thought of asking you if you'd had any previous experience of this sort of thing!" Norman laughed, as his friend settled down in the corner seat facing Lindsey.

"I haven't. I'm absolutely green, and more nervous than I was at my first operation!"

Lindsey sat very still, her small, gloved hands tightly clasped before her in the lap of her strawberry-pink suit. Richard's appearance had been so utterly unexpected, and she sat watching him, trying to keep the revelation of emotion out of her eyes, though completely unable to still the wild clamor of her heart that was like some small, fluttering bird beating impotent wings against the bars of a cage.

As the journey progressed their eyes met again and again, and even when she looked away with a pretence of interest in the scenery she held the vision of him sitting there, long legs crossed and almost touching her knees, his dark head leaning back against the cushioning.

"I should have travelled last night," he remarked as they neared Thornton Junction, "but that abdominal didn't go so well yesterday, Norman, so I stayed in town just to make sure."

"What happened about the furniture at Sutherland Crescent?" asked Norman, while Lindsey felt all the color draining from her cheeks as she awaited Richard's reply.

"I bought a good deal of it, and there are one or two fine pieces still to be had at the sale. I didn't like to appear too greedy, and I was quite surprised by the gift of some books, mostly medical volumes which we'll find interesting in the future."

"When we find time to read them, I hope you'll add!" Richard laughed, and his eyes held Lindsey's.

"I found something for you, too, Lindsey—a quite recent treatise on occupational therapy." He opened his case to produce the little leather-bound volume and passed it over to her. "There you are, that's the voice of absolute authority!"

She took the book from him with a murmured word of appreciation. He had not forgotten her even in the midst of his happy planning with the vision of another woman in his heart. He had given her a present in the way of friendship because he recognized her deep interest in her work, which was his work also. Foolish tears rushed to her eyes, tears which she tried in vain to check, and it was with a feeling of relief that she felt the train draw in to the platform.

Ina was there to meet them, driving the Birkha' car; but she took Norman and Richard to Craigmiles, because 'it was unlucky for a bride and bridegroom to see each other before they met in church.'

"You're looking lovely," she said to Lindsey as they drove away from the farmyard gate. "That shade of pink suits you so well, and your coat's lovely."

"How about mine?" James Hamilton teased. "This is the new semi-green shade of honorable old age! Its last outing was at Lindsey's christening, I do believe."

"Dad, it can't be that old!" Lindsey chuckled. "Moths aren't all that considerate."

"Well, it looks very nice no matter how old it is," Ina declared gallantly.

There was a new buoyancy of spirit about Ina today, Lindsey mused, a deep happiness radiating from within, yet subdued, too, even when a wedding in the family might be some excuse for it.

"Is Hattie very excited?"

"No, just quietly happy." Ina turned the car into the main road. "Jennifer is the most excited member of the family. I expect it's the new frock and grandma's fur cape which Mother insists she wears over her coat to go down in the car."

"What's Hattie wearing?"

"Pale grey, with very dark red carnations. It looks most effective, especially as Mother has given her a squirrel coat to go away in."

Hattie herself came out to meet them when the car drew up at Birkha', and the travellers were hurried away for a meal, while Ina ran upstairs to dress.

"We'll all go down in the car together," Mrs. Cargill said.

Jennifer was the most excited member of the party which set out for St. Andrews that Easter Saturday. Her small, blue-clad figure, with the cloud of fair hair set free from its confining plaits for the occasion, was like a marionette jerked by strings as she bobbed up and down on the car seat between Lindsey and her grandmother, who kept a permanently detaining hand on one small, bare knee.

"When will we see Uncle Doug?" was her most frequent demand, and it sounded in Lindsey's ears like an echo of her own thoughts.

When would she see Douglas? He had not appeared when they had pulled the car up at Craigmiles, but he would surely be at the wedding. Ina had not mentioned him, but they had not had much time for personal conversation before they left Birkha'.

The car slowed down before the church, and a sudden burst of sunshine caught the budding trees in a circle of light, like an omen of happiness for the bride, who waited in the car by her mother's side.

"You'll come with Aunt Lindy, won't you dear?" Lindsey coaxed Jennifer. "We'll see Mummy again inside the church."

For a moment Jennifer hesitated, clinging to her mother's hand, and then, gently urged forward by her grandmother, she followed Lindsey from the car.

"Aunt Lindy," she whispered solemnly as they crossed the pavement and went up the short, flagged pathway, "why do we have to go to church to get my new Daddy?"

"Because God has given him to Mummy and you," Lindsey explained simply, holding the little, white-gloved hand tightly as they entered the dim church.

She was conscious of Jennifer throughout most of the ceremony, a quiet, awed little girl in a dress as brilliantly blue as her eyes; but once she found herself looking in Richard's direction, aware of the old pain again and wondering if one day it might grow less acute.

At last Hattie was coming down the aisle on Norman's arm, smiling at the whispered words of congratulation, but seeing only Jennifer, and instantly the little fingers relaxed their hold on Lindsey's hand and the child ran to her mother. Norman lifted her and they walked together into the sunshine and a new life.

It was only then that Lindsey became aware of Douglas. He had come out with his father, the old man leaning heavily on his arm, and the likeness between them struck her with almost overwhelming force. In these few short weeks Douglas seemed to have grown in stature until he had all the farmer's height and breadth. Shoulders which had looked thin at St. Ronan's had filled out, and even in the conventional morning-suit his arms looked muscular and exceedingly powerful. He seemed almost a stranger, standing there in the shadow of the porch, a man grown out of the boy she had known.

Gavin Harvey crossed to her side.

"How are you, lass? Did you have a good journey from Glasgow? Rick tells me your father's here, and I think I saw him sitting beside you and the bairn in the kirk."

Lindsey turned to introduce her father, who had come out with Daisy Cargill, and Douglas came over to her side.

"I thought you were coming through last night," he began without any formal greeting. "You've stayed away a long time, Lindy."

There was neither reproach nor anger in his tone, only an unfamiliar restraint which seemed wholly in keeping with his swift development from boy to man, and she answered him steadily:

"I had to stay away, Doug. There was so much to think over—decisions to make."

"We're piling as many as we can into the car," Ina said, coming up behind them with Richard, who was doing his best to be an efficient best man. "We haven't a lot of time, because Hattie and Norman are going south with the four-o'clock train."

They got into the car: Hattie and Norman and Jennifer, with Daisy Cargill and James Hamilton in the back seat; and then the taxi drew up and Lindsey found herself sitting on one side of Douglas while Ina took the place on his left. Richard handed in Jean Creighton, flushed and excited in her best black, suffering a little under the strain of new shoes, and then he got in beside the driver and looked back at them.

"All set?"

"All set, Rick!"

They drove to Birkha', where the wedding luncheon was to be served in the long, gracious old dining-room, which was used so rarely these days. It glowed now with warmth and splendor and Hattie sat at the head of the table beside her husband, smiling down its flower-filled length at them all, the remote look gone from her eyes, her fingers linked firmly in Norman's for all to see.

'I've never seen him look so happy,' was Lindsey's secret thought as she watched her brother. 'Not even when he knew he could operate again.' And then her eyes sought Richard, and she found him looking at her across the table.

He had little time to seek conversation with her, however, for soon they were proposing toasts, and Jennifer was demanding 'a big glass,' in her high treble, and there was much laughter and, behind it, a few tears, which is the way at most weddings.

Norman and Hattie had what Richard rightly termed 'an amazing send-off,' the younger members of the wedding-party accompanying them to the Junction in spite of their most spirited protests.

When they returned to Birkha', Ina drove the car rather deliberately away from the house towards the outbuildings.

"Come and see our progress," she invited. "Doug. has been doing marvellous work on the silos, Rick."

They walked round the estate for half an hour and in that time Lindsey saw a new side of Douglas Harvey. It was a side she had suspected, although she had never fully realized its possibilities, the amazing enthusiasm with which he threw himself into a job once he had become interested. And that he was genuinely interested in farming there could be no doubt. He talked fertilizers and silage and yield per acre as if flying had never entered into his scheme of things, and in all his talk there was a long view of the future—rotation of crops, breeding, the possible establishment of a pedigree herd one day, while through it all ran a pride in possession, a love of Craigmiles, which could surely only be equalled by Gavin Harvey's itself.

Then, as they turned into the pathway leading along the edge of the wood, she saw that they were alone. Richard and Ina had walked on ahead and only the gleam of Ina's light coat could be seen through the trees.

Resolutely she turned to her companion.

"Doug.," she began, "there's something I must say to you. There's no use letting it go on unsaid indefinitely."

She faced him, seeing something in his eyes of which she would never have dreamed him capable, tenderness that was not love, insight and a resoluteness of purpose which brought speech to him easily.

"I know what you're going to say, Lindy. I've known it for a long time, I think, but I was so damned arrogant and determined to have my way that I believed I could beat it down in time. I've overridden a few obstacles in the past and I suppose I thought I could trample down a woman's better judgment, but I see now that I hadn't even the right to try to make you love me."

This new humiliation in him was almost embarrassing.

"You knew?" she repeated. "Then, why——?"

"Why did I persist? Because I was determined to have my way at all costs. What *I* wanted must be right because I had been handed a poor deal by life in other ways. I had sunk as low as that, Lindy, and you came along when I most needed sympathy and understanding. You came willing to give it, and I fought against it pretty strongly at first until I began to see you in a new light. You became the woman I wanted—the one woman—and I was determined to have you by hook or by crook. What did it matter that you showed me as plainly as you could that your interest in me was mainly professional? I wanted you, and there was an end to it."

"Doug.," she said gently, touching his arm, "don't blame yourself too much. I was to blame, too, because Rick warned me even in the beginning about the personal approach."

"Rick?" There was a flicker of pain in his eyes. "He stood aside pretty gallantly, didn't he, letting me have my way? I saw that, too," he added bitterly, "but I thought that the world owed me something, everyone in the world —even Rick. Possibly more Rick that anyone, because I had given in about all these damned operations and the crushing defeat of their aftermath."

"Except the final one," she reminded him.

"You did that for me," he said thickly. "Without you I should never have gone through with it."

"But, Doug., what a difference it has made, even in those few short weeks you've been here." she pointed out.

"Yes, it has made a difference," He smiled wryly. "I heard my father telling the Admirable Creighton yesterday that it had made a man of me. Perhaps it has, Lindy, since I'm offering you back your freedom—if I ever really had your promise. I'm still not quite sure," he added with a touch of the old cynicism.

"I don't know what to say, Doug." Her voice was unsteady.

"Because I've said it all for you? I know you were going to tell me all—or part—of what I've just said, and I know it was going to be difficult for you, knowing you so well. I'm not trying to pretend that I can give you up easily. It hurts like hell, because, for what it is worth, I still love you, but neither you nor I could ever put up with a makeshift, Lindy."

"I know," she said. "That was why I felt I must tell you today as soon as we were alone."

They stood for a while watching the sun setting over the ploughed fields of Birkha' that were so like the rich, red fields of Craigmiles, and both their thoughts drifted to Ina Cargill.

"Ina's helped me a lot in this, Lindy. I guess she's helped to lead me along the way back. She's so straightforward and fine, and she thinks the world of you." Douglas said.

"And of you, Doug."

She had spoken without impulse because she felt sure that it was no secret she was revealing. She knew that he must be aware of Ina's love for him, that selfless love which had stood aside so patiently waiting until he should need some part of it.

"I know," he said quietly, "and I feel a worthless skunk about the whole business because, just now, I can't feel like that again—not in the right way, Lindy. It may come, and I know I'd never find anyone that I could get on with as well as I get on with Ina. It's been like that since we were kids, and she hasn't changed in all these years. She's always been like a rock in a rough sea, a stable bit of land when everything else was giving way underfoot, and maybe I've taken her too much for granted. I keep trying to think of her as Ina Cargill, the celebrity, to balance things up a bit, but I guess she'll always be just 'wee Ina' to us all at Craigmiles."

"I think she'll want to be that always."

"Lindy," he continued after a pause, "it's difficult to ask, but has Rick spoken to you?"

She raised questioning eyes to his and found them darkly searching.

"Has he told you that he loves you?"

"No."

The word held all the echo of her despair and the deep hurt which lay close to her heart.

"I wondered."

He did not continue, and presently she forced herself to move, walking slowly back along the path which Richard and Ina had taken before them.

"I knew you were in love with him," he said, almost roughly. "I knew it instinctively, and then, that night in the nursing home when Norman came for you to go to Rick, I was sure. But even then I meant to fight. I was determined I wasn't going to give you up easily. That's the sort of person I am, you see, utterly selfish to the last breath in me."

"You know that isn't true," she said quietly. "You meant to give me up, didn't you, even before I tried to tell you?"

He laughed briefly.

"Did I? I'm not so sure, but I'll let you invest me with that virtue if it pleases you, though maybe it would be nearer the mark to say that I was indirectly persuaded." He was looking ahead to where Ina stood with his brother waiting for them to come up. "Some people have the knack of making you want to do the right thing without preaching, and I guess that wins with me every time. I'm not sure whether I ought to apply for a halo or consider myself a fool for being so easily swayed."

"I don't think you want either the halo or the cap and bells," she returned softly. "Neither would suit you, Doug."

"You seem to know a lot about me."

"I do—a great deal."

Ina was smiling as they came up.

"Well, what do you think of our effort?" she asked.

"It's—a very good effort," Lindsey answered, aware of that one swift glance of Richard's which had gone from her own pale face to his brother's serious one and then back to Ina Cargill's.

"Shall we go in now?" Ina suggested. "The remainder of the wedding-party will be thinking we have eloped!"

Gavin Harvey hailed her with enthusiasm.

"We've been waiting for a wee tune, Ina, to wind up a grand day!"

They played and sang and talked well into the evening, and it was long after nine o'clock before supper was served, and the party began to break up.

"I'll send you over in the car, Gavin," Mrs. Cargill suggested, "seeing that it's not every day you come to a wedding at Birkha'."

Gavin, and a few glasses of Johnny Walker, had the audacity to wink at her.

"I'm thinking it might no' be so very long before I'm back again for another," he observed, his eyes on Ina and his younger son where they stood beside the door. "My, Daisy, it would be a fine thing that, seeing that she's done so much to help him back on to his feet."

"Wheesht, Gavin! A man never likes to think he's been helped on to his feet. He likes to believe he's struggled there of his own accord!" Daisy laughed.

Ina drove them across to Craigmiles and was invited in for a cup of tea 'to tak' the chill off the drive back,' as Jean Creighton put it, and Douglas went to the door with her when she left.

"Well," said Gavin with a satisfied yawn, "that was a great day! It puts ye in the notion o' weddings, Jean."

"They say one makes another," replied Mrs. Creighton, "and I'm thinking the next one won't be too far to seek."

She was looking at Richard and he took his pipe out of his mouth, seeming to bring his thoughts back from a considerable distance to look at her.

"Your father was just sayin' that weddings are in the air," announced Jean as she lifted her tray and disappeared kitchenwards.

CHAPTER SIX

LINDSEY woke at Birkha' on Easter Sunday to find her room bathed in pale golden light as the sun filtered in at the sides of the heavy velvet curtains.

Dressing quickly, she ran downstairs to find Ina and her mother busy with the breakfast preparations while Jennifer ran to and fro, eagerly salvaging relics of the festivities of the day before from the dining-room table. During breakfast she plied them all with eager questions, chief among them the important one about 'Uncle Doug.'s' gift of a pony. Her mother had relented about the gift, and so, in her young mind, there was now no reason why the pony should not immediately be her property.

"Couldn't I even *see* it?" she begged.

"Later, perhaps. You can't always be worrying the people at Craigmiles. This morning you can take Aunt Lindy and your new grandpa for a walk and show them Deep Dene."

Jennifer hesitated and then smiled brightly.

"I know the way. It's not far."

It was on the road to Craigmiles, Lindsey was to discover when she finally set out with her father and their small guide, and before they had gone very far it was evident that Jennifer remembered that fact only too well.

"We could go to Craigmiles, Gwan'pa," she said, using the new and unfamiliar word shyly as she tugged at James Hamilton's hand. "We could see their cows and sheep, an' Uncle Doug, has made a new duck pond."

"But you can't just drop in on people like that," her grandfather pointed out. "They may have gone to church or be very busy."

"But we could still go," persisted Jennifer with all a small child's naive disregard for logic. "Just to see my pony, Gwan'pa."

James Hamilton hoisted her on to his shoulder.

"You win," he said. "How far is it from here?"

"Not far." Jennifer pointed. "Down there."

"It's about a mile," Lindsey explained. "It's really too far. . . ."

Reproachful blue eyes were turned instantly upon her.

"Just for a wee while, Aunt Lindy. Uncle Doug. said we could always come, 'specially to see the pony." Jennifer announced.

"Do you suppose they'll mind?" James Hamilton asked.

Lindsey could not quite meet her father's eyes.

"You take her down. I don't think we should all go," she said.

"Please, Gwan'pa!" There was no denying Jennifer.

"We needn't go up to the house, and we have to be back at Birkha' for lunch," her grandfather said.

"All right."

Lindsey followed them down the hill. It would be no harder to meet Richard today than in the days which would follow, and perhaps he might even have gone back to Glasgow. He had not told them his plans, but it was reasonable to expect that he would have to return quickly now that Norman was away on holiday.

"Look, Gwan'pa, there's Uncle Rick—and Uncle Doug!"

Jennifer in her excitement had pulled James Hamilton through the white gate before which he had set her down, and it clanged shut behind them, leaving Lindsey standing still on the other side. She could see Richard and his brother in the stable-yard, yet she made no effort to follow the others to the house.

Jennifer ran headlong down the slope, her little legs in their long green breechettes covering the ground to where Douglas stood at amazing speed, and Lindsey caught the first excited "Uncle Doug., where's my pony?" before she turned away.

She looked out towards the cliffs, yet she was conscious of Richard leaving the little group in the stack-yard and coming swiftly towards her, covering the ground in the time it took for her heart to steady itself.

"You wouldn't come down, Lindsey," he said.

"It's not exactly the correct hour to pay calls," she answered.

He said: "I was wondering if we would meet today."

He walked on and she turned with him as naturally as if they had arranged a rendezvous for such a morning when all the world had suddenly turned young again and the birds sang and lambs skipped gleefully across the new grass. The sun was on the sea, turning it green inshore and a wind broke it in white foam against the rocks, a wind that came across the headland with a shout of joy, stirring the little leaves on the thorns to a happy murmur and moving the grass in the ditches beneath them to reveal the pale yellow star of a primrose and the fleeting glimpse of a violet.

They walked in silence till thorn and beech thinned, leaving only the gorse and the sea, and here Richard halted, turning to her in that brief, decisive way of his which had so endeared him to her from their first meeting.

"Lindsey, you know what I want to say to you, what I almost said that day a few weeks ago when we were at St. Ronan's."

She remembered that other scene, which seemed the same now, although it had been by a more gentle sea with the soft western wind caressing their cheeks, and suddenly she was looking into his eyes and seeing so much. Richard loved her. He had always loved her, and she had been so utterly blind.

Without movement, it seemed, she was in his arms and the firm, warm pressure of his lips was against her mouth.

"I love you, Lindsey," she heard him say, and the joy that had been in the morning was suddenly flooding into her empty heart. "I didn't think I'd ever have the right to tell you," he went on, "because it looked as if Doug. had first claim, and then I found myself wondering, almost knowing . . ."

"I have loved you, Rick, right from the beginning, but I thought — it seemed that you wanted me to marry Doug. . . ."

"*If you loved him.* I knew he was deeply attached to you, Lindsey, and I could see what your sympathy and understanding meant to him. I had tried with Doug., but a man couldn't give what you offered so freely. I realized that Ina could, if she had been on the spot, and it was then that I began to wonder about you." He was looking down steadily into her eyes. "There was never any question about my love for you," he confessed. "That was an established fact from the first day at St. Ronan's, but there was Doug. to think about, and I honestly believed that you were attached to him and that love would come quite naturally."

"You made it very hard for me," she said softly, "standing always in the background, so far in the background, Rick, that I felt I could never reach you!"

"And now?" he said, smiling.

She put her hands up to caress the dark hair.

"You're here," she whispered.

"For always, Lindsey, if you want it that way."

"If I want it!" she echoed, and then she laughed, and her laughter held the quality of everlasting happiness and the quality of tenderness and love and the newness of life when the year has first turned to spring. She slipped her hand into his much as a child might have done, drawing him towards the narrow cliff path that went down to the shore.

"Tomorrow," he said, "we'll go home together."

"You're travelling back to Glasgow tomorrow?"

"Yes, and you're taking the day off to come to Sutherland Crescent. There's an auction sale I want you to attend with me."

"Richard," she confessed tremulously, "I had visions of you there alone—or with someone else."

He caught her in his arms, brushing the straying tendrils of hair from her brow with his lips.

"Why should I live there alone? Do you know that I even had an idea about—this when I started to buy a houseful of furniture? It all began with Norman telling me that you were an authority on period stuff," he laughed, "and I believe he even suggested that I should consult you!"

"So, that's why you're taking me to Sutherland Crescent?" she smiled.

"That, and a few other reasons," he told her, "chief among them, my darling, the fact that there would be no Sutherland Crescent or no home anywhere if I had lost you!"

THE END